LOST ZENDORI

LOST ZENDORI

MELAINA RAYNE

Original publication: June 2013

Cover Design by M.R.

Images from Jerzy Gorecki and Elena Pimonova

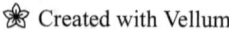 Created with Vellum

NOTE FROM THE AUTHOR

Lost Zendori was previously published in 2013, when I was just a budding new author. After ten years of doing this, I decided it was a good time to go back and revisit Ali and Nicolai's story. To give it a new voice and new structure. There were a lot of ups and downs during the process. So many frustrations. Writer's block. Second-guessing. But in the end, I was glad I did it. I love how it turned out this time around, and I hope you do too.

FOR THE TWO OF YOU

It only took me ten years, but I finally got your story right.
Glad you were so patient with me while I figured shit out.

Ali's tired eyes burned. She'd been up for two days now, and though she desperately needed sleep, she could never voluntarily succumb. Dread weighed heavy on her knowing that the dreams would be there waiting for her when she finally gave in.

Though Ali had lived her entire life in a city in northern Missouri, she dreamed of the jungle. In the beginning, only frightening sounds came to her in the dark. But a dim glow soon grew in the blackness, casting faint shadows.

Massive animals crept around her periphery, and voices echoed like hazy memories. Some nights, Ali heard a woman crying. She never saw her face clearly, but she could feel the woman's sadness and fear as if it were her own.

At fifteen, she dreamed of a strange man with eerie dark eyes and long, flowing hair the color of the palest corn silk. Despite his unusual beauty, something about him terrified her.

Since then, she'd dreamed of him often. Stalking her. Chasing her. Cornering her. She'd wake trembling with fear, knowing that if he ever caught her, horrible things would happen.

She fought hard every time she felt the pull of sleep trying to drag her under. She knew when she finally closed her eyes again, he would likely be there waiting. The other dreams could be scary enough, but he was the reason she dreaded sleep. She didn't want to see his beautiful, frightening face or his hollow black eyes.

Feeling the inevitable sleep coming, Ali lurched to her feet and paced the length of her living room. As a distraction, she counted her steps and forced herself to take slow, deep breaths. It wouldn't help, but she tried anyway, clinging to the hope that one day something would give.

As expected, a surge of anxiety swept in like a tsunami, knocking her off balance yet again. Gripping the doorframe, Ali breathed deep and fought against the lump rising in her throat. Her stomach churned like a washing machine, and no matter how hard she fought it, she knew she would be sick.

Rushing to the bathroom on unsteady legs, Ali dropped to her knees in front of the toilet. Like countless times before, she let wave after wave roll through her as her body rebelled against itself yet again.

The retching seemed to go on forever, but when it finally subsided, Ali gave in to exhaustion. She collapsed against the tub, letting her body slide limply to the floor. Hot tears seeped from the corners of her eyes. And as sleep claimed her, she wondered how much longer she could endure the torture her troubled mind created for itself.

Something changed that night. When the dream came,

Ali knew it was different from the others. Gone were the hazy glimpses of unknown creatures skulking in the darkness. This time, she saw everything with such clarity it no longer felt like a dream.

As she strode through the dense foliage, everything assaulted her senses. The humid air clung to her like a second skin, the earthy scents invaded her lungs, and the chaotic drone of nocturnal animals echoed all around her.

Her skin prickled with awareness. Something or someone followed her. She could feel eyes watching her every move. But for the first time in her life, she didn't feel afraid.

NICOLAI WATCHED the intriguing female glide down the overgrown path on bare feet. Her fluid, graceful movements fascinated him, and he kept his pace even with hers as she traveled deeper into the forest.

The wind rushed through the trees, tugged relentlessly at her hair, and sent the thick, golden waves flailing around her. Nicolai found it mesmerizing the way the wild strands stroked her shoulders and slapped at her lower back.

When the breeze shifted, it brought her mouthwatering scent straight to him. She smelled incredible. Like honeysuckle and raw feminine musk. He wanted to bury his nose against her delicate throat and take in her undiluted essence. But for the time being, he would settle for seeing her face.

As if hearing his thoughts, the woman turned, and Nicolai's heart nearly stopped. He'd never seen anything so beautiful in all his twenty-eight years.

Her glowing honey eyes widened when she spotted him. For a moment, confusion flooded her features. Then she took a tentative step in his direction.

Nicolai woke with a jolt, disoriented and all his senses on fire. Struggling to catch his breath, he sat on the edge of the bed and pushed the sweat-soaked hair from his face.

He hadn't felt so overwhelmed since his Awakening. It had been nearly five years, but he could still recall every vivid detail. The internal shifting, the physical distress, and the agony of heightened senses were brutal.

This felt nothing like that. The restless feeling humming in his every nerve ending could only mean one thing. His mate would be with him soon.

Too excited to sit still, Nicolai dragged himself out of bed and into the bath. Even as he washed up and dressed, his thoughts remained on the woman from his dream. His woman. He wanted to speak to her, but their mental link had yet to fully form. Until that happened, he must settle for replaying the dream in his mind and savor the moment their eyes met in the darkness.

Nicolai drove the twenty minutes to his family home in a daze, his thoughts on his perfect mate. She was tall and lean with smooth, toned muscles. Her long honey-blonde hair begged to be touched, but it was her fierce golden eyes that struck him hardest.

"Nicolai."

Startled by his brother's voice, he turned to see D'mitri standing beside the truck.

"Are you coming inside?"

Nicolai pushed open the door and climbed out, clapping his brother on the shoulder. "Good to see you, *irmão*."

D'mitri stepped close and pressed his forehead to Nicolai's in greeting. "It has been too long, brother."

Nicolai's smile widened. "Yes. And your English is much improved."

"I try."

D'mitri was the last in the family to learn English. Their father insisted they all learn. Said it was important if they planned to travel the world. D'mitri had always argued it pointless if he never intended to leave Barizya.

Nicolai was just the opposite. Where his brother had no desire to stray too far from home, Nicolai craved adventure. Even as a child, he'd loved exploring.

D'mitri was content to stay in his own little bubble and work on his wood carvings. He'd even built himself a workshop down the hill from their family home when he was just a boy. He spent most of his time there, chiseling and sanding one project or another. As a result, he always smelled of sawdust.

Where D'mitri was down-to-earth and loved working with his hands, Nicolai preferred to be in the clouds. He'd loved heights since he was a boy, always climbing trees to be closer to the sky. As an adult, he chose an appropriate profession and earned his pilot's license.

His first job, he worked for a small travel company that flew exclusively to locations in South America. Most often, he flew wealthy couples to lesser-known vacation spots and private getaways.

Two years ago, the company expanded and so had Nicolai's flying experience. Now, he flew regular clients all over North and South America.

Somewhere along the way, he picked up the habit of bringing trinkets home from every destination he visited.

At first, D'mitri showed a slight interest. But over time, mild curiosity turned into routine. Nicolai would come for dinner and the brothers would sit and talk about all the unique and beautiful things he saw in the new city.

Eventually, D'mitri asked Nicolai to teach him English. He wanted to go to the US but didn't want to be dependent on his brother to communicate with others.

They worked on it when Nicolai was home, but their adopted sister, Kaela, took up the slack while he was away.

This last trip had kept Nicolai traveling for over a month and he could hear the progress the two had made since he was last home.

"Are you having daily lessons?"

D'mitri chuckled. "Yes, and Kaela is patient. More than I."

Nicolai snorted. "Anyone is more patient than you, brother."

"True."

As they made their way up the front steps, Nicolai asked, "How is Pai?"

"Stubborn, but well."

Nicolai smiled. He supposed his entire family shared that particular trait. Their father had been the most stubborn male he'd ever known, even before his illness. Now, he could be downright impossible at times.

A few years back, Burian fell ill and after recovering from the bizarre infection, he was never the same. On occasion, he would act out of character or have major slips in his memory.

His doctor eventually diagnosed him with dementia. Though he had days of total confusion and heartbreaking emotional meltdowns, he was quite lucid most of the time.

The problem was never knowing when the bad days would come.

Because of that, D'mitri gave up on his dream of traveling with his brother and exploring new cities. That is, until Kaela put her foot down. She assured him she could take care of Burian on her own. And if she needed help, she could always call her Uncle Grandi.

Grandi was Burian's best friend and like a second father to Nicolai and his brother. Grandi and Burian were much like brothers themselves. They'd grown up together, the best of friends throughout their entire lives. They'd been through many happy times, and shared tragedies that only strengthened their bond. Including the loss of both their mates.

Standing in his father's den, Nicolai felt a twinge of guilt knowing he would be with his mate soon. His father had been without their mother for thirteen years and D'mitri still had to wait for his own mate for who knew how long.

The guilt was ridiculous, of course. They would be happy for him.

"Well?" D'mitri arched a brow, his sea-green eyes searching Nicolai's. "Tell me what happened."

Nicolai smiled. Of course, D'mitri could sense the change in him. Whether instinct or twintuition, as Kaela called it, D'mitri always knew when something wasn't quite right with him.

"I dream of her, brother. I saw my mate last night and she is beautiful."

D'mitri's eyes widened. "*Verdade?*"

Nicolai nodded. "Truly."

He watched the shock turn to excitement in a matter of

seconds and D'mitri sat forward. "How is your mind bond? Do you speak to her yet?"

Nicolai shook his head. He had tried to connect with her, but he was met with only silence.

D'mitri gave him an encouraging grin. "Soon, brother."

ALI WOKE, disoriented and aching all over. The faded gray ceiling slowly came into focus, the narrow wood planks growing clearer as she blinked up at them.

She lay on the bathroom floor, the cold tile unforgiving against her back. But despite her physical discomfort, Ali felt more at peace than she had in years.

Dragging herself off the floor, she cranked the shower on and waited for the hot water to take the chill from the air.

Her hands shook as she peeled off her sweat-soaked clothes, doing her best to avoid the mirror. She didn't need to see her reflection to know how terrible she looked.

She stepped into the shower and let the warmth of the confined space envelop her. With her forehead against the rough tiled wall, the water cascaded over her shoulders and did magic on her aching muscles.

Once she felt somewhat revived, Ali dressed in her cozy cotton shorts and an old baggy t-shirt. She threw her bedding in the wash and straightened her bedroom. Eventually, she wandered into the kitchen and poured herself a glass of water before settling at her desk. With one leg tucked beneath her, she woke the laptop and busied herself with her morning routine.

Twenty-three unread emails sat in her inbox, including one from her agent. Victoria had nothing new for her. Only the weekly check-in to ask about the progress on Ali's current manuscript. Honestly, nothing much had changed in the last week.

Sometimes writing was the perfect distraction, the escape she desperately needed from all the crap in her head. Other times, she felt so overwhelmed by life, even immersing herself in a world she created wasn't enough. Some days she sat for hours, the words spilling onto the page. And others, she stared blankly at the screen.

The latter happened more often than she cared to admit. And in recent weeks, it happened more than ever before.

Thankfully, Ali currently had no obligations to a publisher. She'd already fulfilled her contract for the three-book deal. Now she had to figure out where the hell she would go from there.

She sent a quick reply, informing Victoria that there were no significant changes since their last check-in. Then she scanned over the remaining emails; trashed some promotional junk mail and caught up on monthly newsletters from her favorite authors.

She thought about attempting to write, but her concentration was currently shit. She wouldn't be able to get much done. Not with her thoughts drifting constantly back to last night's bizarre dream.

Instead, she closed her computer and checked her phone. She had one missed call from her best friend. Maggie had called just before midnight and left a message. Though awake at the time, Ali hadn't heard her phone vibrate. She'd been too caught up in her mental chaos to notice.

When her anxieties rose, not much got through the haze of panic. Her mind blocked everything out until she could center herself again.

Fortunately, Maggie understood. She'd been around long enough to know that Ali sometimes needed space.

Playing the message, Ali leaned back in the chair and listened to her friend's ever-chipper tone.

"Hey girlie. Guess what. I'm having a party next Friday night, and though I know you don't like crowds, I'm still inviting you. You know me. I'm always hopeful that this will be the day you finally have a breakthrough and come join the fun. Did I mention Greg will be there? He's in town, and he really wants to meet you. Anyway, let me know if you decide to come and I'll send the car for you. Talk to you later. Love ya, girl."

Ali should call Maggie back but didn't know what to say. What could she say? Sure, it sounded fun, but her worst fear was having a panic attack in front of Maggie's other friends. Not only would she embarrass herself, but she'd also ruin the party.

With a heavy sigh, Ali tossed her phone on the desk and scrubbed her hands down her face. Sometimes she hated her life. She often craved human interaction, but her anxiety could be such a hindrance.

She went out when she needed to, but the fear of having one of her episodes always lingered just beneath the surface. The attacks still came when they wanted. But at least at home she didn't have to worry about witnesses. She felt perfectly content staying in her cozy little apartment, but sometimes she wished she could just be normal.

Rolling her head to the side, Ali's gaze landed on the early morning sky through the open window. Over the top of the neighboring building, a faint orange glow lit the horizon.

Dawn was her favorite time of day. She found the stillness of the morning quite soothing. Sunrise was the one thing she had no control over that always seemed to calm her. And as she stared out at the slow, shifting colors, she didn't have a care in the world. Until the thoughts crept in again and her anxieties flared.

Though Ali preferred to be left alone, she made friends with the two girls in the apartment across the hall. Not by choice, of course. They'd inserted themselves into her life that very first week she'd moved in, somehow knowing she needed someone even when she hadn't realized it herself.

Victoria, the laid-back, sweet one, had just finished college and was working at a coffee shop down on Main Street when they'd first met. Five months later, she landed an internship with a well-known literary agency and moved to New York to start her career. That had been three-and-a-half years ago. Now she had a decent client list of her own, with Ali's name somewhere in the mix.

With encouragement from Victoria, Ali had put her first book out there. It did well enough, but books two and three soared. Both reached the top ten on *The New York Times* Best Seller list, and Ali didn't know what to do with herself.

Maggie was the party girl of the two roommates. She'd tried to drag Ali out of her shell in the beginning, but when it didn't work, she'd settled for simply hanging out. And after Victoria moved away, Maggie spent more time at

Ali's apartment than her own. Until a year ago, when Maggie moved back to her family home that her parents had left her in their will. As an only child, she received the house and her father's family fortune at the ripe age of twenty-four. Not that she needed the money. Maggie had her own interior design business, and given her talent and upbeat personality, the business thrived.

This time of year, when the nights grew cooler, Maggie stayed busy. Between working and hosting parties, she didn't have a lot of free time. Still, she always made time for Ali.

Maggie's first party of the season was for her old college friends. They all flew in or drove up for the week-end, and according to Maggie, things could get a little rowdy. She always called the next day to fill Ali in on all the gossip. And with that wild bunch, there was always an entertaining story or two.

Ali loved hearing her friend talk about the weekend fun, but as much as she wished she could be normal and join them one day, she couldn't imagine being around so many people at once.

2
_____

Two nights later, Ali woke to the sound of a door slamming. She sat up so fast, she nearly fell off the bed. Her eyes darted around the room, searching the darkness for the source of the noise. It took a moment to recognize her surroundings. She was in her room. And judging by the yelling down the hall, the couple in 2B was fighting again.

Slumping forward, Ali placed her hand flat against her chest. She could feel the hard, frantic thumping of her heart against her palm. She hated being startled awake. It put her body in full panic mode and took her hours to settle down afterward.

She trembled uncontrollably and sweat saturated her t-shirt. The slight breeze ghosting through the open window made the room feel like a meat locker. No way could she go back to sleep. She could only climb into the shower and hope it would soothe her enough to lessen the inevitable panic attack.

Ali made her way into the bathroom on shaky legs and

cranked the shower as warm as she could stand it. Peeling off her sweat-soaked clothes, she climbed under the hot spray and sank to the tiled floor. She wrapped her arms around herself, and tilted her head back, letting the water cascade over her trembling body as the chaos rolled through her.

In moments like those, she lost track of time and space, but felt hyperaware of her internal struggle. She couldn't stop it, so she simply let it overtake her.

When the attack was over, exhaustion held her in place. She just hoped her strength returned before the hot water ran out.

Adrenaline sped up the process the moment she heard a faint voice coming from somewhere in her apartment. Her eyes popped open, and she halfway expected to find someone standing in the doorway. But nope. She was alone in her steamy bathroom.

With her heart pounding, she reached up and shut off the water. She held her breath, listening for the voice again, but she heard nothing above the echoing drip from the showerhead.

Ali stepped onto the fluffy bathmat without a sound and tucked a towel around herself. With cautious steps, she slipped into her bedroom, and grabbed her stun gun from the drawer of her bedside table. Creeping to the doorway, she peeked into the living room. Nothing. She searched the entire room, even looking on the far side of the kitchen island to be sure no one crouched behind it.

Confused, Ali moved to the door and looked through the peep hole. No one out there either. All was quiet and even the argument down the hall had ended. Still, she knew she heard someone speak. Another neighbor, perhaps? It was possible. There always seemed to be someone coming and going all hours of the day and night.

The walls weren't exactly thin, but sometimes she could hear Mr. Valencia's TV through her bathroom wall. He tended to turn it up too loud in the evenings. But she didn't think that's what she'd heard this time.

Forcing herself to relax, Ali made her way back to her bedroom and dressed. Just as she pulled the t-shirt over her head, she heard a deep, heavily accented voice.

"Hear me, my female."

Ali gasped, spinning around only to find no one there. Still, she lunged for the stun gun she'd laid on the corner of her dresser. Her hand shook so bad, it slipped from her grasp, landed on the rug with a muffled thump and then skittered under the bed.

Frozen in place, she held her breath and waited.

"Hear me," he said again, his tone holding a faint edge of impatience.

No one was there, but she could hear him as if he stood right beside her. Though terrified, she felt compelled to answer him. So, with her heart in her throat, Ali reluctantly whispered, "I hear you."

He let out a relieved chuckle. "It is good to hear your voice."

Tears stung her eyes. This was it. She'd gone off the deep end. As if she didn't have enough problems, the universe decided she needed to be crazy too.

"Sweet female," he purred. "You are not crazy. I assure you I am as real as you are."

Ali covered her ears. "Stop. Please. I can't deal with this."

There was a long silence before he whispered, "Tell me

where you are. I will come to you, and you will see that there is no reason to be afraid."

Shaking her head, Ali breathed, "Just leave me alone."

She waited, expecting to hear him again, but he said nothing more.

Eventually, she dragged herself into the kitchen and made a cup of lavender chamomile tea. She used to drink coffee, but she learned early on that it stimulated her too much and made her attacks more intense. Victoria had introduced her to herbal teas not long after they met, and Ali'd drank them ever since. Sometimes they helped. Other times, she could do little else but let the panic attacks run their course.

Ali sat at her tiny kitchen table, her legs drawn close to her chest and her chin resting on her knees. She stared at the steam rising from her cup and played over and over the short conversation. She prayed it had only been a dream. Dreams, she could handle. Even panic attacks. But voices? That was the last thing she needed.

Squeezing her eyes shut, she wanted to cry. She didn't know if she could handle much more.

Her phone rang, startling her out of her thoughts. Ordinarily, she might not answer it, but she needed the connection to reality.

Before Ali could speak, Maggie's chipper voice came across the line. "Hey girl. What ya doing?"

"Not much. Just sitting here, drinking some tea." That was a lie. She hadn't touched the cup since she'd sat it on the table twenty minutes ago, and now it was as cold as she was.

Maggie hesitated before she asked gently, "Are you all right?"

She thought she'd schooled her tone, but Maggie must have heard something in her voice.

"Ali?"

She couldn't tell her friend about the voice. Maggie would only worry more. "Yeah. Just another dream."

"I'm sorry, sweetie."

Ali heard the sympathy and worry in Maggie's voice, so she assured her friend. "I'm okay."

"Do you want to talk about it?"

"Not really." Honestly, she just wanted to forget about it.

Maggie didn't push. That's one of the things Ali loved about her. She knew Ali would talk when she was ready. And she wasn't ready.

"So," Ali changed the subject, injecting a bit of cheerfulness into her voice. "Tell me about this party."

Maggie sighed again but dove into the details. She loved hosting parties and Ali happily listened to her ramble on and on about who planned to show. And how she hoped Greg didn't fight with Trevor again. Ordinarily, Ali hated drama. But for the moment, she welcomed the distraction.

ALL DAY and all the next night, Nicolai had a tough time concentrating on anything. All he could think about was his mate. Their first interaction hadn't gone so well. At first, he felt such relief to finally speak to her. His heart had skipped a beat when she whispered that first soft reply into his mind. Relief and excitement bubbled up from deep inside him. Just hearing her voice gave him such joy, and he couldn't stop grinning like a fool.

Then he quickly realized she didn't understand their connection. She didn't recognize him for what he was. His beautiful mate thought she was losing her mind. And he had a sinking feeling that she knew nothing of her heritage.

Nicolai wanted to go to her like he promised; prove to her that he wasn't just a figment of her imagination or a newly developed psychosis. He tried coaxing her to tell him her location, but he would have to wait for their connection to strengthen and rely on the mate bond to draw him to her.

He didn't want her to go through her Awakening alone. He needed to be there to help her through her first transformation. But did he have time to find her and tell her everything she needed to know before it was too late?

After his last mate dream, he saw a little hope on the horizon, and it was glorious.

She sat on the edge of the bed, peering at him over her shoulder. Nicolai lounged on the bed, admiring her beauty. Her smooth, tanned skin glistened in the moonlight, and her tousled hair rested against her bare back. The scent of honeysuckle and raw male pleasure hung thick in the air. Their combined scents and the look of complete satisfaction on her face filled him with pure contentment.

Nicolai dragged himself across the bed and slid his arm around her waist. Pushing her silken hair aside, he pressed a tender kiss to her spine and murmured, "Alessandra."

"Yes, Nico?" she asked with a hint of amusement in her velvety voice.

He pressed another kiss to the lovely curve of her spine. "Hurry back, amor."

She wiggled from his grasp and Nicolai's gaze followed the sway of her hips as she sauntered into the bathroom.

The moment he woke, Nicolai called his boss and arranged a flight to North America. Missouri, to be exact. He wasn't sure how he knew, but he could feel it in his bones. Once he landed, he felt the pull of his mate bond even stronger.

He followed the draw for hours, letting it guide him down dim-lit streets in a city he wasn't familiar with. All the while, he played that last dream over and over in his mind. He would be with his mate soon. That very night. She was so close he could almost taste her.

Near the corner of Milton and Shepherd, Nicolai stopped, unable to take another step. His Alessandra was close. He could feel her essence drawing him to the second floor of the building in front of him.

He'd travelled a long way to see her, but reality quickly set in. She didn't know who or what she was. He couldn't just walk up to her door and introduce himself. If she even opened the door, what did he expect her to do? Be happy to see him? Odds were, she'd slam the door right back in his face the second she saw him.

Things would be so much easier if she knew what was happening to her, who he was to her, and the significance of their dreams. Nicolai didn't know what to do. But walking away wasn't an option. He'd come this far, and she was just inside the building in front of him.

Closing his eyes, Nicolai drew a deep breath and tried

to clear his mind. But everything in him demanded he go to her.

Without conscious thought, he stepped into the narrow alley beside the three-story apartment building and followed his instincts. Reaching with all his senses, he searched the area for anyone who might be aware of his presence. The last thing he needed was to be arrested for skulking around in the dark in the early hours of the morning.

The adjacent structure appeared the victim of an abandoned remodel, so no worries of nosey neighbors spotting him from that direction at least. And at such an hour, there wasn't much movement in her building. All the windows were dark or had the curtains drawn. All but hers.

The window was raised a few inches and a dim light shone from inside. Was she still awake?

Reaching out to her, Nicolai gently brushed his thoughts against hers. Nothing but a wall. Concerned, he avoided the ladder and jumped stealthily onto the fire escape. He sidled up to the open window, standing still for a moment, listening for movement inside the apartment. When he heard nothing, he slipped inside without a sound.

He knew the moment he stepped into her personal space he was done for. Their dreams did nothing to prepare him for the delectable fragrance that saturated the air around him. Now he understood what the elders meant; the sheer intoxication you could feel just being surrounded by your mate's scent. It called to Nicolai, drawing him to the open doorway to his right.

His heart skipped a beat when he found the bed empty, but as he reached out with all his senses. He could tell by her uneven breaths she wasn't conscious, and just the thought got his heart pumping faster.

He crossed the bedroom to the open bathroom door. And the moment he saw her, his heart stuttered. She lay on the bathroom floor, her lean body curled in on itself. Her deep golden hair fanned out behind her, and her creamy skin appeared to glow in the dim light of the vanity.

Her Awakening quickly approached, and Nicolai could see her nature trying to surface. Her jaguar would emerge soon, and he couldn't wait to see her.

Her scent called to him, seeping into him, and it drove him crazy. But he must be patient.

Alessandra would be ferocious. Her passion would be wild, but for the time being, she needed him close. Nicolai could feel her discomfort and mental cloudiness, and more than anything, he wished he could ease her.

Lifting her from the cold floor, Nicolai carried his mate to the bed and gently covered her with the blanket near her feet.

Unable to help himself, he leaned down and pressed a soft kiss to her forehead.

Alessandra reached for him and groaned, "Nico."

Her voice stirred something deep inside him, and he couldn't deny her. Even though she was asleep, he took her hand in his and brought it to his mouth. Placing a gentle kiss to her palm, he whispered, "I am here, amor."

He felt her ease, her body and mind calming as she drifted into a deeper sleep. Standing there, holding her delicate hand, Nicolai closed his eyes and savored the feel of having her so near him.

ALI SETTLED into her comfy chair by the window and stared out into the night. Or rather early morning, according to the blue-green numbers glowing on the stove. From the way she'd angled her chair, she could watch the flare and fade of lights as the occasional car passed. Still her thoughts drifted back to the gorgeous man from that last dream.

In all honesty, it felt more like a memory than a dream, but that was impossible. She knew she'd never met a man that delicious before. Much less had him sprawled naked atop her rumpled covers looking so satisfied.

His raspy, sex-roughened voice. The loving expression on his handsome face. And the way his pale green eyes shone with such affection. Ali wanted that. Too bad he couldn't be more than just a figment of her imagination.

She loved the way his dark, wavy hair lay loose on her pillows and the shadows accented his hard, masculine features. But most of all, she loved his voice whispering to her as she looked at him over her bare shoulder. Why couldn't she dream of him more and dream less of the confusing, frightening things?

Sure, the thought of being that close to someone scared the hell out of her. But she hoped one day she could really feel the way she had in the dream. It was more than just the way he made her feel and the pure contentment of the moment. She longed for her mind to be that calm.

But she had to be honest with herself. One or two good dreams didn't change the undeniable truth. Between the nightmares and the panic attacks, she was getting worse. Dr. Stevens was right. If she ever wanted to get better, she needed to talk to someone about her problems. She'd put it off for long enough.

When the sun finally rose, Ali called the therapist that Dr. Stevens had recommended. She'd had the number on the fridge for months. And after a brief conversation, she had plans to meet up with Jeff for coffee at the little café around the corner.

Ali got there a good fifteen minutes early. The morning crowd hadn't hit yet, but the place wasn't empty. Three men sat at the counter, drinking steaming cups of coffee, and chatting quietly amongst themselves. They didn't so much as glance in her direction when she walked through the door.

The older woman behind the counter called out, "Have a seat anywhere, hun. I'll be with you in a minute."

Ali offered her a small smile and picked the table in the corner by the window. She sat facing the door with her back to the old brick wall and forced herself to take a deep breath. She couldn't believe she was doing this, but she had no other choice. Something had to change, or she wasn't sure she would make it.

The woman approached with a welcoming smile. "What can I get you this morning? Coffee?"

Ali shook her head. "You wouldn't happen to have herbal tea, would you?"

"Sure do. Chamomile, lavender, lemon ginger, raspberry, peppermint, and green tea."

"Peppermint sounds great."

"You got it. Be right back."

"Thank you."

No sooner than she walked away, the bell over the door jingled, drawing Ali's attention. The man who walked in had to be in his mid-thirties and he carried himself with confidence. He glanced around, hesitating a beat before approaching her table. "Are you Ali?"

She nodded.

He offered his hand. "Jeff Donaldson."

Ali looked at him, shifted awkwardly in her seat. Before she could convince herself to be polite and shake his hand, he gave her a knowing smile and sat in the chair across from her.

Immediately, the woman was back with Ali's tea and a cup of coffee for Jeff.

He smiled up at her. "Thanks, Dee."

She arched a brow at him. "Just let me know if you two need anything else."

Ali hadn't seen a nametag. Did Jeff know the woman?

As if reading her thoughts, or her expression, he explained. "She's an old family friend. Went to school with my mama. That, and I come in here almost every morning."

"I've never been," Ali admitted. "I'm not big on crowds."

"There's nothing wrong with that. People can be a bit much sometimes. Trust me, I understand. That's the reason I got into psychology. I suffered from severe social anxiety as a teenager and well into my twenties. If I'm being honest, I still have my moments."

Judging by his open smile and relaxed posture, she never would have guessed.

"So," he began, wrapping his hands around the mug in front of him. "Tell me a little about yourself."

Confused, Ali frowned. "What do you mean? My problems or did you mean me in general?"

"Whatever you want to talk about."

Honestly, she didn't want to talk to him at all, but that's why she was there, wasn't it? Taking a deep breath, she exhaled slowly and then took a drink of her tea.

Jeff waited.

"Well, I just want to be normal. I want to be able to go out in public without worrying about having a panic attack."

"I can help you with that, Ali. I can give you pointers on preventing it, but most of all, I can give you some quick tips on how to get through them when they do come."

"That would be great."

Jeff took a sip of his coffee, studying her for a moment. "Tell me something. What usually triggers the panic attacks? Is it the anxiety of being around people or are there other contributing factors?"

He watched her intently, taking in the way she fidgeted with her hands, but he didn't mention it. Something in his warm, mahogany eyes made her feel seen without making her feel judged.

Still, Ali calmed her restless fingers and sat back in the chair. "Dreams."

Jeff pushed his cup away and folded his arms on the table. "What kind of dreams? Nightmares?"

Ali nodded. "Sometimes."

"How long has this been going on?"

Ali shrugged. "Most of my life. But they got worse when I was about fourteen or fifteen."

He looked thoughtful for a moment and then asked, "Do you mind if I ask what they're about?"

She debated whether to tell him, but figured, what could it hurt? Maybe he could give her some helpful insight. Even tell her why she couldn't stop dreaming of the same crap over and over again.

Tracing along the underside of the table, she shifted her gaze to the people passing on the sidewalk. Jeff didn't speak. He waited patiently for her to respond.

"It was hazy in the beginning. Mostly darkness and strange sounds. A deep roar in the distance, like a raging river or heavy rainfall. Big animals skulking in the shadows. Voices. Both furious and terrified. A woman crying. Sadness."

Giving herself a shake, Ali met Jeff's curious gaze, finding his brows slightly drawn down in concern. "That sounds awful."

"It was," she admitted. "And when I was fifteen, I dreamed about a man. I've never seen anyone like him in my life. He had unusually sharp features and pale skin. Cold, black eyes. He looked hungry. Evil." Ali chuckled nervously. "I think I may have watched too many vampire movies when I was a kid."

Jeff looked around the café and Ali did as well. No one paid them any attention. The men at the counter had already gone and a young couple sat in their place. They ate their muffins and chatted away while Dee leaned over the morning paper.

"Ali," Jeff said, his tone soft and even. "What was your homelife like growing up?"

She shrugged. "It was just me and my mother until I was almost sixteen. Other than the dreams, there was nothing out of the ordinary. When she died, I went to live with her best friend, Deanna, and I stayed with her until I turned eighteen."

"I'm sorry to hear about your mother. That must have been hard for you. Especially at that age."

Ali tried not to think about it. Filipa Sumaro was the most loving, most understanding and supportive mother in the world. When she died, Ali felt like she lost a part of herself.

"What about your father? Where was he?"

"I never really knew him. He and my mother adopted me when I was a baby, and he died before my first birthday."

The sympathy in Jeff's eyes made her throat feel tight. She didn't like to think about how tragic her life had been.

"No men in your mother's life after that?"

A bit taken off guard by the question, Ali laughed. "No. I never saw her so much as look at another man. I asked her about it once, but she told me it was pointless. She gave her heart to my father when she was young, and it wouldn't be fair to pretend she had even a morsel left to give someone else."

Jeff nodded thoughtfully. "What about Deanna?"

Ali frowned. "What do you mean?"

"Was she married?"

"Not until after I moved out. I always suspected she was a little in love with the lady next door, but never saw them together. Not until after I graduated." Ali couldn't help but grin when she thought about the day Deanna told her about Rosalinda. "They've been married for almost three years."

Jeff smiled. "How is your relationship with Deanna now? Do you keep in touch?"

"Not as much as I should, if I'm honest." She felt a little guilty when she thought about how long it had been since they last spoke. "But she has her own life now. I try not to disrupt it by worrying her with my problems."

Jeff gave her a knowing look. "I get it. I don't call my mother as often as I should either. It's easy to get caught up in our own lives and forget to check in with those we're closest to. Especially if we live far apart."

Dr. Stevens was right. Jeff was easy to talk to. Something about him calmed her nerves. It could have been his boy-next-door looks and his kind, mahogany eyes. Or his deep but gentle voice. Whatever it was, she felt comfortable talking to him.

She couldn't believe she told him so much. But she held one thing back. She didn't want to tell him about her most recent dreams and the voice that came to her even when she was awake. She was worried about what admitting those things might mean for her.

As promised, Jeff gave her a few pointers on how to deal with the panic attacks. It turned out that he didn't care too much for medication. Said it was a last resort. He preferred to try natural methods for teaching his patients how to deal with their issues and how to calm down with simple breathing and focus exercises.

"These will help when you are in any given situation. Just take things slow, but you need to push your boundaries a little."

"Like how?"

"Get out of the house more. Go spend time with your friend. Even if it's just for an hour or two. Then slowly build up to more."

"I think I can do that."

3

That night, Ali lay in bed, her mind busy playing over the conversation she'd had with Jeff. She was nervous about going to sleep, but with the help of his breathing exercises, she fell asleep before she'd even realized it.

At first, the dream was hazy. She was in a forest again, but it was different. More like the dreams she'd had when she was young. Vague impressions and hazy images seemed to float through her mind...and then a voice. A different voice, one she recognized but couldn't place. His words were indiscernible, but she knew instinctively to run. She needed to get away from him.

She ran for her life, her heart pounding, her breath rushing from her lungs as she made it through a blurred landscape.

"*Alessandra*," she heard faintly, and that voice she instantly recognized. Her heart thumped frantically as she skidded to a stop.

Suddenly, vibrant colors filled her vision, and everything came into sharp focus. A chill ran up her spine. She could feel the eyes on her. Whoever or whatever followed her was close. As she slowly turned, careful not to make any sudden movements, she froze.

Not twenty feet away stood a massive black jaguar. The frightening but beautiful creature stared straight at her, its glowing, iridescent green eyes watching her carefully.

Ali tried to back away, but with every step she took, the enormous cat drew closer. Its long strides quickly ate up the distance between them.

Panic rose in her belly, but before she could turn to run, she lost her footing. Ali stumbled backward, her ass hitting the ground with a jarring thump.

It took her a moment to focus, but when she finally oriented herself, she recognized her surroundings. Instead of the dark forest rising around her, Ali found her dimly lit bedroom. She lay sprawled on the floor with sweat-soaked sheets tangled around her legs.

Standing in the doorway across from her was the man she'd seen lying so comfortably in her bed a few nights ago. With a pounding headache, and her heart racing like mad, Ali closed her eyes and forced herself to draw slow, steady breaths.

She was still dreaming. She had to be. And if she woke, she could prove that all of this was just in her head and none of it was real.

The low, purring, male voice came again. *"Alessandra."*

Squeezing her eyes tighter, she whispered to herself. "You're dreaming. It's just another dream. You're gonna wake any minute. Just a dream. Just a dream."

When she opened her eyes again, she sat next to her

bed with her sheets twisted around her. The stillness of the night felt eerie, but Ali untangled herself from the covers and eased quietly from the hard floor. On shaky legs, she moved to the doorway, and with her heart still beating at a frantic pace, she peeked into the main living space.

Relieved to find nothing out of the ordinary, she made her way to the fridge and grabbed a juice. Her throat and mouth were always so dry just after waking from one of her vivid dreams.

She drank deeply, downing half the bottle before turning to lean against the counter with a heavy sigh. What the hell was going on with her brain? Who was this guy and why was she suddenly dreaming of him?

But she knew his name, didn't she. Nico. She'd called him Nico in her dream before.

Her senses tingled. A subtle scent hung in the air, one that didn't belong in her space. Whatever it was, it smelled incredible. When the breeze shifted, she realized the scent blew in from the open window. Looking at the alley below, she wondered where it came from and why it seemed so familiar. It was better than any cologne she'd ever smelled, and she stood there breathing it in, taking it deep into her lungs.

Giving herself a shake, she finished off the juice and decided to give Maggie a call. It was late, but knowing her friend, she was either working tirelessly on her newest project or working on last-minute details for the upcoming party.

Feeling a bit stiff, Ali went into the bathroom and cranked on the faucets. She could relax in the bath while she chatted with her friend. No way was she getting more sleep. She might as well do something to relax. She even dropped in a homemade bath bomb that Deanna gave her last Christmas.

While she waited for the tub to fill, she grabbed the phone off her desk and made the call.

Maggie answered on the second ring. "Hey girl."

"Hey." Ali leaned against the doorway. "I know it's late, but are you busy?"

"Not terribly. Everything okay?"

Ali could hear the hint of concern in her friend's voice. "Yeah. I'm good. Just strange dreams."

Maggie was quiet for a moment before she asked. "Different from the others?"

"I don't know. Kind of. I mean, some scare the hell out of me, but others…" She trailed off, not knowing what to say. The ones of the dark-skinned guy standing in her doorway were a bit unnerving, but the ones where he lay sprawled naked across her bed weren't unwelcome. Those were nice.

Maggie chuckled. "Others, what? Dirty dreams?"

With a slight smile, Ali laughed. "Not exactly."

She heard shifting papers and the creak of Maggie's desk chair. "Girl, you better tell me all the juicy details right now."

Ali fought back another laugh. Maggie never insisted she talk about her dreams. Most of the time Ali did anyway. Eventually. This time was different though. Ali could hear the curiosity in her friend's voice.

"Come on. You gotta tell me. That's why you called, right?"

"Yeah." Glancing into the bathroom, she saw the water level was about where she wanted it. "Give me a second."

"Okay." Maggie sighed but waited patiently.

Ali shut the water off and hit the speaker button. "How's this?"

"Good."

Setting the phone on the lip of the tub, Ali wiggled out of her sleep shorts and tossed her worn out old t-shirt on top of them. She stepped into the steaming water and groaned as she sank into the bath. "Man, this feels amazing."

Maggie chuckled. "Come on. Don't leave me hanging over here. Tell me about this dream."

Ali lay her head back and sighed. "I don't even know where to start."

"The beginning would be nice."

Ali closed her eyes and told her friend all about the dream from a few nights ago. "And his voice. It's so familiar to me, but I know I've never heard it before these dreams started. It's like I know him. But I don't. If that makes any sense at all."

Maggie made a curious sound.

"And tonight, I saw his face so clearly. He stood in my bedroom, saying my name in that velvety, seductive voice of his. The last part of the dream was so vivid, I wasn't sure if I was still asleep or if he was really standing in my doorway."

"Did you check to be sure no one was there?" Maggie asked, her tone heavy with worry. "I told you about leaving your windows open at night."

"Of course, I checked. I guess I just wasn't fully awake yet." Ali was quiet for a moment before she admitted, "I know this sounds weird, especially coming from me, but I kind of wish he'd really been here."

As the silence stretched between them, Ali listened to

the slow drip of the faucet and watched the ripples spread across the water's surface.

Eventually, Maggie cleared her throat. "So, what do you have planned for this weekend? Any writing?"

"I don't know. Maybe. I was thinking about coming to your party tonight."

"Really?" Maggie all but shouted, unable to contain her shock and excitement.

Ali winced, hoping she made the right decision. Jeff was right. She needed to step outside her comfort zone. She couldn't spend the rest of her life afraid of what might happen. She had to take chances if she had any hope of living a normal, happy life. But that didn't mean she wasn't scared shitless.

"What made you change your mind?"

Ali hesitated, wondering how her friend would react. But why was she worried? Maggie tried many times to convince Ali that talking to a professional would help her tremendously. Of course she would be relieved.

"I finally called that therapist Dr. Stevens told me about. And I met with him this morning."

"Oh, wow."

"Yeah. Shocking, right." Ali laughed at her friend's stunned tone.

"How'd that go?"

"It was nothing like I expected. I don't know why I put it off for so long. He actually gave me some helpful tips on how to get through my meltdowns a little easier."

"That's great, sweetie."

"We already set up another session for next week," Ali added. "But let's talk about this party. Is it just going to be your college friends?"

Maggie hesitated a beat before she reluctantly admitted, "Not exactly."

Great. "Lots of people?"

"Yes, but it'll be okay. You'll have fun. And if it gets to be too much for you, we can go upstairs and relax for a while."

Ali wasn't convinced, but she wasn't backing out now. "Okay."

"Awesome! You can come early, and we can get ready together."

"I'm not sure I have anything to wear."

Maggie scoffed. "I've got you covered. I have plenty of party dresses."

That, she did. Maggie loved to entertain, and her massive closet proved it.

Part of her regretted the decision to go, but even if she changed her mind, Ali couldn't back out now. Maggie would be so disappointed.

WHILE ALI LOUNGED in the bath and chatted with her friend, Nicolai snagged the little purple address book off the corner of the desk near the window. Surely, she had her friend's address written in it.

Nicolai thumbed through it and found a Margaret (Maggie) Driskal located on a military base in Alaska. With no talk of flights, Nicolai knew that wasn't the right one. He continued flipping through the pages, hoping to find a local address. And he found it in the "J" section. Maggie Jennings, 2116 Clayton Boulevard. Right there in town.

Nicolai spent the rest of the day pacing his cramped hotel room, trying his hardest not to reach out to Alessandra through their mental connection. He was determined their next contact would be face-to-face, but he worried about her reaction. It hadn't gone so well in her apartment, but how would she react to his presence when she knew for certain she was awake?

According to Maggie, the party was going to be huge. And Alessandra didn't sound overly enthused about that fact. Nicolai, on the other hand, was thrilled. The bigger the party, the bigger his chance of sneaking in unnoticed. He only hoped Maggie wasn't greeting people at the door. Surely with a house that size, she must have someone to handle that task while she enjoyed her guests.

Nicolai felt a bit relieved when he saw the number of cars lining the driveway leading up to the enormous house. With people still arriving, he hoped slipping in wouldn't be a problem.

All the guests were decked out in elegant dresses and nice suits. Nicolai was glad he'd thought to wear his best suit, one he'd bought from a sweet elderly woman at a little shop in southern Italy.

When the driver came to a stop in front, Nicolai thanked him and climbed the marble steps with his heart in his throat. He could barely contain his excitement. He would get to see Alessandra again in a matter of minutes. Only this time, he would get to talk to her.

Taking a deep breath, he rang the doorbell and took a step back.

An older woman opened the door with a warm smile. "Good evening."

Nicolai returned the greeting with a gentlemanly nod.

"Everyone is in the library. It's straight back and to the left."

"Thank you," he said politely and headed that way.

A plethora of scents filled the home, but Alessandra's sweet honeysuckle fragrance found him and drew him toward the stairs. She hadn't joined the party yet. His instinct demanded he go to her, but he fought the impulse and continued down the hall.

He entered through the library's double doors and casually surveyed the room. People gathered in groups, filling the grand space with chatters and laughter. Beyond the bodies, shelves covered every inch of available wall space. A grand piano sat to one side of the oversized French doors and a bar on the other.

Nicolai didn't often drink, and that night was no different. He wanted a clear mind for his first interaction with his mate, so he committed to the corner by the floor-to-ceiling windows nestled between two tall shelves.

Curious, his gaze drifted over the books, finding many old leatherbound first editions and obscure reads. Most were in excellent condition, likely handed down for generations, but others appeared quite fragile, as if they might crumble were they so much as breathed on.

"Hey."

Nicolai turned to greet who had spoken and the guy offered his hand.

"I don't think we've met. I'm Greg."

"Nicolai." He answered and they exchanged a firm handshake.

"How do you know Maggie?"

Nicolai thought of the only truth he could come up

with. "Through Ali," he said, using the name Maggie had called her.

"Ali?" The guy's eyes widened. "How do you know Ali?"

Unable to hold back a smile, he answered, "I was in her building."

"Is she your date tonight?" When Nicolai shook his head, Greg's shoulders visibly relaxed. "Maggie's been trying to set us up for over a year, but she never shows. I was beginning to think she wasn't real. I'm glad she's here tonight though. I can't wait to meet her."

Not liking Greg's interest in his woman, Nicolai forced a calming breath.

Greg looked around. "You seen Maggie yet?"

Nicolai shook his head. He wouldn't know if he had.

"They'll probably make an entrance. You know Maggie," Greg chuckled.

Nicolai turned back toward the window, watching the gathering in the reflection while he patiently awaited Alessandra's appearance. What would she look like in a dress? Far better than the other women in the room, no doubt, but he couldn't wait to see her.

Beside him, Greg muttered under his breath. "Holy shit!"

The expression on his face had Nicolai turning to see what had the guy so dumbfounded. The moment he saw her, he nearly lost his breath. There she was. His Alessandra. She walked through the double doors, her arm linked with the arm of a tall brunette woman. He saw the other woman, but his focus was on Alessandra.

His mate looked incredible. The black and gold dress hugged her graceful figure lovingly. His gaze drifted over her, drawn to the smooth skin of her neck and arms. He longed to run his fingertips over the tempting expanse, but that would have to wait.

"Is that Ali?" Greg asked, his awe clear in his voice.

Without looking away from her, Nicolai made a vague sound of assent.

"Excuse me, man." The guy was gone before Nicolai could respond.

He stood motionless as Greg approach the two women. Though his protective instincts kicked in, Nicolai pushed them down and watched Alessandra's face as she noticed all the curious eyes turn her direction.

Her wide honey eyes surveyed the room, and even from so far away, he could see her nervousness. The urge to go to her overwhelmed him, but Nicolai knew she wasn't ready for that yet. Instead, he slipped through the French doors and into the shadows on the patio. Soon. They would meet soon.

4

By the time Ali worked up enough nerve to join the party, the library was packed. Well, packed by her standards. She looked around, feeling overwhelmed and awkward with so many eyes on her. There must be at least fifty people in the room, but she drew on Maggie's energy and let her friend lead her forward.

Thankfully, Maggie didn't say more than a quick hello to people as she passed by them. Instead, she had a specific destination in mind. Ali felt a bit of unease creep in when she saw the tall, athletic guy making his way through the crowd, heading straight for them.

He greeted Maggie with a hard hug and a kiss on the cheek. Even as socially awkward as Ali felt, she was oddly good at reading people and picking up on subtle nuances. This guy cared a lot about Maggie, but the way his intense chocolate eyes strayed to Ali showed undeniable curiosity.

"I'm Greg. You must be Ali." He offered her a crooked little grin but not his hand.

Grateful, Ali gave him a small smile. "It's nice to meet you."

He shoved his hands into his pockets. "Glad you came. I was beginning to think Maggie made you up."

"No. I just don't get out much."

"Well, I hope you enjoy yourself tonight." He leaned in and mock whispered, "You know how Mags is. She can go a little overboard on these things."

"So," Maggie said overly loud. "Greg, how's your family?"

He smirked and gave Ali a wink before answering Maggie. "They're good. Georgia got married last month on a whim, and the folks are getting ready to take a vacation to Hawaii."

As they fell into conversation, Ali felt a measure of relief. With Greg's focus on Maggie, she took her time studying him. Why Maggie thought setting her up with him was such a brilliant idea, she hadn't a clue. She had to admit, he was attractive, but not at all her type. Not that she had a type. She hadn't exactly dated anyone before.

Feeling bad for staring, Ali turned her focus elsewhere. She took in the rest of the room, glancing at the people near her, smiling politely at those who made eye contact. Honestly, being around so many people wasn't as bad as she'd expected. Still, she had her limits.

Taking a breath, she focused beyond the people, to the bookshelves she could see over their heads. It was her favorite room in the house when only she and Maggie occupied it. Those were the days they relaxed on the over-stuffed sofa with a cup of tea in one hand and a good book in the other.

Maggie linked arms with her again. "Come meet some of my other college friends."

Ali let her guide her toward a lively group near the bar. To Ali's surprise, Greg settled on her opposite side. He never once touched her, but the way he moved around the room, he acted as a buffer between her and everyone else. It was nice to have someone understand her aversions and not draw attention to them.

She gladly stayed between Maggie and Greg while she struggled through introductions. Once focus shifted from her, Ali managed to relax a bit. Everyone seemed nice, but the constant chatter soon grew to be too much.

With everyone's focus elsewhere, Ali slipped away, making her way to the piano in the corner. She admired its beauty and ran her hand slowly along the edge as she circled around to the bench. She wanted to play, but she was too shy to do it in a room filled with people.

What had she been thinking coming to this party? She didn't like being around people. Especially so many. Looking around the room, Ali couldn't shake the feeling that everyone was staring at her. They weren't, of course, but panic reared its ugly head anyway.

She tried to take Jeff's advice and find something else to focus on. But she didn't want to be around others if the breathing trick didn't work to derail the coming panic attack.

Ali glanced at Maggie, who was in full conversation. She didn't want to interrupt, so she took advantage of the clear path to the French doors and slipped outside. The moment she stepped onto the massive patio, she took a deep breath and felt instant relief.

She slowly drew the fragrant air into her lungs and

enjoyed the calming effect it had on her. Something about being outside, away from the prying eyes of Maggie's friends, soothed her. Her friend meant well, trying to drag her out of her shell, but Ali should have started smaller.

Tuning out the muffled chatter coming from just inside, Ali let her gaze drift over the lush garden. It was a sanctuary filled with flowers in every imaginable color. And the towering trees lining the perimeter sometimes made her forget the property was nestled into the middle of a neighborhood.

Ali loved the outdoors. It eased her nerves and calmed her like nothing else could. She could spend hours among the plants, enjoying the quiet away from the overwhelming human presence. There was no pressure to carry on conversation. No awkward attempts at socializing. Nobody giving her funny looks or feeling sorry for her. Just her enjoying nature.

Ali took another deep breath and when the wind shifted, it brought with it a new scent. An oddly familiar, masculine scent that she couldn't place. Then she saw him. A breathtaking man stood on the opposite side of the patio, the full moon shining down on him like a pale spotlight. Had he been there the entire time?

He looked deep in thought as he stared out across the garden below. With his shoulder-length hair pulled back from his face, and the moonlight accenting his gorgeous features, Ali studied the perfection of his profile. His sharply angled cheekbones, his strong jaw, and his full bottom lip. Flawless.

As if feeling her stare, he turned and looked directly at her. Ali's breath left her in a rush. It was him. Nico, the man from her dreams. He looked different with his hair tamed and clothes covering his glorious body, but she would know those sea-green eyes anywhere.

Her thoughts ran wild. How was it possible? How was he standing there? Had she finally lost her mind or had the last sixteen hours been one long, vivid dream? Would she wake soon to find herself alone in her bed, tangled in the sheets and sweat coating her body? Or had her dreams been something more? Had they been premonitions?

Deep down, Ali wanted it to be true. The idea of him lounging naked on her rumpled covers overwhelmed her, but the undeniable intimacy between them and the way he said her name with such devotion was inspiring. She wanted that to be what the future held for her. For them. But that would never happen if she couldn't even force herself to talk to him.

She didn't have the guts to speak up first, and just the idea of talking to him made her feel nauseous. She couldn't do it. She wasn't that brave. Besides, other than a polite hello, what would she say? Conversation wasn't exactly a strong point on a normal day, but she didn't know how she'd manage to form coherent words with him staring at her with such intensity.

Overwhelmed, Ali turned her focus back to the garden, but it wasn't enough. She needed space. Stepping off the patio, she followed the stone path that wound through the garden. And when she reached the first bend, she glanced over her shoulder. Part of her expected to see the patio empty and that she'd imagined the man there.

But no. He was real. And a peculiar sensation bloomed beneath her skin at just the sight of him. Like heat and wind rushing below the surface, sweeping through every cell in her body. It stole her breath, and she didn't know how to react. It felt much like the onset of her panic attacks, yet strangely pleasant.

Light-headed, Ali reached out for balance, placing her palm on the waist-high retaining wall edging the walkway.

The gorgeous man studied her with rapt curiosity. And when he stepped off the patio, Ali watched, fascinated, as he strode toward her with calm, graceful movements.

Giving herself a shake, Ali eased further down the path, trying to keep distance between them. But as she reached the next bend in the trail, she turned to see if he still followed, and her heart leapt. He was nearly upon her, and she couldn't take her eyes off him as he stalked forward with such confidence and determination.

He was even more gorgeous up close. Impossibly so. What was a guy like him doing following someone like her? Of all the women at the party, why was he so fascinated by her? Ali knew she should be terrified that a strange man followed her into the dark garden. Yet, she only felt excitement mixed with a hint of arousal stirring in her belly.

What the hell was wrong with her? She was the girl that couldn't stand people looking at her for more than a few seconds. Why was this guy different?

"Ali?"

Startled, she looked toward the distant sound of Maggie's voice. She stood on the patio, backlit by the dim glow emanating from the massive glass doors behind her. Maggie couldn't see them from where she stood, so Ali stayed quiet. Her interest in the mysterious guy in front of her overrode her need to check in with her friend, even though she knew Maggie would be worried.

The guy took Ali's hand, his warm, calloused fingers

encompassing hers. With unexpected gentleness, he led her into the shadows beneath the massive oak trees just off the path.

A peculiar feeling raced through Ali when he turned to face her again. Her head felt light, her breathing grew heavier, a buzzing rose in her ears, and a flush spread throughout her entire body.

A pulsing sound rose in the back of her throat, and though it startled her, she couldn't stop it. If she didn't know better, she'd swear she was purring.

The moment he heard the sound, his mesmerizing eyes widened. He shifted his weight, and with a slight tilt of his head, he leaned closer, his nostrils flaring as he drew in her scent. He opened his mouth, as if to speak, but something behind her drew his attention.

Ali followed his gaze and felt heat flood her face. Maggie was about to catch her sneaking around with some strange guy in the dark. She felt like a teenager, knowing her friend wouldn't approve of such reckless behavior. Or mayhap she would. Who knew?

Maggie rounded the bend, worry clear in her expression as she approached Ali's cozy little corner of the garden.

Ali turned back to the gorgeous stranger when he dropped her hand and stepped away. He hesitated, his expression full of regret, before he strode quickly back the way they'd come.

When she finally spotted Ali, Maggie called out to her. "Girl, what are you doing out here?"

Ali took a deep breath and looked around. "Enjoying the quiet."

"Are you okay?"

Ali forced a smile. "Yeah. I'm good."

"I'm sorry. This wasn't a great idea, was it?"

"No, it's fine. I just needed a few minutes alone." She threaded her arm in Maggie's and turned toward the house again. "Come on. Let's go back inside."

She hesitated, concern written all over her face. But she let Ali lead her back up the path.

They rejoined the party, sidling up next to Greg and a group of guys whose names Ali couldn't recall. One spoke loud and with exaggerated hand gestures. So immersed in telling his story, he barely noticed when Maggie and Ali joined them.

Ali pretended to listen, but her attention shifted around the room, searching the crowd for the one man she wanted to talk to. She felt like an idiot for staring at him and not speaking. How hard is it to just say hi to someone? What the hell was wrong with her? Aside from the obvious.

She hoped it wasn't too late to make a better impression. Maybe she could get Maggie to properly introduce them. That might be a little less awkward than their encounter in the garden.

Greg bumped her elbow lightly with his, drawing her attention. A small smile tugged at the corner of his mouth. "Are you enjoying yourself?"

Ali shrugged. "More than I expected to, honestly."

"Where'd your friend, Nicolai, run off to?"

Confused, she stared up at him. She barely had time to form the question when Maggie cut in. "Who's Nicolai?"

Greg gave her a perplexed look. "You know. Ali's friend with the accent."

Maggie shook her head.

"About my height, dark hair, unusually bright green eyes."

Yes. Ali knew who he meant, but what gave Greg the impression the guy was her friend? Had he witnessed their bizarre encounter? Even though nothing happened, she imagined it looked much more intimate than it had been. Especially with him holding her hand and gazing at her with such intensity.

Maggie raised a single brow at her. "Since when do you have a guy friend?"

Feeling heat flare in her face, Ali glanced between Maggie and Greg.

Maggie watched her carefully, something shifting in her expression. "I'll let this go for now, but we are definitely talking about this later."

Ali nodded, grateful her friend didn't make a big deal about it in front of everyone else, but she didn't look forward to that chat.

Over the next few hours, Ali tried to enjoy herself, despite having so many people in such tight proximity. Conversation flowed around her, but she quietly observed Maggie's other friends and how they interacted.

One guy, Derek, managed to get Ali talking. Sort of. He asked her where she was from. What did she do for a living? How did she know Maggie? Standard questions, but they felt invasive. Ali didn't like sharing much about herself with anyone. Especially people she just met.

Maggie was the only exception. She knew everything about Ali. All her quirks and anxiety issues. She even knew about her family history. Or lack thereof.

Still, she forced herself out of her comfort zone and

answered Derek's questions. Even if they were short vague responses.

She'd never been great at carrying conversation, so Ali felt grateful when Maggie filled in more details when the conversation lagged. Eventually, Derek got bored. But Ali wasn't offended when he shifted his attention elsewhere. She gladly turned her focus back to the main conversation.

Greg sat at the end of the sofa with Maggie perched on the arm beside him. Her foot swung slowly back and forth as she chatted and laughed with the others.

Ali stood quietly observing them all, envying their carefree nature. She wanted to be more like everyone else, but she knew it would take a long time to gain that level of comfort herself.

By the time midnight rolled around, only Maggie's college buddies and a handful of local friends remained. Though the crowd had thinned, Ali was beyond ready to go upstairs and be alone for a while.

Maggie, observant as always, leaned in and whispered next to her ear. "You want to call it a night?"

"Yeah. I think I'm gonna head upstairs." When her friend's expression shifted to worry, Ali assured her. "I'm fine. Really. Just gonna soak in that incredible tub of yours and relax for a bit. Don't feel like you have to shut down the party or anything."

Maggie studied her for a moment and nodded. "I'll be up to check on you in a little while."

"No rush. Enjoy your time with your friends. You only see them a couple times a year."

"Maybe we can watch a movie later. I mean, after I make sure everyone has a ride home and the rest of these guys get settled into their rooms."

Ali smiled. "Sounds good."

Greg shifted on the sofa. "You want me to walk you up?"

"Thanks, but I'm good." Ali appreciated the offer, and she knew he was only being polite. Still, she didn't want to give him the wrong idea. Besides, she wasn't interested in company. She just wanted to be alone for a while.

Ali said goodnight and made her way upstairs to her second favorite room in the house. Her tension eased the moment she shut the door. The bright, airy décor always calmed her. The pale blue walls reminded her of the summer sky, and the fluffy white bedding so plush you'd swear it was made of clouds.

She would climb into the lush comfort soon enough. But first, she wanted to soak in the giant jetted tub and decompress while Maggie entertained her remaining party guests. She'd give Ali plenty of time to unwind. But getting around the inevitable conversation about her secret guy friend? Impossible.

Ali hoped it would wait until morning, but she knew better. Maggie would be upstairs well before the sun came up, so Ali needed to take advantage of every second she had alone. Starting with a relaxing bath.

Ali cranked on the faucet, and while the tub filled, she gathered everything she needed. Towels were in the cabinet behind the door, along with a vast selection of soaps, salts, oils, lotions, and shampoos.

Maggie thought of everything to make her guests comfortable and then some. It was like being in a lavish spa. The towels were fluffier, the scents richer, and she kept a fresh robe hanging by the door. After a night at her friend's house, Ali always felt revitalized. Why didn't she visit more often?

Setting her choice of products on the ledge beside the deep bath, she dipped a foot into the steaming tub, testing the temperature. Perfect.

After shutting off the tap, she slipped out of her borrowed dress and hung it on the hook by the door. She climbed into the tub and sank into the water up to her neck, letting the warmth envelop her. Hopefully, she could clear her mind and let the tension seep from her tight muscles.

The bath was exactly what Ali needed, and she stayed in the tub until her fingertips resembled prunes. Despite her best efforts, her thoughts kept returning to the odd interaction with Nico. Or did he prefer Nicolai?

Once she dried off and wrapped herself in the lush robe, Ali hit play on her mellow time playlist and sat cross-legged on the king-size bed. By the time a soft knock broke through the relative quiet of the room, Ali felt ready to curl up and go to sleep. Instead, she drew a deep breath and called out, "Come in."

Maggie eased the door open, a faint smile making an appearance. "I wasn't sure if you were still awake. It took a little longer getting things situated than I thought."

"You know me. I rarely sleep anyway."

Maggie stood in the doorway. "You still up for hanging out for a little while? I'm not feeling much like going to bed yet."

"Restless?"

"Yeah. It usually takes me a bit to wind down after these things."

Ali patted the bed. "Come sit."

Maggie settled on the edge, one leg tucked beneath her and the other slowly swinging back and forth. "I know some of the guys can be a bit much, but did you have fun at all?"

"Surprisingly, yes." Other than a few awkward moments, it hadn't been terrible. Ali really did enjoy listening to everyone's stories and watching them all interact. "Everybody seemed nice."

"I told you they were great."

Ali hadn't been worried so much about everybody else. She was more nervous about getting overwhelmed and having a full-blown meltdown in front of a bunch of people she'd just met.

"Hey, what's this?" Maggie reached over and ran a finger over the quarter-inch mark on the ball of Ali's foot at the base of the middle toe. "I didn't know you had a tattoo."

The feather-light touch made Ali's foot flex involuntarily. "It's been there for as long as I can remember."

"Hmm." Maggie hummed thoughtfully. "From your previous life, you think?"

Ali shrugged. "Probably. I just don't know what kind of person tattoos a baby's foot."

"You ever thought about getting it removed?"

"Not really." Ali studied the familiar blue-black symbol, rubbing her thumb over it like she'd done countless times throughout her lifetime. "I've had it this long. Why get rid of it now? Besides, it's on the bottom of my foot. How many people are gonna see it?"

Maggie nodded thoughtfully. "True. I just wonder what it means."

Ali shifted her position, stretching her legs out. "Who knows."

"Speaking of mysteries, can we talk about this Nicolai guy?"

Ali snorted. "Like I have a choice."

Maggie gave her a chiding look. "You know I have a million questions, but I'm not going to drill you."

Somehow Ali doubted that. With Maggie's overprotective nature, and Nico as an unknown, the questions were coming whether she wanted to answer them or not. Ali figured she might as well get the conversation over with.

Maggie must have seen her resolve, because she scooted to the center of the bed and settled in like she expected juicy details. She couldn't wait to learn more about the mystery guy. Or the light in her eyes could have just been the result of all the wine she'd drank.

Ali took a deep breath and let it out slowly, hoping her friend didn't think she'd finally gone off the deep end. "I know this is going to sound bizarre, but you know those recent dreams I've had about that gorgeous guy in my apartment?"

"Yeah."

"Well, it was him. Nicolai is the guy from my dreams."

Maggie stared mutely at her, a blank look on her face.

"While it's a relief to get a break from the nightmares, I was a bit shaken up when I saw him here tonight. I don't know what to think or what the hell is going on, but it's the same guy for sure."

After a painful stretch of silence, Maggie gave her head a shake. "Wait. What do you mean? You didn't invite him here?"

"No. When I first saw him tonight, I just assumed he was one of your friends."

Her brows furrowed. "Greg said he was your friend."

"I know. But before tonight, the only place I've seen him is in my dreams."

When Maggie's gaze shifted to the comforter between them, her thoughts clearly chaotic, Ali's unease grew even more.

"Look, Maggie. I know I'm not normal, but this? This is crazy, right? I feel like I'm losing my mind. This can't be possible."

Maggie's gaze jumped to hers again, and she reached for Ali's hand. "Sweetie, I don't think you're crazy."

Ali believed her. Maggie had always been supportive and didn't treat her like a freak, even though Ali felt like one sometimes.

"I'm sure there's an explanation for this. I mean, you could have seen him before. Like at the store. Or on the street somewhere."

"Then how would I know his name? Explain how I've never talked to him, but I know his voice and his accent and every inch of his body like we've been together for years."

Ali could almost see the gears turning in Maggie's mind. And then she asked something Ali didn't expect. "Are you clairvoyant?"

"I don't know." Was she? She'd had strange dreams for as long as she could remember, but she couldn't recall a time when she'd seen something before it happened. Aside from the nightmares, most of her dreams felt more like hazy memories from another life. Not visions of the future. Until Nico.

Maggie leaned back on her arms. "So, now what?"

Ali frowned. "What do you mean?"

"Are you going to see him again?"

"I hope so. I just don't know how."

5

Oddly enough, the rest of the weekend passed without incident. Well, anxiety was plentiful, but no nightmares and no dreams of Nico. No dreams at all. She had a hard time going to sleep, and how frustrating was that? The one time she wanted to get sucked into dream land, her racing thoughts wouldn't allow it.

What the hell was she supposed to do? She couldn't just wait and hope he showed up again. Except, she had no idea how to find him. Maggie didn't know him. Neither did any of her friends.

Who was Nico and where had he come from? Why hadn't she just opened her mouth and spoken to him while he stood right in front of her? Any normal person would have at least said hi to him. Instead, the two of them had stared intensely at each other and played a slow, silent game of chase.

How bizarre to have a strange man stalking her through the dark garden without Ali launching into a full-blown panic attack. Instead of freaking out, she'd felt uncharacteristically calm throughout the whole ordeal.

She didn't understand why she felt such a strong draw to be near him, but she couldn't deny it. Something about him called to her. The attraction. The tingling in her mind. The heat radiating throughout her body. All of it should have frightened her, but it didn't.

Instead, she just felt frustrated because Maggie had interrupted and scared him off. She couldn't be mad at her friend for caring, but she needed to understand how and why Nico had just stepped out of her dreams and into her life.

Ali had the presence of mind to know the moment she spiraled into obsession. She had to get a hold on her curiosity before it grew out of control and became habit just like everything else. She couldn't let Nico be her latest on the lengthy list of fixations. She had to do something.

Ali shot Jeff a text and asked if they could meet up sooner than they'd planned.

He replied immediately. *My eleven o'clock canceled for today. Is that time good for you?*

Ali glanced at the clock. Five hours away. Could she wait that long?

Or we could go for coffee again if you'd prefer. My first appointment isn't until nine.

Ali agreed to meet him at the café in fifteen minutes. She rushed into the bathroom, brushed her teeth, and made a haphazard attempt at yanking her hair into a ponytail. She knew she looked a mess, but she didn't care. She needed to talk about her latest dilemma and get some unbiased advice. Professional advice.

By the time Ali got to the café, Jeff had already

arrived. He sat at the same table as before and Dee stood beside him, chatting about the weather as Ali slid into the chair across from him.

The friendly waitress turned to her. "Morning. What can I get you, hun?"

"Peppermint tea would be great."

"You got it."

Before she could walk away, Ali spoke up. "Actually, could you make that chamomile instead?"

"Sure can."

Ali waited until the woman was out of earshot before she turned to Jeff. "Thank you for meeting with me. I know it's last minute, but I need your advice."

He offered her a warm smile. "It really wasn't a problem. What did you want to talk about?"

"Well, I thought about what you said last time. And I went to Maggie's party."

"That's great." Jeff sounded genuinely proud of her. "I know it was a huge move for you. But stepping out of your comfort zone can be good."

Ali agreed. She was glad she'd gone, but for more reasons than simply pushing her limits. Sure, she wanted to function like a normal person. Seeing Nico again and figuring out what the hell was happening would be nice too.

"How was the party?"

"Not the worst experience of my life, but after a few hours, I got overwhelmed and went upstairs."

Jeff nodded. "Taking a break is good."

Ali agreed. "It helped a lot."

"How are your dreams? Any changes there?"

"They've sort of shifted."

"What do you mean?"

Ali hesitated, unsure just how much she should tell him, but she settled for giving him a brief recap on her dreams of Nicolai. "I don't know who he is, but I can't stop thinking about him and how real the dreams felt."

"It's normal to cling to pleasant dreams when you've been plagued by nightmares for so long. Savor it, but don't let it become another obsession. Think of it as a sign that things are getting better for you. Your subconscious can heavily impact every area of your life. Including your dreams."

He looked thoughtful for a long moment, his eyes drifting toward the window when a stiff breeze shook the trees lining the sidewalk outside.

"After what you told me about your experience at the party, I believe the change of scenery helped you grow a bit more comfortable with being around others. But I feel like you may have jumped the gun a little."

Ali agreed. But she couldn't regret it. Not after the encounter with him. With Nicolai.

"I wonder if some time away would do you some good."

Ali stiffened, her breath freezing in her throat. This is what she'd been afraid of. Talking led to concern. And concern led to "suggesting" a long stay in a place with bars on the windows.

Jeff must have seen the panic in her eyes because he quickly explained. "I only meant to suggest a vacation. Somewhere surrounded by nature. I think the fresh air will do you good."

Ali's shoulders eased a fraction.

"It will get you out of your stagnant routine and give

you a chance to recharge. And I know the perfect place. My aunt owns a bunch of cabins up in the Ozarks that she rents to vacationers. It's beautiful up there this time of year. If you're interested, I could give her a call and see if she has any availabilities."

Honestly, that sounded fantastic.

ALI ARRIVED JUST AFTER NOON. In the center of a small clearing sat a modest one-story cabin. It had an old tin roof, and the porch ran the full length of the front.

As she parked next to the worn-out blue pickup truck, Jeff descended the front steps. He greeted her as she got out of the car. "How was your drive up?"

"Once I got outside of town, it was nice. Peaceful."

He lifted an armful of firewood from the back of his truck. "Come on in and have a look around."

She followed him inside, her eyes instantly drawn to the fireplace across the large room. Judging by the rustic exterior, she expected a wood-burning stove tucked in the corner. Not the floor-to-ceiling stone face with the chunky mahogany mantle.

Not a touch of country décor anywhere in sight. No deer heads adorned the walls and no bearskin rugs lay in front of the fireplace. Instead, a cozy suede couch sat on one side and two matching chairs on the other. In the middle of the seating area, a simple coffee table sat on a charcoal gray handwoven rug.

Off to the right, an equally beautiful kitchen with dark cabinets, a cast-iron sink, and ample counterspace. A table just big enough to comfortably seat four people separated the kitchen and living room. The open floorplan was great for pacing if Ali needed it, but she suspected her panic attacks would be minimal during her stay.

Jeff glanced over and grinned. "Nice, right?"

"Yeah. My friend Maggie would love it here."

"Aunt Lucy bought up a dozen of these places about ten years ago and completely renovated them. And between the cabin rentals and her husband's real estate company, they are sitting pretty."

"I can imagine."

Jeff finished stacking the wood in the cutout beside the fireplace. "This time of year, it can get cold up here at night, so it's good to have plenty of wood in case the electricity goes out. There are also candles and matches in the black box on the mantle."

Ali nodded. "Thanks."

"The bedroom and bathroom are back there." Jeff indicated the narrow hallway. "Aunt Lucy came up this morning and put fresh sheets on the bed. And there are extra blankets and towels in the hall closet."

"Thank you. I really appreciate everything."

"The key is on the counter in case you decide to run into town or go exploring. But don't wander too far at night. It's easy to get turned around out there after dark."

Beyond sitting on the porch, she didn't plan on going out at night.

Jeff glanced at his watch. "I need to get going. I'm meeting up with a friend in town. If you need anything else, you have my number, and Aunt Lucy's is on the fridge along with the local emergency numbers. Cell signals are hit and miss out this far, so you can use the landline if necessary. It's on the table over there."

Ali looked the direction he indicated, noting the phone perched atop the vintage half-circle table against the far wall.

Once they said their goodbyes, Ali watched Jeff drive away. Standing on the porch, she looked around the yard as the rumble of his truck slowly faded into the distance.

She should've grabbed her bag from the car and settled in. Instead, she sat in the oversized rocker, enjoying the fresh mountain air and the soothing sounds of the forest. She liked her little cozy apartment in the city, but at the cabin, she didn't have to worry about people intruding on her solitude. According to Jeff, there was no one around for miles. Such a relief.

Eventually, Ali brought her things inside and put them away. The bedroom was nothing fancy, but the bathroom was something out of a dream. If she didn't have plans to explore the outdoors, the highbacked clawfoot tub would be the ideal place to hole up for the weekend. With the massive bay window overlooking the small meadow behind the cabin, it could easily be her new favorite sanctuary.

Instead of letting herself get sucked into yet another comfortable convenience, Ali broke the cycle and decided to go exploring.

She took a walk down the dirt road, heading back in the direction of town. Half a mile down the winding drive, she came across a narrow trail that led into the dense forest. But she kept going.

Ali ambled along the road, kicking at loose rocks along the way. She enjoyed being so far away from civilization. Her stress levels decreased the moment she left the city but being surrounded by nature calmed her even more.

Despite the worsening episodes or the odd shift in her nightmares, Ali had a feeling her life was changing for the better. Logically, it made no sense, but after her conversation with Maggie, she didn't know what to think. How could a man step right out of her dreams and into her life? Could her friend be right? Could Ali be clairvoyant? Whatever the case, she wanted to understand what the hell was going on.

Ali made it to the fork in no time. Left led back toward town and right went deeper into the Ozark wilderness. If she kept going, she'd eventually find another cabin. Eight and a half miles, according to the sign. But no way would she travel that far. She didn't have time for that kind of trek.

Just as she planned to turn back, she rounded a bend and spotted an old wooden bridge up ahead. The closer she drew to it, the more a feeling of déjà vu grew.

Ali stopped near the center of the bridge and peered over the weathered railing. Ten feet below, clear water trickled gently in the rocky creek bed. All around her birds chirped happily, and little feet scurried in the surrounding trees.

Still, as peaceful as it was, Ali couldn't linger too much longer. She shifted her gaze to the thin strip of sky peeking through the trees above her. Night was quickly approaching, and she needed to get back to the cabin.

Though unsure about the local wildlife, Ali didn't think wolves or mountain lions were common in the area. But she did remember reading about hikers spotting bears on occasion.

Walking a quicker pace than her previous leisurely stroll, Ali headed back the way she came. Now and then, she heard footsteps that were not her own echoing off the trees. Since she never saw anything, she assumed it was only a deer and kept moving.

By the time she reached the trail again, it was mostly dark. Ali hadn't realized she'd traveled so far and part of her regretted not waiting until morning to go exploring.

She made it a mere twenty yards onto the trail when she sensed she was not alone. She could feel eyes on her, and it sent a shiver up her spine. Looking over her shoulder, she saw nothing, but she quickened her pace, hoping she'd at least make it back to the main driveway. No such luck. A noise behind her stopped her in her tracks. Something big had stepped onto the path and she had a feeling it wasn't a bear.

With her heart in her throat, she reluctantly turned around. There, in the middle of the path, stood an enormous wolf. Ali's breath left her in a rush. Her first instinct was to run, but she knew better than to instigate a chase with something much quicker and much stronger than herself.

Forcing a shaky breath, she took a deliberate step back. The wolf curled its lips into a wicked snarl, and the sight of those huge teeth made Ali feel as though she couldn't breathe.

Intense yellow eyes followed her as she slowly inched backward. She had to get out of there and quick, because if the wolf ever got a hold of her, she was done for.

She managed to gain a thirty-yard gap before it advanced on her. With its longer strides, the distance between them closed rapidly. The closer it drew, the faster Ali's heart thumped in her chest. This was it. No way was she getting out of the woods alive. She'd never see her friend again and she'd never find out what might have been with Nico.

Just as she thought, *screw this* and tried to make a run for it, Ali heard something behind her, approaching at an incredible speed. Her first instinct was to curl into the fetal position and try to protect herself, but she had no time. Before she could even move, a massive black blur streaked past her and slammed into the wolf.

The fight was terrifying. She could feel the vibrations in the ground as they fought. She should be running while they were distracted, but she couldn't tear her eyes away from the ferocious tangle of bodies or the claws and teeth tearing at exposed flesh. Frozen in place, Ali watched in awe.

Was that a jaguar? How was it possible? She'd never heard of jaguars so far north. Where did the thing come from and why was it in Missouri of all places?

Suddenly, a yelp sounded from the fight. Everything went silent except for her breathing and the rumbling sound coming from the massive cat. It stood between Ali and the wolf. The wolf lay on the ground, eyes focused on the jaguar. After a tense few seconds, the wolf inched backward until it gained a good distance. Then it wheeled around and hauled ass in the opposite direction.

Once it was gone, the jaguar turned toward Ali. She couldn't move. She could only stare with wide eyes.

Do not be afraid, a familiar voice whispered. The voice from her dreams. Nico?

Ali glanced around. She saw no one nearby. Just her and the frightening, beautiful animal in front of her. Forcing a breath, Ali closed her eyes. She was dreaming. She had to be. But she couldn't recall ever going to sleep.

None of it made sense. The wolf might have been believable. But the jaguar? And the voice...*that* voice. She had to be dreaming.

A subtle huffing sound drew her attention. The big cat hadn't moved. It just stood there watching her. Ali held its stare for who knows how long before she took a tentative step back. She hoped it would stay put and let her go back to the cabin. No such luck. It followed her, mirroring every move she made.

Hopefully, it wasn't hungry. Did jaguars eat people? As scared as she felt, she couldn't remember a single fact she'd learned about them in school.

Do not be afraid, the voice whispered again.

Unable to contain herself, Ali choked out a laugh. Right. How could she not be scared? A wild animal stalked her. The second one of the night.

Ali backed away until her heel hit something on the trail, and she lost her balance. Her ass hit the ground hard, jarring her back and rattling her teeth. By the time she recovered, she looked up and saw the big cat hovering not ten feet away, its iridescent green eyes focused intently on her.

Ali couldn't breathe. Up close, it was terrifying, but an incredibly beautiful creature. After a heartbeat, it stretched its neck toward her. She knew she was about to become dinner. But instead of sinking its gigantic teeth into her like she expected, it eased closer and rubbed the side of its face against her arm. When she didn't move, the big cat lay down beside her, shifted its weight, and nudged her hand with its nose.

In shock, Ali slowly lifted her hand and watched in disbelief as the jaguar bumped her palm with the top of its head as if wanting her to pet it. What in the Twilight Zone was happening to her?

When it bumped her palm again, Ali took a steadying breath and slowly slid her hand across the top of the massive head. Her fingers drifted down the thick, muscular neck, and she watched in awe as it leaned into her touch. She wanted to laugh at the strangeness of the situation, but she didn't want to startle him. She just sat there petting this enormous, beautifully frightening wild animal.

Surprising her, a thrumming sound started low in its chest and Ali could feel the vibration against her leg. "Wow," she whispered. Was it purring? As if hearing her thought, the cat looked up at her with those iridescent eyes and the sound increased.

Ali sat stroking the sleek, black fur until well after dark. She felt uneasy about being in the middle of the woods, but she suspected she needn't worry about anything with her new friend around.

As if it knew she wanted to go, the big cat eased to its feet. Ali sat there for a little too long, and it nudged her. When it stepped back, Ali took the hint and eased off the forest floor.

He made a chuffing sound and pushed against her hard enough to make her stumble. Startled, she asked quietly, "What was that for?"

He turned his focus toward the trail and gave her another nudge. Ah. He wanted her to go. Excellent idea. No matter how much she might enjoy just sitting there with him and stroking his fur, she needed to get back to the safety of the cabin, just in case the wolf came back.

Climbing to her feet, Ali headed back, and the jaguar fell into step beside her.

Now and then, she looked over at him, still a little in shock over what had happened. She'd always loved jaguars, but she never thought she'd see one in person. Especially not under such unusual circumstances. How odd was it that she traipsed through the forest with a wild animal at her side like they were old friends just out for an evening stroll? Could her life get any weirder?

As they walked, the jaguar focused on the surrounding forest, his eyes constantly searching the darkness. Logic told her she should be terrified, but after what had happened, Ali felt safe with him at her side. If he'd wanted to eat her, he would have done so already.

He walked her all the way back to the cabin, and Ali hesitated at the bottom of the steps, grateful to have had him show up when he did. "Thank you."

He stared back at her, his eyes sparkling with too much intelligence, as if he somehow understood her. But how ridiculous was that? Wild animals couldn't communicate like that. Could they?

As if proving her wrong, he sat on his haunches and chuffed at her again. His eyes shifted toward the porch and then back to her. Okay. Okay. She could catch the hint.

Ali turned and climbed the steps, glancing back at him before she closed the door. He sat at the bottom of the stairs and waited patiently for her to go inside.

"Goodnight."

No surprise, Ali couldn't sleep. Even after a long soak in the giant claw-foot tub, she still couldn't fully relax. For over an hour, she lay in the comfy bed staring at the rough wood ceiling while her mind ran wild.

She couldn't stop thinking about all the odd occurrences in her life and how much it seemed like an elaborate work of fiction. Then a thought occurred to her. Writing about it might help her make some sense of it all. If not, she'd at least have a good start on a story unlike anything she'd ever written before. At the very least, it could give Jeff a better understanding of her issues. Then maybe he could figure out a way to help her.

With a plan in mind, Ali kicked off the covers and headed back into the main living space. She grabbed a bottle of water from the fridge, flicked on the dim lamp, and then curled up on the couch with her laptop.

She opened a fresh document and dove right in, letting

the details of her dreams flow onto the page. Starting with the first one she could remember.

She was so focused on her new project she didn't realize how much time had passed, until her body shouted at her to take a break. Her back ached from hunching over her computer and her fingers cramped from overuse.

Sitting up straight, she stretched her arms overhead and arched her back. She shifted left to right several times to loosen her tight muscles and get a little relief.

Scrolling back to the beginning of the document, she scanned over her progress. She'd typed page upon page of endless details, noting everything she could recall. A good bit of it didn't make much sense, but she couldn't ignore the obvious similarities between Nico and her new jaguar friend.

She'd dreamed of both man and beast. Then they both showed up in her life shortly after. Coincidence? Or was Maggie right? Could the dreams, in fact, be visions? Ali didn't know what to believe.

Setting her laptop aside, she stood and stretched again. Her entire body felt stiff from sitting in the same position for far too long. She needed to move around and get her blood flowing properly. Maybe go outside and get some fresh mountain air.

After the encounter with the wolf, Ali didn't know if she wanted to leave the comfort of the cabin. But she couldn't let fear rule her. That was one reason she was on her little getaway in the first place.

As she turned, she spotted a shadowy figure through the window. Was that someone sitting on the porch? With her heart in her throat, Ali quickly shut off the lamp and moved closer to the window.

Relief washed over her. Not a person, but her jaguar friend sat at the top of the steps. After their earlier encounter in the woods, she felt comforted by his presence. In fact, she felt drawn to him.

Pushing open the door, Ali stepped outside. When the cat's dark head turned toward her, she offered a gentle greeting. "You want some company?"

He didn't move, so she took it as a yes.

She padded barefoot across the porch, settling on the top step beside him. "Are you guarding me?"

He made a soft chuffing sound and his focus shifted toward the tree line.

Ali grinned, propping her elbows on her knees. "I'm not sure I need looking after right now but I'm glad you're here. I just wish you could talk to me and distract me for a little while. Sometimes it's a bit much being alone with my own thoughts."

His iridescent sage-green eyes met and held hers as if he understood perfectly.

"I know. I'm a freak, right? Here I am befriending a giant wild cat like it's nothing unusual. But leave me alone with my thoughts for five minutes and I'm verging on a full-fledged meltdown."

He made an odd sound in the back of his throat and nudged her hand with his nose. Ali took the hint, reaching out to gently stroke the side of his muscular neck. She smiled as he leaned into her touch and rubbed against her hand like an enormous house cat.

"I have to admit. I don't normally talk to anybody this much. Except for my friend, Maggie. Everybody else makes me nervous, but your presence is sort of soothing."

Ali's gaze shifted to the dark forest as she absently ran her fingers over the jaguar's soft fur.

"There is this one guy I wouldn't mind talking to, but I'm not sure how that would go. I'm not so great with people, and he's probably the most beautiful person I've ever seen. I wouldn't even know what to say to him."

Her jaguar friend turned toward her again, but she kept her focus forward.

"I have no idea if I'll ever see him again, but if I'm honest, conversation should be the least of my worries. My life has been anything but ordinary, but lately, there's been some weird stuff happening. The strange part is, I think I'm more terrified that this whole thing is just a dream. Or worse, I've completely lost my mind and it's all one big delusion."

Alessandra.

Ali's fingers stilled. That velvety, accented voice was back. Cautiously turning, she expected to see the man crouched behind her. But no one was there. She was alone with her guardian jaguar on the porch. Not another soul in sight.

With a nervous laugh, she whispered, "I must be going crazy. I swear I just heard his voice again."

You did hear me.

Though her companion appeared unbothered, Ali felt a bit unnerved. She suddenly didn't want to be outside anymore. Lurching to her feet, she moved with quick steps and slipped inside. With her heart in her throat and her breaths coming erratic, she shut the door and fumbled to flip the lock into place.

Ali leaned her forehead against the hard panel and forced herself to take slow, deep breaths the way Jeff had showed her. But before she could get her heartrate under control, the voice came again.

Do not be afraid.

Easier said than done. Despite her thoughts just moments ago, she feared for her sanity. When she'd heard the voice before, she'd passed it off as the remnants of a dream still lingering. But she wasn't shaking off sleep this time. She was wide awake, and Nico's voice was as clear as if he stood right beside her.

Spinning around, Ali searched the darkness for him. With the help of the glowing clock on the microwave, her eyes quickly adjusted, and she found herself alone in the cabin.

Alessandra.

With her back against the heavy oak door, Ali covered her ears and slid to the floor. She prayed the voice would go away, because if it was real, then so was everything else she'd dreamed about. And she didn't know if she could handle that.

I know it is unsettling, but I assure you, our connection is real.

Even with her ears covered, she heard him plain as day. He wasn't some invisible man or someone lurking in the shadows. He was in her head, speaking to her as clearly as she heard her own thoughts. How was that possible? Was she both clairvoyant and telepathic? Or simply having a complete mental breakdown?

Panic rose in her belly, and she glanced across the room at where her phone sat on the coffee table. She should call Jeff and tell him everything. He could help her. Or take her somewhere to get the help she clearly needed. She could dismiss the first time but having a man's voice echoing in her head repeatedly couldn't be ignored.

There is nothing wrong with you, Alessandra.

Right. She mentally scoffed. *Because hearing voices is perfectly normal.*

Not voices. Only my voice.

What the hell did that matter?

You hear me because of our bond. I understand your reluctance to trust it, but I can explain everything if you will give me the chance.

A soft knock on the door startled Ali. She nearly jumped out of her skin, but she didn't make a sound.

"Alessandra." His voice came in the form of pure velvet.

She didn't know whether to be terrified or incredibly relieved to hear him physically speak for the first time. Either way, it made her heart beat double time. What the hell was he doing out there? And how did he know where to find her? Maggie and Jeff were the only two people who knew about her little getaway.

"I am only here to talk."

Drawing on all her courage, Ali dragged herself off the floor and peered through the peephole. It really was him, and even through the tiny, warped lens, he still looked magnificent. Less like he did at Maggie's party and more like from her dream of him.

"Will you open the door so we can speak face to face?"

A cynical laugh bubbled up from her throat. "Why would I do that? I don't know you. You could be a crazy person." Which would be perfect since she felt as though she'd lost her mind.

"We are both entirely sane. I promise you that."

Right.

He leaned closer to the door and stared directly into the peephole as if he could see her. "Come," he purred.

Ali's heart pounded even harder. The way his voice caressed that single word made her feel inclined to obey him. And not simply by opening the door and joining him outside. Her body stirred, heating in the most delicious way.

Leaning her forehead against the door again, she released a rough breath. What the hell was wrong with her? Some weirdo followed her to the middle of nowhere and her body betrayed her by getting aroused? She had serious issues.

I can give you answers. About our connection, your dreams, and your jaguar friend.

Ali's head whipped up and she peered through the peephole again. "What? What about him?"

He is more than a jaguar.

"What do you mean?"

The truth about him, about us, would make for an interesting story. Perhaps when you learn the truth, you can use that for your next novel.

Chaos filled Ali's mind. On one hand, she felt as if some profound revelation was about to be revealed and he was right. It would be the perfect foundation for her next book. But then it hit her. "How do you know about my writing?"

Your thoughts have been filled with it for the last two hours, and you are so close to making the connection that I could not stay quiet any longer.

"So, tell me."

He straightened. Took a single step back. "Perhaps it would be easier to show you."

Ali shifted her weight to her other foot and swallowed hard. "Then show me."

He beckoned her again. "Come outside."

Could she trust him enough to open the door? Last time she saw him, he hadn't done anything to hurt her. And they'd been alone in the dark garden.

I would never hurt you, Alessandra.

Ali squeezed her eyes shut. Logic told her to stay put and call for help, but curiosity and instinct had her drawing a deep breath and flipping the lock.

When she pulled the door open, the man no longer stood there. But her jaguar friend sat at the bottom of the steps, his iridescent eyes on her as she cautiously stepped onto the porch.

"Where is he?" she whispered.

I am right here.

Before she could respond, the jaguar's entire body shivered and disappeared. In little more than a blink, the massive cat was gone, and in its place crouched a man.

"Nicolai?" Ali breathed.

He slowly stood, his pale eyes watching her as if he expected her to run. But Ali wasn't going anywhere. She stood frozen in place, her eyes raking over every inch of him.

The most incredible display of virility she'd ever seen stood at the foot of the steps, holding her full attention. Thick, toned muscles wrapped in smooth, golden skin stretched across his chest and shoulders. She followed the ripple of muscles down the hard plain of his stomach, further down to... *Oh, damn.*

Clearly, he wasn't shy or lacking in confidence. And with such a remarkable body, he had reason to be proud. The decent part of her screamed for her to avert her eyes, but heaven help her, she couldn't look away.

"I apologize. I should have considered you might be uncomfortable with nudity."

"I...I...um..." she stammered, finally lifting her gaze to meet his.

"My clothes are not in the immediate area. Do you have a towel I could use to cover myself?"

A towel? Ali snorted. *Seriously? You need a freakin' tarp for that thing.*

An amused smirk tugged at his full lips. "You are sweet."

Heat flared in her cheeks. Damn it. She had to stop thinking like that. If he could hear her thoughts, she needed to get them under control.

"Alessandra."

Clearing her throat, she nodded. "A towel. Sure."

She hesitated, pretending not to take one more lingering look at him before she turned and hurried back into the cabin. Forcing herself to breathe, she made quick work of retrieving the towel, snatching one off the stack and heading back out to hand it to him.

Ali averted her eyes until he had the terry cloth tucked tight around his hips. With his vitals covered, Ali could focus on the rest of him. Not that it was much help. He was breathtaking. From his beautiful golden skin to his toned muscles. And the thick, raven hair falling loose around his hard shoulders. Every inch of him was perfection. She wanted to step forward and touch him to be sure he was real. But she fought the urge and met his eyes again.

Nicolai studied her, curiosity tugging at his dark brows. "If I am honest, I find it perplexing that you handled the shift better than my lack of clothing."

Ali's face heated again at just the thought of what the towel concealed. She cleared her throat again. "Well, it was certainly jarring. But it's hard to deny something I watched happen right in front of me."

"Very true." When she only stared at him, he added, "Shall we stand here the rest of the night quietly admiring one another? Or would you like to sit and talk?"

Either option was fine by her, but she needed answers and he'd promised to give them to her. Moving to sit on the top step, Ali looked up at Nicolai expectantly until he settled beside her.

He raked his fingers through his hair, pushing the wavy strands from his face before shifting his attention to her.

"So, tell me," Ali urged him. "Why did I dream about you? And why are you here?"

"Because of the mate bond."

Ali blinked at him, uncertain how to respond. Mate bond? Was that what it sounded like?

Seeing the question in her expression, he nodded. "You and I were destined to be together."

Her thoughts went instantly to the dream of him. The one with him in her bed, looking comfortable and satisfied. The contentment she felt and the pure happiness in his eyes as he watched her. It terrified her, but she wanted that more than she'd ever wanted anything.

"It will be that way between us."

Ali's voice trembled. "How do you know?"

He reached out and his fingers brushed her temple. "Because we dreamed it."

"We?" She stared up at him. "You mean, we shared the dream?"

Nicolai nodded.

"How is that possible?"

"The same way we speak mind to mind. I do not know why or how. It is just the way of our people." As if reading her next question before it even fully formed in her mind, he continued. "We are Jagara. An ancient race of shifters who have lived deep in the South American jungles for countless generations. When it is time, we dream of our mates. That is how we find one another."

"Wait." Chaos flared in her mind. Her thoughts running wild. "Are you saying I'm like you? That I can do what you just did?"

"Yes."

Ali's breath left her in a rush. "I'm not crazy then. I'm just not human."

"No. You are Jagara. A beautiful bi-natured woman."

That explained so much, yet still left her confused. She had so many questions.

"The coming of your *Despertar* is what sparked our mate bond."

"*Despertar*?" She stared at him. "Awakening?"

He smiled. "You speak the language."

"My mother taught me. She was from South America. Her family moved to the States when she was a teenager."

Nicolai looked deep in thought, and when he spoke again, his voice was low but held a thick curiosity. "What else did your mother teach you?"

"None of this, that's for sure." Ali searched his luminous eyes. "What is the Awakening exactly?"

"A time of transition when a Jagara's senses grow stronger, and their jaguar emerges."

"Emerges? That sounds painful."

Nicolai hesitated, his expression giving away his unease.

Though she dreaded the answer, she asked anyway. "Does it hurt?"

"I wish I could tell you no, but I cannot."

Great.

"Thankfully, it is only painful in the beginning."

Ali sat quietly contemplating the information. She was overwhelmed. How could she be relieved, yet so terrified at the same time?

"I do not mean to frighten you, but you need to understand what is happening and what to expect as your Awakening progresses. It will make things easier for you."

Ali nodded, even though she didn't know if she was ready to hear what he had to tell her.

"Alessandra, you sense the changes taking place inside you. You see it. Feel it. Even if you do not understand it."

He was right. She'd known for a while that something was different, but she never would have guessed what that was.

"When your Awakening began, it changed something inside you. It opened the link between our minds. And because I found you before the full change comes upon you, I can help you through your first transition."

Ali sat quietly, staring at Nicolai. It was a relief to not have to go through such a thing on her own. Still, she couldn't help wondering what it would be like.

"What are you thinking?"

"What does it feel like to change? To shift? I know you said it's painful at first, but what about after?" Ali studied his handsome face, curious about his personal experience. "Tell me what it feels like for you."

It was Nicolai's turn to look across the yard. He leaned forward and propped his heavy arms on his knees before he began. "It is hard to explain. It is a freeing of sorts. Like your human form opens, and your true self bursts from the folds."

"That sounds nice. Violent, but nice."

He smiled at her. "You are nothing like I thought you would be the first time I saw you."

"What did you think I would be like?"

"Afraid. I did not want you to be, but I worried you might fear me."

Ali resisted the sudden urge to comfort him, but she admitted, "I was scared shitless. Still am. But I'm also incredibly relieved that I haven't lost my mind."

Nicolai frowned. "I am surprised your mother kept this from you. She should have known you were close."

"Well, that would be kind of difficult. She died just before I turned sixteen."

His eyes grew sad. "I am sorry. I know how hard that is. I lost my mother as well."

Her heart ached for him. "Sorry."

"It was a devastating loss for my family, but at least I still had my father and my brother."

Ali felt a twinge of jealousy. She didn't have any other family that she knew about. Sure, Deanna took her in and cared for her, but Ali had tried not to get too attached. Instead, she'd treated those two years as more of a count-down until she could go off on her own. Even if it was to just lock herself in her apartment and rarely venture out, at least she wasn't a burden on her mother's friend anymore. She knew Deanna didn't feel that way about having her around. Deanna loved her. Ali knew she did. Still, she'd felt like a burden.

Nicolai broke the silence. "Did your mother never tell you about your heritage? About your lineage?"

"I asked her once when I was around ten years old, but she didn't know. There was no info about my birth family in the system."

His curious expression shifted to understanding. "You were adopted."

"I was only a baby when I got placed with her."

"It was only the two of you?"

Ali nodded. "She was married, but he died soon after they adopted me. I never really knew him. But the way she used to talk about him, I feel like I did."

They sat and talked for hours. And when she yawned so big her jaw popped. Nicolai smiled. "I should go so you can get some sleep."

"Yeah," Ali laughed. "That's going to happen." *I have too much to process. Too much to write about.*

"Then go write." Nicolai stood. "I will leave you to it."

Before she could argue, he dropped his towel beside her and descended the steps. The shift from man to animal happened so fast, she barely caught a glimpse of his perfect backside before he was a jaguar once again.

Ali watched his graceful movements as he prowled across the yard. Then he took one last look at her before he disappeared into the thick trees.

Once he was out of sight, Ali went back inside and

made her way over to the couch. Tucking her feet beneath her, she opened her laptop.

Overwhelmed by the information Nicolai unloaded on her, Ali had so much to process, but she had no idea where to start.

Try the beginning.

Nicolai's teasing tone made her smile. *There's an idea.*

His amused laughter echoed in her mind. And feeling a bit better, Ali turned her attention to her work.

7

The sun streaming through the lightweight curtains left a faint crosshatch pattern on the burgundy duvet. Stretching, Ali rolled onto her back and craned her neck toward the light, soaking up the muted rays and letting them gently warm her skin.

Sprawled across the bed, Ali closed her eyes with a contented sigh. It had been a long time since she'd felt so relaxed. And even though she'd been up late and had less than four hours sleep, she felt oddly well-rested. Guess that was an accurate example of quality over quantity.

She felt a gentle stirring at the edge of her mind. Focusing on the familiar feeling, she heard a low purr. *Good morning, Alessandra.*

With a small smile, she replied. *Good morning.*

How had she so quickly become comfortable with him in her mind? It could be the relief she felt knowing she didn't have an undiagnosed mental illness. She was simply different.

Do you have plans for today?

She didn't. She just wanted to relax and enjoy being away from civilization.

Would you like to join me for a walk? I have something I want to show you.

While intrigued, Ali needed to mentally prepare herself for seeing him again.

Nicolai's laughter danced in her mind. *No rush. We have all day.*

Ali dragged herself out of bed and made her way into the bathroom. She didn't know why she procrastinated. Still, she drew out her morning routine for as long as she could, staying in the bath until her fingers pruned and the water cooled.

She had no reason to worry about seeing Nicolai again, but whether anxiety or excitement, her nerves were shot. She felt like a teenager waiting for a boy to pick her up for their first date. But this wasn't a date. Only a walk. And she needed to calm the hell down.

She took her time smoothing on her coconut mango body butter and then dressed in something comfortable. When she finally made her way outside an hour later, Nicolai sat on the porch looking as if he didn't have a care in the world.

Thankfully, this time, he was dressed. He wore a pair of low-slung well-worn jeans and a t-shirt that looked ridiculously soft. "Where did you get the clothes?"

He smiled, flashing his white teeth. "Once you finally went to sleep, I went back to my hotel and retrieved them."

"Oh."

Nicolai had to see her awkward unease, but he didn't mention it. "Do you want to sit for a bit? Or are you ready for a little adventure?"

"Where are we going?"

"There's a trail behind the cabin. It leads to a beautiful spot I think you might enjoy."

A hint of anxiety crept to the surface as she followed him around back. Wandering into the forest with a perfect stranger had to be the dumbest thing she'd ever done. He could be a serial killer for all she knew. She could see the headlines now: *Woman's Body Found by Hikers.*

Nicolai glanced at her, a faint smile on his face as they headed down the trail. "You have no need for such worries with me."

Mortified that he'd heard such ridiculous thoughts, awkward laughter bubbled up from her throat. "I desperately need to figure out how this works so I can stop embarrassing myself."

Nicolai held a branch out of her way. "First, you need not be embarrassed. I am glad for your cautiousness. And second, it is new to me as well. We will learn together."

Interesting. "So, the connection is something that only happens between mates? Not anyone else?"

"Mostly, but strong bonds have been known to form between siblings. Like the bond I share with my brother. I cannot hear his thoughts but have sensed his emotions on occasion."

"Oh wow. Like twins?"

Nicolai smiled. "Exactly."

Being an only child, she couldn't imagine a bond like that. Must be nice having someone in your life you care about that much.

When the path narrowed, Nicolai walked ahead of her, acting as a buffer between her and the overhanging limbs. Even held them out of her way when necessary.

Ali listened to the sounds of the forest. The wind blew through the trees, the squirrels and birds chattered as they scurried about, and in the distance, she could hear the faint echoing trickle of a creek.

Nicolai glanced over his shoulder. "I sense your love of nature."

Ali looked around, taking a deep breath, drawing in the fresh earthy scents around her. "Yeah. I don't know why I never moved to a place like this. I hate being crowded or surrounded by people. Honestly, I don't much care for being around most people. Maggie is fine and you…"

When she didn't continue, Nicolai looked thoughtful. "What about Greg? Do you not like him?"

She shrugged. "I don't really know him very well. He seems nice enough, but the party the other night was the first time I've met him."

"I believe he is trustworthy. He gives off a strong protective aura."

Ali arched a brow curiously. Protective aura? He sensed that too?

Nicolai gave her a double take. "What?"

"Nothing." She grinned. "How much farther?"

"Nearly there."

Five minutes later, they came to a bend in the path that took them around the face of a huge boulder. Off to the left, water burbled at the bottom of a sheer drop. Up ahead, the creek veered to the left, away from the path.

Slowing, Nicolai stopped and hopped down to the creek bed as if the ten-foot leap was nothing. When he held his hands up to her as if he expected her to jump, Ali shook her head. "You are crazy."

Curling his fingers, he motioned for her to jump. "Come. I will catch you."

She frantically shook her head. "I can't."

He held his arm out. "You can. Trust me. I will not drop you."

Ali snorted. "The last time someone told me to trust them, I ended up with a broken arm and stitches in my chin."

"Alessandra, I would not ask this of you if I felt you were in danger."

The sincerity in his tone and his eyes made her feel a little better, but she didn't easily trust people. Especially those she didn't know very well. Still, she took a deep breath and whispered. "Okay. But if you don't catch me, I'm never talking to you again. If I survive."

He stepped closer. "Sit and put your legs over the edge. Then you will not have so far to jump."

Ali did as he said and with her legs hanging over, Nicolai reached up and put his hands on her calves. "Come. I will catch you."

She laughed nervously and asked him if he was ready.

"When you are." He smiled up at her.

She closed her eyes for a second to calm herself, and then she went for it. Instead of jumping like he wanted, Ali pushed off the edge and let herself slide down until her feet hit the ground. And the journey was breathtaking.

Nicolai's eyes held hers, his firm but gentle hands helping steady her as she slid down his front. Breathless, Ali stared up at him, her entire body warmer with him pressed against her and his masculine scent invading her lungs. He smelled incredible. It took restraint not to lean in and run her nose up the column of his throat.

Reluctantly, she dropped her arms and Nicolai hesitated before stepping away.

"Come." Nicolai took her hand and she let him lead her down the creek bed. "Not much farther."

The stream zigzagged through the narrow ravine, winding deeper into the forest. In several places, they were forced to hop to the opposite side to keep their feet dry, Nicolai helping her across when necessary.

Ali stopped in her tracks when they rounded the bend, and the waterfall came into view. It wasn't some grand rush spilling dramatically into a massive plunge pool. The modest cascade tumbled over the rocky lip, rippling the surface of the shallow leaf-lined pool not fifteen feet below. Still, he was right. The little secluded spot was undeniably beautiful.

"This is great."

A satisfied smile spread across Nicolai's face. "I thought you might appreciate it."

She did. She'd seen places like it in movies, online, and in magazines. But none of it compared to witnessing such beauty with your own eyes.

While she stood taking in the serenity of her surroundings, Nicolai leapt with ease onto the massive boulder near the water's edge.

Ali stared up at him in awe. No way could she have done that. Hell, she probably couldn't even climb up with hand holds and rigging. She'd never been all that physically inclined. She'd spent most of her time indoors, reading or watching TV. The most physical she got was yoga on her living room floor.

"Come on." Nicolai crouched and offered her a hand. "I will help you."

Ali hesitated, uncertain whether she wanted to join him.

"The view is better from this height," he promised.

His encouraging tone had her clasping his open palm. She wasn't a slight woman by any means, but he hauled her up as if she weighed no more than a small child. Could the guy be any more perfect? Wasn't it enough just to be gorgeous and gracious? Did he have to be effortlessly strong as well?

Shifting her focus, Ali surveyed the area. Nicolai was right. The higher vantage point drastically altered the view. From up there, she could see the colorful rocks that covered the bottom of the rippling pool.

A crisp breeze whistled through the branches overhead, drawing her eyes upward. All around them leaves shook loose and floated to the forest floor.

Ali tilted her head back and drew a deep breath in. She loved the smell of fall. While the other trees began to shed their summer foliage, the evergreens remained lush and fragrant. That sweet, refreshing scent of pine never failed to soothe her.

Ali stretched her legs out, and as her gaze roamed over the tranquil little spot, she decided she could grow accustomed to living in such a place. No people for miles. Just her and nature.

Then she glanced over at Nicolai and corrected herself. She didn't mind his company. And if everything he said was true, if everything played out like in her dreams, they would be enjoying more than just each other's company soon.

Suddenly remembering that he could read her thoughts, Ali shifted her focus back to their surroundings. It was a beautiful day, and the last thing she needed was to embarrass herself. She just wanted to relax and enjoy her time away from all the city noise.

If he had picked up on her thoughts, Nicolai didn't mention it. He just settled beside her, his arms crossed and resting on his raised knees. Oddly, Ali didn't feel obligated to speak and Nicolai didn't seem to mind. They just sat quietly enjoying the beauty that encircled them.

As the sun reached directly overhead, Ali lay back on the boulder, basking in the balmy comfort shining down on them and soaking up the warmth radiating from the rocky perch beneath them.

"Feels good," Nicolai rasped.

"So relaxing," she agreed. "It makes me want to take a nap."

He reclined next to her, and she could see by the faraway expression that came over his features, he was no longer beside her. When he spoke, he was miles away. "Where I come from, the sun does not find us often. As a child, I recall travelling great distances to find open sky when the rains were not upon us. D'mitri and I would play in the river while our parents lounged on the bank."

Ali caught glimpses of his memories as he spoke, but one stood out as clearly as her own. A boy with wild hair and pale sage-green eyes frolicked in a sparkling pool surrounded by towering trees. Sunlight shone down through the break in the natural canopy and danced on the water's surface like a million tiny diamonds. Ali had never seen such a luscious, tropical place, but sharing Nicolai's thoughts, she felt as if she'd been right there with him.

"There is nowhere I love more than my home, but because I saw the sun so rarely, I appreciated it more when

I did. Of course, I see it much more often now that I travel."

Ali envied people like Nicolai that got to travel the world. She had always liked the idea of experiencing the natural beauty of distant lands and remote locations. But her disinclination to be around others put a damper on that dream.

Although, with Nicolai by her side, she felt a modicum of hope. Maybe she wouldn't spend the rest of her life in self-imposed isolation after all.

As Nicolai stared up at the sliver of clear blue sky above them, Ali studied his profile. His sturdy jawline. His chiseled cheekbone. The perfection of his lower lip. Truly a work of art. Add in the way the sun made his deep-bronze skin appear to glow. Perfection.

The bluish sheen licking through his dark hair reminded her of a raven's feathers, and her fingers itched to touch it. Instead, she restrained herself and lay beside him, admiring the view.

Without warning, a low growl broke the comfortable silence between them. Ali's hand flew to her stomach in a failed attempt to muffle the sound, but it was too late. Judging by the arch of his dark eyebrow, Nicolai heard it as well.

Ali could feel her face heating with embarrassment. "Maybe we should head back and get something to eat. Are you hungry?"

"Starving." Nicolai hopped down from the boulder and offered her a hand. "Come."

8

Ali stared at the contents of the fridge, racking her brain over what to fix. She didn't cook often because she had nowhere near the skills her mother had in the kitchen. Despite the know-how, nothing ever turned out as good as she remembered her mother's food tasting. Maybe it was the love the woman put into everything that made all the difference. Or perhaps, Ali just didn't have the same passion for cooking.

Another loud growl broke through her thoughts. Whatever she decided, she needed to make it quick because her talkative stomach grew more persistent by the minute.

"Would you like me to prepare something?"

Ali looked over her shoulder at Nicolai. He lounged against the counter with his arms crossed over his chest and an amused smirk tugging at his flawless lips.

Irritated by his calm demeanor, Ali scoffed. "No. You're my guest."

One thing her mother taught her, even at an early age: Take care of your visitors. If someone comes to your home, don't make them fend for themselves. Make sure they know where all the toiletries are. Get them blankets and pillows before you go to bed. And most importantly, feed them.

Food was always a huge part of her mother's hospitality. Too bad Ali wasn't as good a cook as her mother. Then she could feed Nicolai something delicious.

"Anything you make will be much appreciated." he assured her.

A muffled, rhythmic beeping drew her attention. For a second, she wondered where it came from. Then Nicolai slipped a thin cell phone from his pocket and glanced at the screen.

Seeing the hard frown marring his dark brows, Ali asked, "Something wrong?"

"I need to make a call. Do you mind?"

"Of course not. Do what you gotta do."

"Thank you."

When Nicolai slipped outside onto the porch and put his phone to his ear, Ali turned her focus back to the stocked fridge. She made up her mind and took out all the needed ingredients. There was one thing her mother used to make that never failed to bring her a little comfort.

Thankfully, there was a package of pre-boiled eggs. So, that would cut out boil time and she wouldn't need to chill anything. She could just whip it up quick and have it done in no time.

Nicolai was outside for quite a while, and when Ali glanced out to check on him, she could see the tense line of his shoulders. She couldn't see his face, but she could feel the worry and sadness rolling off him in waves.

Curious, but not wanting to intrude, Ali turned her

focus back to her task. She managed to finish just when Nicolai finally ended the call and returned.

"Everything okay?"

"Sad day for my friend." He gave her a weak smile. "Nothing you need to worry over."

"Do you need to leave? Go be with your friend?"

Nicolai shook his head. "He only wanted to update me on the situation. I am right where I want to be."

The way he looked at her, the way the sadness in his eyes eased a bit, made Ali glad he was there with her.

Clearing her throat, she grabbed a couple water bottles from the fridge and the covered bowl from the counter. "Would you mind if we ate outside? Maybe have a little picnic out back? I would rather not be stuck inside on such a gorgeous day."

Nicolai smiled. "That sounds perfect."

NICOLAI GRABBED the quilt off the back of the sofa and followed his mate to the grassy patch out behind the cabin. Once Ali settled cross-legged on one side, he stretched out on his side and propped himself on an elbow. Curious, he eyed the container between them. "What is in there?"

Ali popped the lid and tilted it toward him, revealing little triangles stacked neatly inside. "Egg salad sandwiches."

"Egg salad?" He frowned. "I have never had that."

Ali's brows shot up. "Really?"

"Never."

She held the bowl closer to him. "Try one. It's one of my go-to comfort foods."

Nicolai took one of the little triangles and gave it a sniff before he took a bite. As he chewed, Ali's unease grew. She was anxious about his reaction. "The flavor is interesting. Like nothing I have ever tasted. It is very delicate."

Ali flinched a little and sat the bowl down between them. "I could fix you something else if you don't like it."

"No. It is good," he assured her and took another bite.

"You don't have to be nice." She pushed her hair back from her face and sat back on her heels. She watched him chew for a few seconds before she added, "If you don't like it, I could get you something else."

Nicolai stopped with his sandwich on the way back to his mouth, and he lifted his eyes to hers.

Ali shifted uncomfortably. "What?"

"I like that you want to please me, but I promise you, this is perfect because I know the care you put into making it." When her cheeks flushed with the prettiest shade of pink, Nicolai nodded to the stacks of little half sandwiches. "Eat, Alessandra. I can feel your hunger."

Her blush grew a tad darker, but she did as he said, bringing her own little triangle to her mouth to take a timid bite.

As he popped the last bit into his mouth, he watched her relax as she chewed. He couldn't help but wonder what it was about the food that brought her such comfort. "Tell me why this is your comfort food."

Ali looked toward the forest as she finished chewing. "My mom used to make them for me every Saturday. It was one of those unspoken, unofficial traditions, I guess. We would sit in the kitchen and talk about our week or anything that might be bothering me. She was always there for me, giving me advice, cheering me up no matter how terrible the week had been. She always knew what to say, and by the end of our lunch, I always felt better."

Ali looked down at what was left of her sandwich and picked at the crust.

Nicolai could sense the emotion swirling beneath the surface. The sadness she felt just by thinking of her mother.

"You miss her."

Ali lifted her amber eyes and nodded. "Every day."

"You still do this every Saturday," he whispered, knowing she did. "I am happy you shared it with me."

She finished another sandwich in silence and then leaned back on her elbows. "I never thought about it before, but food has always been a source of comfort for me. Because Deanna, my mother's best friend, always had these freshly baked treats when we'd go to her house on the weekend. Sometimes it was her homemade yeast rolls and honey butter. But most often, it was her famous sweet apple cinnamon bread."

Nicolai smiled. "Both sound delicious."

"Oh, they are. My mouth is watering just thinking about them." Ali shifted her warm amber eyes back to him. "What about you? Do you have anything that comforts you?"

He didn't know if it was too much for her to hear, but he had to tell her the truth. With his eyes steady on hers, Nicolai answered, "You."

Ali frowned, confusion dancing over her expression. Clearly, she didn't understand what he meant.

"I know we only just met, but I always knew you would come into my life one day. That was a tremendous comfort on the nights I ran alone or felt the need for companionship. I have waited my entire life for you, and finally, here you are."

He couldn't hear her thoughts in the moment, but he saw the shift in Ali's expression. Skeptical. Nervous. She tucked a few stray hairs behind her ear. "And what if I don't live up to your expectations?"

"Impossible." Nicolai assured her. "You are my mate."

Ali contemplated him, the moment stretching out as he awaited her response. Finally, she admitted, "I honestly thought I would be alone forever. I didn't think I'd ever be able to have a normal relationship. I could only hope to find somebody who would accept me for who I am, issues and all."

Nicolai's eyes bore into hers. "You are more than accepted, Alessandra. We were made to be two halves of the same whole."

Ali's relief and skepticism were at war. Nicolai could see it in her eyes. If he said more, he might overwhelm her, and he didn't want that. He needed to have patience, because only time would show her the truth in his words.

Nicolai rolled onto his back and lifted his gaze to the sky instead of focusing on her. "So, tell me more about your mother. What was she like?"

Once Ali began talking, the tension left her slender shoulders. She told him stories from her childhood and just listening to his mate talk about her mother made him miss his own.

Eventually, Ali grew quiet and moved to lie beside him. They lay for a long time, staring at the sky and watching the clouds roll slowly by.

Her thoughts drifted and Nicolai could feel her

concern over his earlier phone call. He didn't want to tell her about it. She didn't need that kind of sadness touching her life, not after everything she'd been through, but he couldn't shelter her from such things forever. She would be a part of his life. And with the tragedies that often befell their people, she would experience them eventually. What was the point in hiding anything from her now?

Without looking at her, Nicolai said, "I know you are curious about what happened with my friend."

In his periphery, he saw her shift focus from the sky to his profile. She didn't speak, but she made a soft sound of agreement.

"It is not a good day for Marius. His sister is missing and her mate, Zavier, has declared that he is ceasing the search for her."

"Why?"

"Mina has been missing for nearly eight months, and Zavier has held onto hope for this long. Marius still believes that she will come home one day, but Zavier thinks it is time for him and their daughter to move on."

Nicolai felt the wave of sadness roll through Ali before she asked softly, "How old is his daughter?"

"Nearly four."

Ali took a breath and closed her eyes. "That's so sad. I can't imagine losing my mother so young. Fifteen was bad enough. Four is just heartbreaking."

"Yes." Nicolai agreed. "The sadness over losing a mother, a daughter, or a mate is devastating for all our people. Every loss is felt throughout the entire community. The connections among the tribes run deep, much like the thick intertangled roots tying the massive trees together in the jungle. Especially with so few Jagara left. One of us suffers, we all feel the echoes."

"But why has Zavier given up hope?"

Nicolai let his head roll toward Ali. "She has never spoken to him."

Ali frowned, not quite understanding. But before Nicolai could explain, it dawned on her. "Their mental connection."

He nodded. "Since the moment he realized she was gone. Zavier has always hoped that one day she would speak to him, but he has heard nothing. If she were alive, there would be no way for her to keep quiet. There is no way she would."

Ali searched Nicolai's face and he could see the warring emotions written all over her expressive features. And then she said something he didn't expect. "I don't know that I could ever give up."

Nicolai felt the same. "Now that I have heard your sweet voice in my thoughts, I believe it would be disconcerting to be in such silence again. I understand why Zavier has chosen this path, but I do not think I could stop searching for you either."

9

Ali shoved her dirty clothes into the washer. Though she'd got back to her apartment hours ago, she couldn't stop thinking about her week alone with Nicolai. She'd gone out there to get away from her usual routine and came away with far more than just a soothed psyche.

The unbelievable had happened in the mountains. She'd not only found the man that had haunted her dreams, but she discovered that he was her destined mate. She wasn't as overwhelmed by that knowledge as you would think. Instead, she felt immense relief.

She wasn't completely nuts. According to Nicolai, she wasn't even human. There was a side of herself she never knew existed, a heritage she wouldn't have guessed in a million years.

If she hadn't seen Nicolai shift forms with her own eyes, Ali never would have believed him. But after everything she'd learned in the last week, she understood the restlessness she'd always felt. It was her jaguar side anxiously waiting to emerge.

She wanted to tell Maggie everything; explain why she'd dreamed of Nicolai and how he'd found her at the party. But she didn't know how her friend would react. Most likely, she'd want to have Ali committed.

She at least needed to call and let Maggie know she'd made it back home. They hadn't talked much over the last week because Maggie didn't want to intrude on Ali's vacation time. Still, she'd texted a few times to check up on her, and Ali promised to call her once she got home and let her know how the week went.

Ali put the rest of her things away, and after chopping some fresh fruit, she settled at the counter for a late lunch. Prepared for a lengthy conversation, she called her friend.

Maggie answered on the second ring with a cheerful, "Hey, girlie."

Her sunny mood was so contagious Ali couldn't help but smile. "Hey. You busy?"

"Nope." Maggie chuckled. "What are you doing? You back home?"

"Yeah." Ali plucked a piece of apple from her bowl and popped it into her mouth. "I just got settled in to eat some lunch."

"How was your trip?"

Ali had anticipated a nice stress-free week away from people. Instead, she'd spent much of the time with Nicolai. But she couldn't tell Maggie that. Her friend worried about her too much already, so she decided to leave out that little detail. "It was good. Better than I expected."

"You sound relaxed."

"I am. I loved it out there. I honestly didn't want to

leave. It was nice being surrounded by miles and miles of wilderness without anyone else around." Except Nicolai.

"You didn't stay cooped up inside the whole time, did you?"

Ali grinned at her friend's motherly tone. "No. I explored some of the hiking trails and had most of my meals curled up in the oversized rocker on the front porch. I even had a picnic on a quilt in the little meadow behind the cabin."

Maggie sighed. "I'm jealous. I'd love to do something like that, but I have so much lined up for the next couple months."

Maggie always had a busy schedule toward the end of the year. She ran herself ragged not only with work, but also various parties and fundraisers for local charities. Her heart was in giving back to the community any way she could. Come the new year, she needed a break. Usually, she would come to Ali's apartment, and they would veg out in front of the TV, binge watching a series she'd been meaning to get to. Maybe they could do something different this time around.

"Well," Ali suggested. "We can plan a girl's trip up there in January, after everything dies down."

"Definitely."

"So, how are things with work? Did you finish the Charleston project?"

Maggie scoffed. "I wish. I'm still waiting on the Rathburne armchairs. I've been getting the runaround all week but finally talked to the manager at the primary location. Turns out there was a mix-up with the order and it never got picked up."

"What the hell?"

"Yeah. He apologized and assured me the chairs would be on the truck and shipped out first thing Monday morning. Luckily, Mrs. Charleston doesn't come back from vacation until next Friday." Maggie sighed. "At least I'll have the weekend to relax."

"Yeah."

"If you want to come and hang out, you're more than welcome. It'll just be me and Greg here tomorrow."

Greg? "He's still in town?"

Maggie hesitated a split second, the pause so quick, Ali almost missed it. "Yeah. He was supposed to go back Monday, but he decided to stay a little longer. Well, he had a little help with that decision. His boss contacted him last Sunday night and informed him that the office would be closed for the week since half the employees are out sick with the flu."

"Oh, wow."

"Thankfully, he's been able to work remotely from here. That way he has something to keep him busy while I'm working."

"That's good."

"He's talking about staying until after my client party, next weekend."

"Wait. What?" Ali glanced at the calendar on the fridge. "Next Saturday is the twenty-fourth already?"

Maggie laughed. "Yes. You think you might want to come?"

Part of her wanted to, but Ali wasn't sure she should push herself too far too soon. She'd already been to one party that month. Honestly, it hadn't been all that bad, but she'd only just returned from her much-needed break from the city. Sure, Nicolai had opened her eyes to the root cause of most of her problems, but she'd spent too many years in near solitude. Was she ready for more human interaction already?

"Hey Ali, can we talk later? A client is calling."

"Yeah. Sure."

They said their goodbyes and Ali sat quietly finishing her lunch while she waited for the spin cycle to end. Once the washer was done, she threw her clothes into the dryer and did some obsessive cleaning to keep herself distracted.

Still, as she swept and mopped the floors, her thoughts drifted to Nicolai again. Had he made it back to his hotel yet? She wasn't sure how long it would take him to get back into town. She didn't know how fast he ran.

She'd offered to give him a ride back to the city, and though he'd admitted his reluctance to leave her side, he'd politely refused. Said he needed the run to help curb his instincts. Ali didn't know enough about him or their kind to understand what he meant, and she was afraid to ask.

Was it some animalistic need that drove him, or did he feel the same restlessness she often suffered? Did running help? Was a good run all she needed to relieve that recurring internal unrest? She had so many questions.

The questions could wait, but Ali was curious about something else. How strong was their mental connection? Could they hear one another clear across town? Farther? Though she felt silly testing it, Ali closed her eyes and whispered Nicolai's name in her mind.

Yes?

His quick response made her smile. *Hi.*

His deep laugh filled her mind. *Hello, Alessandra.*

Did you make it back to your hotel yet?

I did. And I am currently staring at the ceiling, thinking of you.

She felt her face flush, and she was glad he wasn't there to see it. She'd embarrassed herself enough over the last week. *Really? What about me?*

Wondering when I will see you again.

Though they'd spent the entire week together, she understood what he meant. She already had an over-whelming urge to be near him again, and they'd only been apart a couple hours.

She should take some time and process all the informa-tion he'd unloaded on her back at the cabin. But no. She didn't want that. She couldn't understand it, but ever since they'd gone their separate ways, a hollowness had settled in her chest.

She couldn't wait to see him again, but before she could decide whether to invite him over—or if it was too soon—Nicolai asked, *Do you have plans for tonight?*

Ali grinned. *Nothing exciting. Just finishing some mindless cleaning.*

Hmm.

Gathering her nerve, Ali went for it. *Would you like to come hang out at my place? Maybe order takeout and watch a movie?*

I would love to.

Ali couldn't stop her smile from spreading. *I need to finish this up and get a shower. It should only take me about another hour, but you can come over any time after that.*

Sounds good. I will see you at five-thirty.

The second she felt the connection with Nicolai slip

away, she dove back into her chores. She finished up by vacuuming her rug in the living room and then stood in the bedroom doorway to give the whole place one last once-over. Everything looked spotless.

Satisfied, she glanced at the clock. Four-forty-five. Plenty of time to get cleaned up and looking halfway presentable.

On an ordinary day, it took her a full thirty minutes to shower, moisturize, dress, and dry her hair. Her instinct was to rush through her routine, but she made a conscious effort to slow down and stretch it out. That way, she had less time to pace. If she had free time, her anxiety would skyrocket, and she'd be a sweaty mess by the time Nicolai arrived.

He showed up at five-thirty on the dot. Ali had just finished drying her hair and thrown it into a ponytail when she heard him knock. And with butterflies in her stomach, she answered the door.

Nicolai looked gorgeous as always, his comfy-looking jeans and t-shirt fitting him to perfection. Honestly, he looked damn delicious no matter what he wore. And she knew that personally. Over the last week, she'd seen him all dressed up in a fine suit, naked as the day he was born, and everything in between.

He wore his hair down again, and a faint shadow of stubble peppered his strong jaw. Damn. Could the man be any finer?

Nicolai grinned, his pale eyes lighting up the second he saw her. "Hi."

"Hi." Ali smiled, stepping aside to let him in.

Though his wide shoulders crowded the narrow entryway, his presence didn't overwhelm her the way other people did. Not that anyone ever came into her space, aside from Maggie. Even then, it was only because the woman had forced herself into Ali's life and into her heart.

Nicolai moved farther into the room and looked around like he'd never been there before. "Looks different in the daylight."

Ali snorted. "A little bit. Yeah."

Sure, he'd been in her apartment before, but it felt different having him there when she knew for certain she wasn't dreaming. Especially after spending the week getting to know him a little. It wasn't a small space, but Nicolai's presence made it feel that way. Not crowded. Just filled.

He was a big man. He took up space physically, but that wasn't it. His raw, heady scent permeated the room the moment he stepped inside, and it wrapped around her, making her feel like nothing else could ever touch her.

Ali cleared her throat. "I was about to get a drink of water. You want something?"

"Water is fine. Thank you."

Ali poured them both a glass and when she turned back to him, Nicolai's attention had shifted to her knick-knack shelves. Oddly, she didn't have the urge to fill the silence. She simply watched him as he studied her baubles one by one. His fingertips brushed over several, a hint of a smile playing at his lips.

"What's that goofy grin for?"

Nicolai glanced at her over his shoulder. "My brother would love all this."

Ali stared at him. "Really?"

"D'mitri isn't much of a traveler, so whenever I visit

someplace new, I always bring a little something back for him."

"That's nice of you."

Nicolai lifted his shoulder, making a noncommittal sound. "He has a decent collection, but nothing like this."

Ali moved to Nicolai's side, her eyes drifting over her treasures. "My mother got most of them for me."

She could feel Nicolai's eyes on her, but he stayed quiet, waiting for her to say more.

"For years, every time we went into town, we'd stop by her favorite little secondhand shop. She'd grab a few books and I'd scour the glass cases for new treasure. I didn't always find one that called to me, but when I did, she would buy it for me."

Nicolai smiled.

"Sometimes she would find things she knew I would like and just bring them home to me." Ali straightened the little silver bell with the toucan perched on the top of the handle. "This was one of the last ones she gave me and it's in my top five favorites."

"It is beautiful."

Ali was curious about his brother. She had no clue what it was like to have a sibling. "Are you and D'mitri close?"

Nicolai nodded. "We have very different lives now, but we have always had a strong bond."

"Is he younger or older?"

"Older." Nicolai grinned. "By three minutes."

"Oh, wow." Ali hadn't expected that answer. "You know, I've never seen twins in person before. Just TV and movies. Or read about them."

"They were once common among our people. My

grandfather told me that when his father was a child, more than a third of the Jagara population was from a multiple birth. But there are currently only two known sets of twins. Other than myself and D'mitri."

"That's crazy. I wonder what caused such a drastic decline with the last few generations."

Nicolai shrugged one shoulder. "No one knows."

After a long silence, Ali cleared her throat again. "So, what do you like on your pizza?"

"Anything but anchovies."

Ali scrunched her nose. "Trust me. You don't have to worry about that."

Nicolai chuckled.

"Go make yourself at home." Ali nodded toward the sofa. "I'll send in the order, and we can pick something to watch while we wait for the food to get here."

"Sounds like a plan."

While Nicolai sauntered into the living room, Ali snagged her phone off the kitchen counter and opened the app for Joey's Pizzeria. She went straight to the previous orders tab and selected her usual. Half ham and pineapple. Half pepperoni, mushroom, and black olives.

Once she'd placed the order, Ali joined Nicolai on the couch. Feeling a little nervous, she reached for the remote. "Anything particular you want to watch?"

"Something lighthearted."

Ali opened the Prime app and went straight to her watchlist. Something lighthearted. Easy to follow even if they fell into conversation. Something with no sex, preferably. She felt awkward enough just having him in her personal space.

But as she scrolled, Ali quickly realized just how many

on the list contained heavy storylines and graphic sexual encounters. She kept her mental barrier firmly in place and didn't dare look over at Nicolai. She didn't want to know if he noticed the reoccurring theme.

Her heart leapt into her throat when he sat his glass on the table in front of them and angled his body toward her. "I am curious."

Oh shit. She sat quietly, staring at the TV, blindly scrolling while she waited for him to comment about her movie choices.

Instead, he said, "I noticed your friends call you Ali. Is that what you prefer?"

Relieved, she shrugged one shoulder. "Usually. Why?"

"Because in our shared dreams, I called you Alessandra. Would you rather I use Ali instead?"

"Either is fine. But I will admit, I like the way you say Alessandra. Something about the way it just rolls off your tongue makes me feel things."

The moment the words left her mouth, Ali wanted to crawl into a hole and hide. The amused expression on Nicolai's face didn't help any.

She managed to ignore the growing warmth in her cheeks and turn the conversation on him. "What about you? Is it Nico or Nicolai?"

"Aside from you, no one has ever called me Nico. But I do not mind being Nico to you. It feels more..."

He hesitated, searching for the right word and Ali offered, "Intimate?"

He smirked. "I would have said personal, but yes."

"Does that mean everyone else has to call you Nicolai, then?"

"If you like."

Ali knew it was stupid, but that one tiny detail made her feel special.

"How about that one?" Nicolai nodded toward the TV.

Ali looked over, relieved to see the image filling the screen. *The Princess Bride*. Thank the gods for screensaver mode.

Finally. Something appropriate. One of her all-time favorites. If you asked her, it was one of the greatest love stories onscreen. Plus, it had adventure, comedy, and—most importantly—a happily ever after.

Leaning back against the couch, she settled in and hit play.

OVER THE NEXT WEEK, Nicolai and Ali spent more time together than they did apart. Mostly, they lounged on her cozy, broken-in couch, half-watching TV while they got to know each other better.

Nicolai quickly learned that she didn't much care for overly processed foods or chain restaurants. She preferred prepackaged organic meals, fresh produce, and the local family-owned eateries that made homestyle meals.

Though cut off from their people for most of her life, there was no hiding Ali's Jagara side. She clearly loved nature as much as any Jagara. Why she lived in the middle of the busy city, he had no idea. The way she spoke of her solitude made him think she craved connection, but he understood her reluctance to attempt bonding with anyone.

She missed her mother. And he could understand that all too well. Life hadn't been the same since his own mother passed. She'd been the heart of their family. And when she left, she took a part of them with her.

Ali shifted on the couch, turning to face him. "I'm contemplating going to Maggie's party next week."

Nicolai's head rolled toward her. "Another party already?"

"She has them just about weekly this time of year." Ali opened her mouth to say more, then closed it again as she picked at her fingernails.

"What is it?"

Chewing on her lush bottom lip, Ali shifted nervously beside him. "If I decide to go, would you want to go with me?"

"Of course."

The tiniest hint of a smile gave away Ali's relief. He didn't know why she felt so nervous about asking him. She would learn soon enough that he would go anywhere with her.

NICOLAI HAD ONLY LEFT a few hours ago to get ready for the party. But the anticipation of seeing him again and finally introducing him to Maggie had Ali's anxiety through the roof.

Still, she managed to get her hair and makeup done, and shimmied into her dress before Nicolai arrived.

Ali opened the door and froze. Nicolai stood in the hallway looking amazing dressed in all black. The long-sleeved button-up shirt and the well-fitted slacks looked incredible on him. He had his hair pulled away from his face again, and he stood there with his hands behind his back as his eyes drifted over her with blatant appreciation. "You look beautiful."

"Thanks." She blushed. "You don't look so bad yourself."

He gave her a crooked little grin and then leaned in, placing a kiss on her cheek.

She closed her eyes, savoring the feel of his warm, soft lips against her skin even if it was short-lived.

When he straightened, Ali cleared her throat and stepped aside. "Come on in. I need to go grab my sweater before we go. It's a bit chilly out tonight."

She didn't waste time snagging the knitted cardigan off the end of her bed. It didn't really go with her dress, but it was her favorite. Just an extra layer of comfort as she tackled yet another party.

She tugged it on as she made her way back into the living room. "Are you ready?"

Nicolai hesitated, his sage-green eyes drifting over her again, lingering for a moment at her throat.

"What?" Ali breathed.

He met her eyes again. "Before we go, I would like to talk to you about something important."

Ali shifted uncomfortably, his serious tone making her nervous. "Okay."

"Because of our unique circumstances, I planned to wait, but I think maybe now is the perfect time." When Ali remained quiet, Nicolai continued. "As far back as I can remember, I have always wanted to give a gift to my mate the day we found one another. For the longest time, I had no plan of what that might be. But after my Awakening, I went to my uncle and asked him to make a special piece for me. For you."

Ali's heartbeat stuttered when Nicolai reached into his pocket, retrieving a small black box. Her wide eyes jumped to his, panic setting in.

Nicolai chuckled. "This is not what you think. I promise."

Relieved, but also embarrassed, Ali leaned against the back of the couch and released the hard breath. What was she thinking? It was far too early in their relationship for a ring.

Nicolai stepped closer to her and opened the lid. Nestled in the little velvet cradle lay an onyx pendant in the shape of a jaguar in profile. The eye? A pale green stone, the exact shade of Nicolai's eyes.

The necklace was beautiful. She'd never seen anything like it. Ordinarily, she wouldn't accept such an expensive gift so early in a relationship. But the strange connection she shared with Nicolai and the expectant look on his handsome face, there was no way she could refuse it when it clearly meant so much to him.

Reaching out, she ran her finger across the smooth surface. "It's beautiful."

Nicolai let out a relieved breath and smiled down at her. "Will you wear it tonight?"

Ali stared up at him for a long moment before she finally agreed.

Nicolai carefully took the delicate silver chain and lifted the necklace from the box. "May I?"

With her heart in her throat, Ali turned around, gathering her hair to one side so he could slide the necklace into place.

Nicolai's warm fingers brushed her neck as he hooked the clasp, and the ghost of a caress sent a shiver through her entire body.

When his hands fell away, Ali turned to face him again. She nervously lifted her eyes to his and whispered, "Thank you."

10

H and in hand, Nicolai and Ali strolled through the double doors and into the dimly lit library. Though there were more people in attendance than Maggie's last party, Ali appeared less stressed than before. Whether it was simply her confidence growing or having him at her side, Nicolai liked seeing her so much more relaxed.

Don't let it go to your head. Ali glanced at him as they made their way through the crowd. *But having you here helps. Your presence is calming.*

He grinned to himself and gave her hand a gentle squeeze.

As she moved farther into the room, Ali searched for her friend and found her near the bar with a small group of people.

The second Maggie spotted them, she broke away from the conversation and approached them. Her curious gaze raked over Nicolai as she embraced Ali. "Who the hell is this guy?"

Though only meant for Ali to hear, Nicolai easily picked up Maggie's whispered question.

With a bright smile on her beautiful face, Ali introduced them. "Maggie Jennings, this is Nicolai…"

When she hesitated a heartbeat, he provided through their mental link, *Montez.*

"Nicolai Montez."

Judging by her stunned expression, Maggie knew exactly who he was.

Nicolai stepped forward and offered her a hand. Though reluctant, she slipped her palm into his, and he leaned down, touching his forehead to the back of her hand in the customary Jagara greeting of respect.

When he straightened, Nicolai gave her a warm smile. "It is a pleasure to meet you, Maggie."

She held his gaze, a not-so-subtle hardness in her tone. "Well, I'd say the same of you, but it would've been nice if you'd introduced yourself the last time you were here. You know, considering you were in my home. Uninvited."

Ali pinched the back of Maggie's arm and said through gritted teeth, "Be nice."

Though the thought of his new mate defending him made him smile, he didn't blame Maggie for at least being irritated with him. "No. She is right. It was rude of me."

"Damn right," Maggie muttered.

That earned her another hard look from Ali.

The feisty brunette ignored her completely. She stepped closer to Nicolai and lowered her voice. "Look, I don't know who you are or where the hell you came from, but I do know one thing. Ali is my best friend, and she had better not get hurt or I will end you. Do you understand me?"

Nicolai fought back a grin. He liked this woman's spirit and her fierce protectiveness when it came to Ali. "Perfectly. But I assure you, there is no need to worry. I could never harm her."

After a moment, the tension in her shoulders eased a fraction. She appeared satisfied by his response, but he could still see a hint of skepticism in her watchful eyes. Nicolai knew it would take time to fully earn her trust, but he'd accept that.

Maggie turned her focus back to Ali. "You look gorgeous, as always."

A faint hint of pink blossomed in her cheeks. "Yeah, well. Like you always say, it's all about the dress."

Nicolai snorted. "Trust me. It is not the dress."

Both women stared at him openly. But it was true. It wasn't the dress. Sure, it accented her figure and complemented her skin tone beautifully. Still, it was the woman beneath it that called to him. His woman. His mate. His future.

A long silence hovered between them before Maggie cleared her throat. "So, I couldn't help noticing your accent. Where are you from?"

"My home is in a small village near Maylanju."

"Maylanju?" Her brows shot up; her interest piqued. "The ruins in Brazil?"

Nicolai eyed her with curiosity. "You are familiar with it?"

"A little. I wrote a paper on ancient civilizations my junior year of college. While everyone else wrote about Egypt, Greece, and Rome, I focused on obscure places in South America. Maylanju was one of them."

Interesting. Other than locals, he'd never met anyone

else who knew about the ruins. But he supposed you could find anything on the internet these days. "What made you choose your topic?"

"Ancient cultures fascinate me. And it is unreal how many lost cities there are deep in the rainforest. I'd love to go see some of them."

Ali looked taken aback. "I didn't know that about you."

"Yeah, well. I doubt I'll ever go."

"Why not? What's stopping you?"

Maggie snorted. "Despite what you might think, Ali, I'm not that much of an explorer. The biggest adventure I've ever been on was going camping in my best friend's back yard when I was twelve. And that didn't go so well."

Nicolai chuckled. "You cannot let that stop you. I may be biased, but most of South America truly is beautiful. Photos do it no justice. I assure you the experience will be well worth the trip."

He could see Maggie turning it over in her mind, clearly contemplating it. "Maybe one day."

As the girls fell into quiet conversation, Nicolai spotted a familiar face across the room. The guy slowly made his way toward them, speaking to party guests while weaving through the crowd. Greg, Maggie's friend, the guy Nicolai had spoken with briefly at the last party.

As if she sensed his nearness, or saw Nicolai's focus in that direction, Maggie turned just as Greg approached. In an instant, her entire demeanor shifted, and her eyes sparkled with delight. "There you are."

Greg pulled her in for a quick hug and kissed her cheek. "Sorry I'm late. The meeting ran longer than expected."

Maggie smiled up at him. "No worries. I was just chatting with Ali and Nicolai."

Greg clapped Nicolai on the shoulder. "Hey man. Good to see you again."

Nicolai returned the sentiment and Greg shifted his gaze to Ali, greeting her as well.

If Nicolai was the jealous type, he might have bristled with Greg standing so near his mate. Fortunate for everyone, Nicolai was a level-headed man. Mostly.

Besides, even though Maggie had tried to play matchmaker with them before, Nicolai needn't worry. Despite his previous interest in Ali, Greg's attention focused elsewhere. If their body language was any indication, something had changed between Greg and Maggie since the last time Nicolai saw them. And he wasn't the only one who noticed.

As the conversation flowed amongst their little group, Ali didn't miss the way Greg's hand repeatedly strayed to the small of her friend's back. Judging by her expression, Nicolai knew Ali would ask Maggie about it when they were alone.

She didn't get her chance, though. Despite Maggie and Greg's easy-going personalities, Ali's anxiety slowly increased as the night wore on.

Maggie kept a close eye on her, even discreetly asking her if she was okay. Of course, Ali hid her growing discomfort because she didn't want to disturb her friend's party. Still, despite her reassuring Maggie all was well, Nicolai could see right through Ali's calm façade.

He didn't have to be privy to her thoughts to know when she'd had enough. She wasn't the only one who needed a break from the ceaseless chattering around them.

Nicolai's senses were overstimulated, much like the onset of his Awakening, and he needed room to breathe.

The blend of scents—natural and perfumed—was tolerable for a brief time. But combined with Ali's growing unease, Nicolai didn't think he could take much more.

Leaning down, he whispered next to her ear, "Would you like to come get some fresh air with me?"

Ali looked up at him, her amber eyes sparkling with gratitude. *Yeah. It's a little stuffy in here. Some air might do me some good.*

ALI FOLLOWED Nicolai through the double doors and onto the back patio. Her tension eased a fraction the moment the crisp midnight air surrounded her. Getting a little distance from the party helped, but she had a feeling it wouldn't be enough this time.

Nicolai gave her hand a gentle squeeze, drawing her attention to him. "Can I ask you something?"

"Sure."

"If being around so many people is too much for you, why come here tonight?"

She let out a gush of air, turning her focus toward the garden. "I don't know. I guess I'm just pushing myself. Trying to be normal."

"For you or for everyone else?"

She didn't know how to answer that honestly. Sure, she didn't like being known as the weird girl who lived in the apartment down the hall. But what did that matter? It was her life, however unusual. Why should she care what other people thought of her? Especially strangers.

"Not to be an enabler, but if you preferred to curl up on your couch and watch movies all night, I would be content with that."

Ali gave him a halfhearted laugh. Did she want to be a functioning member of society? Sure. But considering her newly discovered heritage and all that came with it, Ali supposed normal wasn't a word she could ever really use to describe her life.

Just thinking about how much and how fast everything was changing, she felt as if she couldn't get enough air. She attempted to force it down, but a fresh wave of anxiety washed over her. And despite the cool breeze drifting through the yard, Ali's temperature rose.

She could feel the panic attack building, but it was nothing like the others. Still, she took another slow, deep breath before opening her eyes again. Instead of peering out over the garden at the view that usually calmed her, she found Nicolai's sage-green eyes studying her with concern.

"Alessandra." His warm hands enveloped hers. "I both see and feel your growing unease. Let me help you."

Ali stared up at him, wondering what the hell he could do to take away that increasing restless feeling in her gut. But if he was offering, she'd take any help she could get. Breathless, she asked him, "How are you going to do that?"

"Tell me what is happening in your head. Better yet, take down that barrier you have put between us. Let me in."

Shaking her head before he even finished, Ali breathed, "I can't."

"Why?"

"Honestly? Because my thoughts are bouncing all over the place and I'd be embarrassed if you heard them."

Nicolai stepped closer, his eyes full of sympathy. "I understand. It can be scary to open yourself up to someone, but I will never judge you for your thoughts. I am your destined mate. I will be your partner, your other half, for the rest of our lives. I promise you that nothing you have going on up here"—he gave her temple a gentle tap—"could ever change that for me."

Ali pulled away and stepped around him. She knew his words were meant to reassure her, but they had the opposite effect, making her anxiety multiply.

"Alessandra. Talk to me. What is making you panic?"

"You," she reluctantly admitted. She didn't want to hurt his feelings. She liked him, but everything about the situation overwhelmed her.

When he didn't respond, she turned to face him again.

"Part of me is relieved that I have an explanation for some of my issues. The idea that fate or genetics or whatever has determined who I am meant to be with is sort of a relief. But at the same time, not being in control of yet another aspect of my life terrifies me. We barely know each other, but I feel like you've already staked your claim on me, and I'm not sure how I feel about that."

Nicolai released a long breath, clearly feeling the effects of her stress. "I did not mean to upset you. That is the last thing I want. But let me be clear, Alessandra. I do not need to claim you. You are already mine. Just as I am yours."

Feeling the sudden sting of tears behind her eyes, she whispered, "You can't say things like that."

Needing to put some distance between them, she

stepped onto the stone path and made her way into the garden. Surrounding herself with nature was always the best bet when it came to relieving her anxiety, but she worried it wouldn't work this time around.

Nicolai didn't make a sound, but he followed close behind her. She could sense him every step of the way, his nearness feeling like a weighted blanket when she just needed to feel light and free.

Instead, she only felt smothered and moody. Her internal temperature continued to rise, and the jittery sensation in her belly grew with every step she took. By the time she reached the bottom of the curving path, she couldn't take it anymore. She spun around to face Nicolai, and the words all but exploded out of her. "Can you back off for a minute? I just need a little room to breathe!"

The startled look on his face made Ali instantly regret her outburst. It wasn't like her to raise her voice and she felt terrible for lashing out at Nicolai.

"I'm sorry. I don't know what's wrong with me."

Nicolai took a cautious step forward, his tone soothing as he spoke. "Do not apologize. Nothing is wrong with you. You are only overwhelmed, but all will be well soon."

Ali stared at him. How could he be so sure? He didn't understand what it was like to not be in control of his own body.

Reading her thoughts, he nodded. "I do, Alessandra. I have been where you are in this moment, so I know how overstimulated your senses have become."

Her senses? Frowning, she searched internally. Was it her senses? Not just her usual panic attack? No. She already knew this was different. But...

"It is your Awakening." Nicolai held her stare and kept

his voice low. "Not only can I feel it, but I can smell it on you."

Her face flushed. Breathless, she whispered. "What the hell is that supposed to mean?"

"As our Awakening progresses, our scent grows stronger. Yours has intensified tenfold in the last half hour, doubled in the brief time we have been outside. I should have realized sooner."

Ali didn't know how to process that bit of information. She stared up at him for a long time, trying to sort out what it all meant. Then a thought occurred to her. "You smell me? Is that bad?"

"Not at all."

She hesitated, reluctant to ask, but curious. "What do I smell like?"

Nicolai's eyes drifted shut, his nostrils flaring as he slowly inhaled. He released the breath and met her eyes again before he whispered. "Heaven."

The pure bliss on his face made her heart race. And then she remembered the way his scent made her feel.

Without thought, she stepped close to Nicolai and pressed her body flush against his. Nuzzling against his throat, Ali ran her nose up the side of his neck, drawing in a lungful of his masculine scent. "I love the smell of your skin."

She couldn't believe that sultry voice was hers. She should be embarrassed by her uncharacteristic behavior, but she couldn't muster the energy to care when Nicolai growled low in his throat.

She should be terrified. Instead, it ignited something in the very center of her being. A restless, clawing need. The way Nicolai shifted his weight, she knew he felt it too.

Because when he straightened, she noted the wild flare of color in his intense eyes as he studied her upturned face.

Something passed between them in that moment, but Ali couldn't be sure what it was exactly. An acknowledgement? An acceptance? Whatever it was, she somehow knew that Nicolai was her new center. She may barely know him, but every cell in her body called to him. And something about the man woke a hunger in her that she'd never felt before.

Rising onto her tiptoes Ali ran her tongue along the edge of his ear and breathed, "Take me home."

Nicolai looked into her eyes for a long moment. Even in the dark, she could see his pupils flare. He quickly took her hand and led her up the path, around the house, back toward the road. She followed happily, knowing that when she got him back to her place and into her bed, she wasn't ever going to want to leave it again.

Sitting in the close quarters of the cab, the intense aroma that seemed to ooze from Nicolai's every pore overwhelmed her. His grip on her hand tightened when she closed her eyes and drew another deep breath, taking the scent into her lungs.

Ali felt an instant dizzying effect. And when Nicolai's palm cupped her cheek, she looked up at him again. The concern in his eyes left her breathless.

"What?" she panted.

With a hint of emotion that she couldn't quite place, he told her, "It is nearly time."

Ali felt flush. Her body shook the way it did when she had one of her episodes. But this time around, a low pulsing vibration radiated through her, and she even felt it throbbing in her gums.

Nicolai was right. The time for her change quickly approached. She could feel it. The ache grew in strength, intensifying until it felt unpleasant. It spread to every joint and muscle in her body.

By the time they reached her apartment, Ali's hands shook so hard she could barely get the key into the door.

Once inside, she could only stand there. She didn't know what to do. How much time did she have left before she was writhing in pain? Would it last a long time? Would it be quick, like ripping off a band-aid?

She nearly jumped out of her skin when Nicolai's arms came around her, but she settled back against him when he dragged her close and whispered against her ear. "I know you feel overwhelmed, but all will be well, Alessandra. I am here with you."

Having his arms around her felt so good it brought tears to her eyes, but as much as his words comforted her, she knew it wouldn't last. Soon the pain would be unbearable and there was nothing he could do to stop it.

"Just breathe."

He ran a gentle hand over her hair and down her back. On an ordinary day, the gesture would have been enough to soothe her. Not that day.

Ali closed her eyes, trying to focus on remaining calm. But no amount of deliberate breathing could have prepared her for when that first wave of pain rocked through her body. If Nicolai hadn't been holding onto her, she would've collapsed to the floor.

It didn't last more than thirty seconds but left behind a lingering ache in her every muscle. As her body eased, Ali let her head fall against Nicolai's chest, her breaths coming in a ragged, panting rhythm.

"Come. You must lie down."

He helped her to the bed, pulling back the covers for her. Once she climbed in and settled on her side, Nicolai crawled in behind her. He snuggled close, tucking his arms around her and drawing her back against his warm body.

They barely got settled in when the next wave of pain hit her. Her body tensed, and she held her breath as it rolled through her, much stronger than the first one.

Ali lost track of time as wave after wave overtook her, assaulting her mind as brutally as it did her body. At some point, she had a fleeting thought that childbirth might be more enjoyable. But her thoughts quickly vanished when her body arched violently.

Through it all, Nicolai held onto her, whispering reassuring words and nuzzling her neck. Having him there with her helped, but her entire body felt like it was on fire.

"Relax, my strong female. You are doing great. Just breathe with me."

She did as he said and took in a deep, shuddering breath. It eased the pain a little, so she took another, following his breathing pattern as well as she could.

She didn't know how long the pain lasted, but when it crested, the discomfort slowly dissipated until her whole body relaxed again.

She savored the moment, warm in his arms, but the reprieve didn't last. Not ten seconds later, her body felt as though it split apart, and the sound of a tormented animal echoed through the room. Her throat ached, dry and raw like the time she lost her voice the summer before her mother passed away. But this wasn't bronchitis. It was nowhere near as pleasant.

Another ragged cry echoed through the room as her

body shook with such violence her vision blurred. With her eyes squeezed shut, Ali silently prayed for it all to be over. She didn't know if she could withstand even one more second of the torture.

She couldn't be sure if she blacked out or if everything suddenly stilled. Whatever the case, the relief was blinding. Ali drifted in and out of consciousness, vaguely aware of her surroundings. But when awareness trickled back in, she lay panting, her body shuddering sporadically. All the while, Nicolai whispered soothing words.

When Ali finally opened her eyes again, everything appeared different. Clearer. More vibrant despite the darkness.

She lay on her side, her head in Nicolai's lap. His warm hand gently stroked her neck and shoulder over and over while her breaths slowly returned to a steadier rhythm. Each inhale and exhale felt strange. Her body didn't respond the same way it had before. She'd changed. As had the world around her. Everything looked, smelled, and felt different. Even Nicolai's touch. Especially his touch.

Then realization struck. It had happened. She'd made it through her first transformation.

Though curious about her appearance, Ali didn't have the energy left to lift her head and see what her jaguar form looked like. But because she was too exhausted to keep her mental walls in place, Nicolai easily read her thoughts.

Caressing her cheek, he assured her. "You are beautiful, amor."

Her eyes drifted shut again. *Show me.*

Ali felt the gentle push of his thoughts and gasped as

the image formed in her mind. Stretched out on her disheveled bed lay a breathtaking golden jaguar with dark rosettes dotting its sleek coat. She didn't know why she expected to be black like Nicolai. She knew melanistic jaguars were much less common than spotted ones. Still, that's what she'd envisioned.

Nicolai's hand glided lovingly over the cat's lean neck and down its side. Ali felt his touch in the corresponding places on her own body, and that was the only thing that made it all feel real.

"I know it is disorienting but you will find your bearings. Give it time."

His soothing tone and continuous touching made her want to drift off to sleep.

"Rest, Alessandra. I am going nowhere."

11

Nicolai lay for hours watching the gentle rise and fall of his mate's chest. She sprawled on her back beside him, sleeping like the dead. Not even the growing sounds of the city that drifted in through the open window disrupted her slumber. After the night she had, he wouldn't be surprised if she slept most of the day away.

Nicolai couldn't wait until she opened those beautiful eyes again, but knowing what a rarity a good, quality sleep was for Alessandra, he didn't dare wake her. She needed the rest. He could only hope this was the new norm for her. No more reluctance to go to sleep. No more fear of what awaited her when she did. Only time would tell though.

Sometime around mid-morning, Nicolai felt the first signs of her waking. Careful not to disturb her, he remained quiet, watching her as she slowly woke.

When she finally opened her eyes, he could see the momentary confusion. Then she turned her head and looked him in the eyes.

Keeping his voice pitched low, Nicolai offered a gentle greeting. "Good morning."

She blinked slowly, her expression unreadable. *You're still here.*

"Of course. Where else would I be?"

Her gaze drifted over the expanse of his bare torso, and Nicolai saw the golden sheen flicker in her amber irises. He knew it was a sign of her jaguar surfacing, but it settled again just as quickly.

Surprising him, Alessandra rolled onto her side and snuggled close, resting her head on his shoulder. They lay for a long time in comfortable silence while she absently traced her fingertips over his exposed flesh. Never in his life had Nicolai been so content to stay in bed all day. But with his mate in his arms, he was tempted.

"Are you hungry?" he asked against her hair.

I'm starving.

"Would you like me to get you something to eat?"

Yes, please, she said as she absently rubbed her cheek against his chest.

Nicolai would rather lay in bed with her all day, but his mate needed sustenance and it was his responsibility to make sure she got it.

Though reluctant to leave her side, Nicolai placed a gentle kiss to her forehead. "Get more rest. I will be back shortly."

As he slid out of bed, Ali made a soft noise behind him. He knew glancing back at her was a mistake the second he turned.

With her arms over her head, Ali's back arched as she stretched. Nicolai had never seen anything so adorable, yet so incredibly sexy at the same time. The way the sheet pulled tight over her chest didn't leave much to the imagination. He could see her nipples through the thin fabric, and he wanted nothing more than to yank it off her to get an unhindered view of her glorious body.

Though he'd seen her without a stitch of clothes on during the night, there had been nothing sexual about the experience. But seeing her in the warm morning light woke the part of him he'd been suppressing for the sake of her comfort.

Climbing back in bed with her felt like the better option, but Nicolai had to remind himself of his mission. Food. His mate needed food.

Tearing his gaze away from her, Nicolai pulled on his shoes and retrieved his shirt from the floor. He made a point to take slow, deep breaths while he worked the buttons into place and rolled the sleeves up his forearms.

He'd reined in his impulses by the time he'd fully dressed, and his mate lay on her side watching him as if she liked what she saw.

Unable to keep the space between them, Nicolai sat on the edge of the bed, gently brushing her wild hair from her face. "What do you crave?"

She hesitated a heartbeat before finally speaking aloud. "Food."

The second the word left her lips, Ali froze, confusion crossing her delicate features.

"Something wrong?"

Ali lifted a tentative hand to her mouth, her catlike eyes wide with surprise. "My teeth. They're so big."

Nicolai couldn't stop his smile from coming. He found it endearing the way Ali's words slurred. He remembered vividly the first time he spoke after his own canines came in. Even when in their resting position, they'd filled his mouth in a way that took him weeks to grow accustomed to.

"Let me see." Nicolai reached out, gently lifting her top lip with his thumb.

Ali instinctively opened for him, allowing him to inspect the sharp little white daggers. They extended beyond her blunt human teeth, and they were beautiful.

"This is normal in the beginning." He promised her. "But they will not always be this way."

Ali's brows furrowed. "They won't?"

"No. They will lengthen like this and more when you are agitated or excited in any way. But most times, they will stay the same length as your other teeth. See."

He pulled his own lip back, showing her his resting canines and Ali quickly sat up. Her hand lightly gripping his jaw as she leaned in for a closer look. "Wow. How have I not noticed them before now?"

Nicolai took her hand, kissed the palm. "You had other things on your mind. Especially last night."

His words triggered her memories of the night before. The images flashed through her mind in rapid succession, and Nicolai sat quietly while she processed it all. Finally, she met his gaze again, her gorgeous eyes wide with surprise. *I did it.*

"And you did well."

She stared beyond him, recalling the moment her jaguar burst free of its confines. It had been a thing of beauty, but he could see a flicker of doubt in her expression. "I remember screaming."

With two fingers under her chin, Nicolai gently drew her attention back to him. "We all have difficulty with our Awakening. The first time our jaguar overtakes us is painful, yes. But with more practice, it comes easier. It is much like working any muscle. The more you use it, the stronger it grows."

"And feeding muscles builds their strength, too, right?"

Her hopeful tone made Nicolai smile. "Of course."

"Then get me some food already. I'm starving."

So surprised by her demand, Nicolai dropped his hand, staring at her in disbelief.

After a short, awkward silence she raised her delicate brows. "Get me some food, please?"

Chuckling, Nicolai stood and placed another kiss on her forehead before leaving her alone with her thoughts.

ALI DIDN'T KNOW what to think. Everything felt different with her senses amplifying her entire environment. The air around her. The way it rushed in and out of her lungs. The scents that came with it. Some delicious, like the smell of stir fry coming from somewhere in the building. Or the lingering scent of Nicolai…everywhere.

Unfortunately, not all the scents were so pleasant. Not only could she catch a hint of the dumpsters in the alley, and the harsh bite of the exhaust from the passing cars, but she could smell the dried sweat on her own skin and bedding. How Nicolai endured it, she hadn't a clue, but she wouldn't make him deal with it again when he came back from the store.

Dragging herself out of bed, Ali stiffened when she felt the cool air on her skin. She looked down at herself, confused as to why she was naked. When had that happened? And how had she only just noticed?

For a moment, panic tried to creep in, but Ali pushed it away. She didn't know Nicolai very well yet, but she trusted him enough to know that he hadn't taken advantage of her. It was just a bit disconcerting waking up naked without any recollection of how it happened.

After gathering her dress off the floor, Ali stripped the bed and shoved everything into the washer. She sprayed her favorite citrus room deodorizer to freshen up the place, then hopped into the shower for a quick scrub down.

Once she was clean, moisturized, hair dried, and dressed, Ali felt much better. She grabbed new sheets from the linen closet and made the bed. Though she could have easily crawled back in and slept another four hours, her stomach was making audible demands. Good thing Nicolai wasn't gone a terribly long time. Still, by the time he returned, she was so hungry she'd eat about anything.

She figured he'd grab something from the deli across the street or the diner down the block. Something quick and easy. What she didn't expect was him to walk through the door carrying two oversized canvas grocery bags overflowing with food.

Ali snorted. "Did you clear out the produce section?"

Nicolai laughed. "Not quite."

She followed him into the kitchen, having a peek into one of the bags. "I know I said I was hungry, but this is a bit much. There's no way I'm eating all this before it goes bad."

"You will."

"Not without your help."

Nicolai propped his hands on the counter and looked over at her. "Alessandra, your body is changing, and as it continues to adjust to your surfacing nature, you will need to eat more to replenish the energy you burn. Last night, you depleted a great deal during your first transformation."

She supposed he was right. She did still feel tired.

Nicolai nodded to the kitchen table. "Go sit while I prepare some food for you."

"You don't have to do that. It's enough that you did the shopping." Besides, he was a guest in her home.

She grabbed a cutting board from beside the stove, but as she reached for a knife, Nicolai covered her hand with his. "Let me. It is important."

Although the independent part of her wanted to insist she at least help him, something about the look on his face made her relent. Crossing her arms over her chest, Ali leaned a hip against the counter. "Okay, but tell me why."

He stared at her, his eyes searching hers for a moment before he explained. "For countless generations, our people thrived by upholding our traditions. But many of those traditions have been lost over the years in our attempt to adapt with the times or overcome tragedies. Still, those of us remaining believe in continuing the customs we most value. Especially those centered around nurturing and caring for our mates."

"And that includes feeding me when I'm perfectly capable of doing it myself?"

"Not the point. I know you are capable. But as your mate, I have the overwhelming need to take care of you. It is something I have looked forward to all my life."

Really? All his life?

"Yes." Nicolai answered, easily reading her thoughts. "It is customary for a Jagara male to see his mate through her Awakening. And when the times come, her mating and birthing cycles as well."

Ali stared at him, unsure how to respond. She barely had her foot into his world, and he was already talking about knocking her up?

"I know there is much to take in, but as your mate, it is my responsibility to teach you everything you need to know about our people. I am happy I get the privilege of being the one to ease you into our way of life." He grinned. "I suppose I could have held off on the reproduction talk."

Yeah. That would have been nice. Having babies with him shouldn't be a part of the conversation yet, but there was no taking it back once it was out there.

Snagging a bowl from the cabinet, Ali set it next to the cutting board for Nicolai and then hopped onto the counter to watch him work. His quick, efficient movements were impressive. He was good with a knife.

Happy to change the subject, Ali said, "I'm just realizing I never asked what you do for a living. I'm assuming you're a chef."

Nicolai paused, glancing over at her. "Actually, I fly for an exclusive travel company."

Ali scoffed and nodded toward his hands. "Never seen a pilot use a knife like that."

He chuckled. "Know a lot of pilots, do you?"

"None, actually."

Nicolai tossed a handful of mangos into the bowl and got to work on a pineapple. "Control over a blade is a common skill among our people. We train at an early age to wield them properly, be it standard use or self-defense. It is a convenient, if not necessary, tool to have. Especially in the jungle."

Ali could understand that. She'd never been, but she'd learned on those nature shows and read about it in those books her mother collected, the jungle could be a dangerous place if you weren't careful.

She grabbed a piece of fruit and popped it into her mouth. The moment the sweet, tangy flavor burst on her tongue, she closed her eyes, humming her appreciation. Never in her life had a mango tasted so good. Nor anything else that she could recall.

When Ali opened her eyes again, she found Nicolai watching her, his knuckles white as he gripped the edge of the counter. Just like that, the mood between them shifted. It felt like all the air got sucked out of the room and the heat in his expression woke a swarm of butterflies in her belly.

"You cannot make sounds like that."

She felt the heat creep into her cheeks the moment she understood what he meant. The raspy, strained quality of his voice and the way he devoured her with those impossibly pale green eyes stole her breath. So much for wondering if he was physically attracted to her.

"Attraction has never been a problem."

His ability to read her thoughts so clearly could be unnerving at times, but sometimes, she was glad he knew what was going through her mind. It was easier for him to read it than for her to work up the courage to speak it.

"The benefits of a mate bond," he agreed. "But there is no need to be afraid to say what you feel."

Yeah. That would take her some time. While she felt more comfortable with him than she did most people, she wasn't accustomed to letting anyone get too close. Aside from the necessary interactions with a select few, Ali rarely even talked to others. Much less shared her feelings.

Even her best friend got a watered-down version sometimes. But that was only because Maggie already worried about her enough. Ali didn't want to bombard her with every little ridiculous anxiety trigger.

The thing was, even though she called or texted regularly to check in, Maggie had never once treated Ali like she was broken. She helped make life easier without making her feel like a burden. That's why Ali had become friends with her in the first place. Well, that, and Maggie's persistence.

Nicolai's eyes softened, the tension in his shoulders easing. "I am glad you have her."

"Me too." If not for Maggie inserting herself into Ali's life, the last few years would have been unbearable. Ali might not have been in a good enough place to let Nicolai in the way she had. And how tragic would that have been?

Though only in the beginning stages of their relationship, Nicolai had already changed her life forever. She still had a long way to go, but she already couldn't imagine a future without him.

Nicolai moved closer, his knuckles brushing her cheek. "No need to worry about such things. I was always meant to be in your life. Neither fate nor our nature would have allowed any other outcome."

Having no choice with where life took her and who she ended up with should have Ali panicking. At the very least, she should feel some level of concern. But that wasn't the case. Nicolai's words along with his gentle touch both calmed and excited her.

A slow smile curved his lips. "Good to know."

Finally tearing her eyes from his, Ali snagged another piece of fruit and popped it into her mouth. This time, she didn't make a sound. Instead, she focused intently on Nicolai's movements, staying quiet while he peeled and chopped the rest of the fruit.

By the time he finished, he'd nearly filled the large mixing bowl. Nicolai sat the knife down and grabbed a small chunk of mango, offering it to her.

Without thought, Ali leaned toward his outstretched hand, accepting the juicy bite like it was the most natural thing in the world for him to feed her.

Ali's lips grazed his fingers, and the low growl that rumbled in Nicolai's throat froze her in place. The guttural, primal sound sent a lightning bolt of arousal shooting through her, and she felt it in every nerve ending in her body.

Slowly chewing the sweet fruit, Ali watched as Nicolai lifted his hand, licking the juice from his fingers.

He held her gaze the entire time, his intense focus making her crave more than just eating from his hand. She wanted to lick every drop of juice from his fingers. Before she could stop herself, Ali reached out and took his hand, bringing it to her mouth. The sweetness of the mango still lingered on his skin, and she savored every drop.

His ragged breaths told her everything she needed to know. She didn't have to read his thoughts to know they aligned with hers. Still, he didn't make a move.

Multiple times over the last two weeks Ali thought he might kiss her, but not once had he followed through. Each time he pulled away, making her wonder if she'd read him wrong. But with him standing so close and the intensity of his focus, she knew he felt the same craving she did. If he meant what he said, if he was so attracted to her, why didn't he go for it? Would she have to make the first move?

Uncertain where the courage came from, Ali looked him straight in the eyes. "Why haven't you kissed me?"

Nicolai drew a deep breath and let it out slowly. "I wanted to wait until you were ready."

Ali was more than ready. She craved his mouth on hers. Needed it more than she needed her next breath. And though nervous, she held his stare as she lifted her chin in invitation. "Then kiss me."

She'd never been so forward in her life, but Nicolai didn't seem to mind. Judging by the resolve in his eyes, her invitation was all he needed. He stepped between her knees, took her face in his hands, and pressed his lips to hers.

It was a gentle kiss. Nothing overly sexual. But Ali's body came alive in an instant. A tingling heat blossomed beneath her skin, spreading until it completely consumed her. She had no idea a simple kiss could elicit such an intense reaction, but she could easily get addicted to the feeling.

Nicolai must have agreed, because his fingers sank into her hair, and he slanted his mouth over hers.

It was a slow, drugging kiss. Nicolai's tongue gently stroked against hers and Ali got lost in the moment, savoring the feel and taste of his mouth. She could sit on that counter for hours with him wedged between her legs and let him devour her if he wanted.

With a throaty groan, Nicolai gripped her hips and pulled her to the edge. Ali's breath left her in a rush the moment his hips pressed against hers. She could feel every hard inch of his undeniable arousal.

In a moment of panic, she pushed him away, slamming the door on her thoughts. What the hell was she doing? She'd only asked for a kiss, but if they continued down their current path, they'd end up back in her bed. And unlike last time, they wouldn't be sleeping.

She could see by the hunger in Nicolai's bright eyes, he was willing to keep going if that's what she wanted. But was she ready to be that vulnerable with him?

Sure, she'd loved every exhilarating second, but she also felt a hint of embarrassment. She'd only been kissed twice in her life. Once by the neighbor boy when she was thirteen, and again on her eighteenth birthday. The first had been innocent enough, but neither had been anywhere near as enjoyable as it was with Nicolai.

"Not that I have much to compare it to, but you are an amazing kisser."

"As are you, amor."

Ali hesitated, surprised by his response, but then smiled at him. She hadn't realized they'd advanced to endearments already, but she liked the idea of him calling her "love."

She never thought herself capable of having a normal relationship with anyone. In a way, she'd mourned the loss of that hope a long time ago. But since meeting Nicolai, all that had changed. There was a bond between them she didn't fully understand yet, one that grew stronger by the day. And whatever was between them, it wasn't your average connection. She looked forward to exploring it more.

After everything that had happened since he'd come into her life, Ali knew she wanted so much more than just the comfortable friendship they'd been building. She wanted the full mate connection and everything that came with it.

12

For as long as she could remember, Ali had obsessed over every decision she'd ever made. But for the first time, she felt sure of herself. She didn't know if it was all the years of pent-up sexual frustration or the mysterious bond between the two of them. Whatever the reason, Ali craved so much more than just kisses with Nicolai. She wanted all of him.

Hopping off the counter, her eyes never left his as she slowly made her way to the bedroom. A hunger that matched her own blazed in Nicolai's iridescent eyes.

Ali's heart thumped with excitement as she stepped into the doorway and beckoned him with a shy smile. For a heartbeat, she thought he might refuse her, but the second Nicolai shifted his stance, she knew he wouldn't tell her no. Instead, he followed her, closely watching her every move.

Ali stripped off her clothes as she backed into the bedroom. And Nicolai followed her, his greedy gaze raking over every inch of exposed flesh. She couldn't decide which she felt strongest. Vulnerable or exhilarated. Either way, every coherent thought drifted away when Nicolai stalked closer, peeling his clothes off as well.

She'd seen every gorgeous inch of the man before, but those times hadn't had quite the same impact. Nicolai was a frighteningly beautiful man and Ali was enthralled.

Standing fully naked in front of her mate, she should feel some inkling of unease. Nervousness, at the very least. But nope. Only a clawing, burning need to have Nicolai's body against hers.

A deep growl rumbled low in his throat, and he shifted his stance. Pale eyes followed her every move, watching her from beneath thick, dark lashes.

Ali didn't know why she did it. Instinct, perhaps? But she turned, offering her back to Nicolai. She watched him over her shoulder, her body feeling warm and lithe as she crawled onto the bed.

As he prowled closer, her vision shifted. Colors grew more vivid. Even the tiniest details sharpened. Ali's body was alive with sensations. Her restlessness increased with every step he took.

His eyes slid over her body like a caress. Delicious images flashed through her mind. Visions of them intertwined. Nicolai's mouth devouring hers and his body claiming what was his.

Ali desperately wanted those visions to be her reality. Her temperature increased, her breaths came in shuddering draws, and a low-level vibration hummed throughout her entire body. Or was it Nicolai's? Their mental connection was so strong, she couldn't tell where her need ended and his began.

With his eyes blazing, Nicolai climbed onto the bed

and claimed her mouth with a deep kiss. Relief washed over her, but it wasn't enough. An overwhelming hunger for more clawed at her insides. A hunger like none she'd ever felt before.

Gripping at his back, Ali drew him closer, and soaked up the feel of his smooth, warm skin against hers.

The kiss went on and on, growing more intense with every swipe of his tongue. The tingling heat that blossomed in Ali's body rose until it overwhelmed her. For a heartbeat, she panicked again and pushed against his chest.

Nicolai growled in protest but instantly eased up, giving her a moment to breathe. Regret washed over her the moment his warm body left hers. Still, she took advantage of the space he'd put between them and rolled onto her belly. She attempted to crawl away from him, but she didn't get far.

She went still the second she felt Nicolai's breath dance over her skin. Ali closed her eyes, a shiver rushing up her spine. All her senses flared, making her painfully aware of every subtle move Nicolai made. Still, she startled when his mouth touched the small of her back.

Easy, love. Nicolai whispered into her mind. The gentle brush of his thoughts against hers soothed her. Nicolai wanted her, but if she chose to stop, he would back off and give her more time.

That wasn't what she wanted though. Sure, part of her thought it was too soon for them to explore the physical side of their relationship. But it was a very small part. Her need for him outweighed any miniscule doubt or nervousness. She wanted him.

Nicolai's tongue traced her spine, from the small of her back to her nape. Though unsure how to feel about the rasping draw of his catlike tongue, Ali squirmed beneath him, her body craving more.

Nicolai growled his approval, pressing open-mouthed kisses along her shoulder as he pushed his knee between her thighs. Ali followed his lead and moved her legs wider, her entire body tingling with anticipation.

The moment his hips met hers, Ali pushed back against him. She could feel every hard inch of him pressed against her overheated core.

Nicolai groaned into the side of her neck and rocked against her, his arousal sliding easily through her slick folds.

Ali gasped into the blanket. The throbbing in her center grew stronger, and she couldn't help herself. She rolled her hips in invitation.

Nicolai hummed his approval, nipping at her neck as he rocked against her again.

Ali couldn't be still. She moved restlessly under him, needing the friction. "Please."

"What is it, love?" Nicolai asked as he brushed over her hot entrance.

Ali whimpered. "Please."

He growled. "Tell me."

"I want you." She released a ragged breath. "Inside me."

Nicolai gripped her hip and pushed forward, their simultaneous gasps filling the otherwise quiet room. Overwhelmed by the delicious invasion, Ali took a moment to adjust.

Nicolai rested his forehead against her shoulder. *You feel amazing.*

She could tell by his shuddering breaths that he fought to maintain composure.

So soft. So hot. So perfect.

Panting, she rolled her hips and begged him, *Keep going.*

Nicolai's arm slipped around her waist, his warm palm coming to rest between her breasts, holding her close. He gave her what she wanted. What they both needed. He fell into a rhythm, keeping his pace slow at first. Ali savored each plunge, rolling her hips against his every time he sank into her.

As the last remnants of the wall between their thoughts came tumbling down, Ali was lost to sensation. The physical pleasure. The connection. The emotion it stirred within her. She could feel it all. Not only hers, but everything Nicolai felt as well.

Though overwhelmed, Ali couldn't hold still. The way she pushed back against him, meeting his every stroke, drove them both toward a release that could be nothing short of explosive.

The sound of their ragged breaths. The tingling, burning heat that rushed beneath her skin. The obscene, wet noises their bodies made as they came together. Every bit of it added to the growing intensity.

Suddenly, the pace changed and Nicolai let out a vicious growl. His hands gripped her harder, one on her hip and the other creeping up to the base of her throat. For a heartbeat, panic wanted to bubble up from the depths. But Ali didn't have time to fully acknowledge it.

She went still the moment Nicolai's mouth clamped onto the back of her neck. Nothing had ever felt so delicious, yet so terrifying at the same time. She was torn between wanting him to stop and needing him to keep going.

With a possessive growl, Nicolai gripped her tighter, his thrusts growing in force and speed.

Ali grasped desperately at the blanket beneath them, attempting to hold onto some semblance of control. But to no avail. A profound mix of sensations coursed through her, building and building with no end in sight.

Just when she thought she could take no more, Nicolai's sharp teeth broke through the tender flesh of her shoulder and set off a chain reaction.

Those four little pinpoints of pain flooded her with the most breathtaking pleasure she'd ever experienced. It was like a dam burst inside her. Wave after wave washed over her, and when her inner muscles convulsed around him, Nicolai went still. Ali could feel the near violent pulses of his release deep inside her as he followed her into oblivion.

They lay panting, lost in a sea of haze while their bodies slowly calmed. And by the time Ali could draw in a steady breath, she felt Nicolai shift over her.

He extracted his teeth from her shoulder with unexpected gentleness. Ali felt a warm trickle ease from the tender wound, but Nicolai's tongue swept over the trail and back up to the punctures.

At the very least, Ali should be angry with him for biting her. Yet, somehow, she wasn't. She'd welcomed the pain because pleasure had accompanied it, a pleasure she could never have imagined possible.

Ali let Nicolai tend to her, enjoying the feel of his tongue rasping against her hypersensitive skin. He lapped at the aching spot, then closed his lips over it, massaging it with his tongue.

He placed a line of soft kisses across her shoulder, and despite his gentleness when he finally slipped from inside her, they both gasped at the separation.

When Nicolai collapsed beside her, his warm fingers brushed her hair back from her face.

Prying her eyes open, Ali found him studying her. The genuine concern in his too-bright eyes made her heart flutter. Not wanting him to worry, she offered him a satisfied smile and dragged herself closer. She draped her arm over his sweat-covered chest and rested her head on his shoulder. Ali felt relaxed to the very center of her being, and she didn't have a single care in the world.

Nicolai's fingers sank into her mussed hair and held her close. "Your thoughts are not clear to me, love. Tell me you are all right."

Ali grinned against his chest. "My thoughts aren't all that clear to me either. But I promise you, I am very much okay."

With a heavy sigh, he gave her a squeeze and pressed his lips to her forehead. "Good to know."

Though happy to lay there for the rest of the day, Ali felt a rising need to make a trip to the bathroom.

"Then go," he whispered against her hair.

Reluctant to leave the comfort of his arms, Ali pushed herself upright and turned to put her feet on the floor. After a good stretch, she looked over her shoulder at the sexy man lying in her bed. She couldn't help but smile. He was a vision. *The* vision, to be exact. He looked exactly like he had in their shared dream.

Nicolai eased across the short distance she'd put

between them. His arm wrapped around her waist, and he placed a kiss to her spine. "Alessandra?"

She laughed softly, knowing how this would play out. She'd seen it. "Yes, Nico?"

"Hurry back, amor." He kissed her once more, his lips brushing her back and eliciting a pleasant little shiver.

When he finally let her wiggle from his grasp, she headed to the bathroom to empty her bladder. Not wanting to be away from him any longer than she had to, Ali hurried to take care of business so she could crawl back in the bed with Nicolai.

As she moved to the sink to wash her hands, Ali caught a glimpse of her eyes in the mirror. They looked much like Nicolai's. Bright irises with that familiar iridescent feline sheen, and her pupils flared as she leaned in closer to inspect them. She was in awe. Instead of their usual soft brown color, her eyes looked like deep pools of warm golden honey.

Beautiful. Nicolai whispered into her mind.

Movement in the doorway caught her attention. Her mate stood gloriously naked, leaning against the jamb with his arms folded over his chiseled chest.

His eyes drifted down the length of her and then back up to meet hers again in the mirror. "How is your shoulder?"

Ali reached up, her fingers brushing over the tender flesh. It wasn't terribly sore, which surprised her. Especially when she leaned in again and spotted the four puncture marks marring the curve where her neck and shoulder met.

Running her fingers over the spot again, she closed her eyes, recalling the sensation that rushed through her when his teeth broke the surface. The intensity she felt in that moment was more than just the mix of pleasure and pain. It was a binding of sorts. She felt the shift deep inside, and though she still didn't fully comprehend the complexity of their connection, she welcomed it.

"Come back to bed, love. You need rest and I need to hold you."

As Ali woke from a much-needed rest, she heard a low, rhythmic buzzing coming from somewhere nearby. It died off and then a few minutes later, it started up again.

Oh! Her phone. Someone was calling.

There were only a handful of people it could be, and she didn't want to talk to any of them. She would rather still be sleeping. She didn't want to move, but she knew that if they were calling, it was for a good reason.

Reluctantly, she rolled over and grabbed the phone off her side table without even opening her eyes. "Hello?"

"Where the hell have you been?" It was Maggie and her voice was thick with worry. "I've been trying to get ahold of you for hours. Why haven't you answered your phone?"

Confused, Ali pulled the phone from her ear and looked at the screen. Fourteen text messages and nine missed calls. "That's funny. I didn't hear it ring."

The line was quiet for so long, Ali pulled the phone

from her ear again to make sure the call hadn't dropped. Nope. Still connected. Finally, Maggie asked, "Ali, are you okay?"

"Yeah." She rubbed her eyes. "Just tired."

"Tired? Dare I ask what happened to you last night?"

Ali frowned. "Last night?"

"Yeah. You disappeared. I'm assuming you went home with Nicolai."

Images of the last twenty-four hours came flooding into her mind. For a moment, panic trickled in. What was she supposed to say?

But after a beat of silence, Maggie asked. "Did you go home with him?"

Ali looked across the empty bed, a twinge of disappointment setting in when she realized Nicolai wasn't there. She sat up, listening for him in the other room. Nothing but silence. Ali eased from the bed, clutching the sheet around her naked body, and padded barefoot to the doorway. Nico wasn't in her apartment. After everything they'd gone through together, after everything they'd done, would he just leave like that?

"Ali?"

She could hear the worry in Maggie's voice, but she didn't know how to reassure her friend without telling her too much.

"That's it. I'm cancelling my meeting and I'm coming over there right now. If that man did something—"

"What?" Ali all but screeched. "No! He would never hurt me, Maggie. I'm fine. Just trying to wake up. I had a rough night. That's all."

"Are you sure? He's not right there making you say that, is he?"

Ali snorted, rubbing her forehead. "Look, I'm sorry. I didn't mean to make you worry. I just wasn't feeling all that great last night, and Nico brought me home."

"Did you get sick or did your social meter just run out?"

Unsure what to say, Ali jumped on the explanation. "Yeah. I got really overwhelmed and my anxiety skyrocketed. I wasn't thinking all that clearly and I just wanted to come home."

"So, you just left without saying anything?" Maggie blew out a frustrated breath. "Ali, I've been so worried about you. You could have said something. Or at least texted me that you were leaving?"

Suddenly irritated by her friend's tone, Ali snapped. "I was a little preoccupied. Sorry."

Maggie exhaled slowly, and when she spoke again, her tone was much softer. "How are you feeling now? You sound kind of rough. Do you need anything?"

"No. I'm fine. I just needed sleep, I guess. You know how exhausted I am after one of my episodes." That's all Ali could say. She couldn't tell Maggie the truth. Not all of it, anyway.

"You sure you're okay?"

"I could use a hot bath, and something to eat."

"Well, I need to go. I'm meeting a new client for dinner. I just thought I'd try calling you again before I left." Maggie let out a heavy sigh. "Get some food in you and get some more rest. I'll call and check on you in the morning. If you need anything, day or night, don't hesitate to call me. Okay?"

"Yeah," Ali agreed. "I'll talk to you later."

The sound of keys drew her attention to her apartment

door. Clutching the sheet tighter, she sat her phone on the counter and stepped around the corner into the entryway just as Nicolai shoved the door open with his foot.

He hesitated when he spotted her and then grinned. "Well, isn't this a nice surprise."

Ali watched him kick the door closed and eyed his bags with curiosity. "Where'd you go?"

"Figured since you were sleeping so heavy, I'd get my things from the hotel like we talked about this morning. And I grabbed more food while I was out." He sat the takeout bags on the counter and let his duffle bag slide off his shoulder before he sauntered over to her.

Ali stared up at him as he drew her close and placed a gentle kiss to her lips.

"How do you feel? Did you sleep well?"

Ali nodded. "Until Maggie called. Which she did a lot, apparently. I'm surprised I didn't hear it before."

"Not me. You were focused on other things. And besides, I found your phone beneath the bed while searching for my clothes. It would not turn on, so I plugged it in before I left." Guilt flickered over Nicolai's features. "I should have thought to let her know, last night, that you were all right. She must have been so worried."

"Definitely. She threatened to cancel dinner with a new client to come over here and check on me."

Nicolai sighed, resting his forehead against hers. "She is never going to trust me with you, is she?"

Ali fought a grin. "I'm sure she'll come around."

14

A week later, Ali stood beside Maggie, chatting with a few of her friends. Well, Maggie chatted. Ali just listened, only joining in the conversation when someone addressed her directly.

At the moment, Charline was bragging about her kid scoring the game-winning point of the final playoff game. And for the life of her, Ali couldn't remember what sport the woman had mentioned. She only half listened, feigning interest when necessary. But for the most part, she kept an eye on Nicolai.

He fascinated her. The way he drew and held people's attention was mesmerizing. He was such a people person, carrying conversation as easy as breathing. The exact opposite of Ali.

Standing near the piano, Nicolai and Greg listened to a man talk about mundane details of his job that, from Nicolai's thoughts, was the most uninteresting thing he'd ever heard.

Bored, Nico?

He threw her a tired look. *Nearly to tears.*

Ali laughed under her breath, earning her a curious look from Maggie. Ali leaned in and whispered, "The boys look almost comatose."

Maggie turned, and Ali knew the moment her friend spotted them. Maggie groaned. "Better go rescue them before Mr. Higgins puts them to sleep. I don't know how he does it, but that man could talk for hours about marketing. Don't get me wrong. He's a genius when it comes to doing his job, but it's a snooze fest listening to him talk about it if you aren't into that sort of thing."

The two of them made their way over to the trio, and Maggie politely inserted herself into the conversation. After a few minutes, she smiled at Mr. Higgins. "Do you mind if we steal these two from you?"

"Not at all."

The second he shifted his focus to the group of people to his left, Maggie linked arms with Ali and led her to the bar.

The bartender sat four glasses in front of them. Ali didn't usually drink, and she'd never had champagne before. But she accepted a drink anyway and took a tentative sip. It wasn't exactly what she expected, but it wasn't terrible.

Tiny bubbles fizzed and crackled in the glass, tickling her nose as she drank. It smelled of citrus and delicate flowers. Tasted crisp and fresh, but with a subtle spicy flavor that lingered on the tongue.

Maggie raised a curious eyebrow. "Good?"

Ali shrugged but took another drink. "Not bad."

Maggie chuckled softly. "Well, don't overdo it. This stuff goes to your head quick."

Two glasses and a half hour later, Ali knew precisely what her friend meant. Every bit of tension she'd felt before had disappeared. She couldn't be sure if that was the bubbly or Nicolai's constant touching. But either way, Ali had never felt so comfortable and carefree. But that wasn't all she felt.

With their proximity, Ali couldn't escape his masculine scent. It made her want to press her nose against his throat and inhale deeply. Maybe even drag her tongue over the exposed flesh so she could taste him.

Maggie and Greg were so deep in conversation, neither of them heard the low growl rumble in Nicolai's chest. *Careful with your thoughts, love.*

Why's that?

Nicolai's pale eyes bore into hers. *Getting me worked up is not the best idea. Not here. Not now. Not when you look and smell so enticing.*

Ali's heart did a funny little flutter. Why was she so surprised by his admission? She felt the same about him. He always looked good enough to eat, and the scent coming off him was intoxicating. She couldn't wait for the night to be over so they could go home and get naked together again.

A spark of hunger lit his eyes, but with his jaw clenched, he managed to maintain his composure. *Patience is not one of your virtues, is it?*

And clearly not one of yours either. Ali shot a quick look over his shoulder, taking in the others scattered around the room. *We could always ditch the party again.*

A low growl danced through her mind. *I am barely out of the woods with Maggie. Do not make me upset your friend again.*

Disappointed, Ali let out a quiet breath and leaned back against the bar. She supposed she could endure the party for a little longer.

Nicolai stroked his fingers down her arm, drawing her attention back to him. *But we can step outside for a little relief while she is distracted.*

Well, that sounded promising.

Maggie was deep in conversation with Greg, but Ali felt guilty about sneaking away. Especially after leaving without a word the last time and making her friend worry.

Ali knew if she waited for a lull in the conversation, they might be there a while. Once Maggie got going, it was hard to get a word in. Fortunately, Maggie paid more attention to the two of them than Ali thought.

The moment Ali shifted toward her, Maggie paused, her expression showing a hint of concern. "Everything okay?"

"Great." Ali offered her a tentative smile. "We're just gonna step outside for a few. We'll be right back."

Maggie looked up at Nicolai, holding eye contact for a moment. Ali saw something pass between them. A silent, mutual understanding. Then Maggie nodded, her shoulders relaxing before she shifted her attention back to Greg.

Feeling a little less guilty, Ali slipped her hand into Nicolai's. She let him lead her through the double doors and onto the patio. The cool, misty night air enveloped her, and it felt good on her heated skin.

Ali closed her eyes and leaned back into Nicolai when his arms came around her waist. She wanted nothing more than to have their clothes gone so she could feel his bare skin against hers. Sadly, it was neither the time nor the place for such intimacy. Unless they could find somewhere no prying eyes could see them, Ali would have to wait until they got back to her apartment.

"Mmm." Nicolai nuzzled behind her ear, inhaling deeply. "Your scent is mouthwatering."

The way his warm breath danced over her sensitive skin sent a shiver through her.

He whispered. "I cannot wait to get you home."

Images flashed through Ali's mind. Images of Nicolai spreading her out on her bed. Wedging himself between her legs. His fantasy was so vivid, Ali could almost feel his hands gripping her thighs and his mouth devouring her.

Part of her wanted just that. Craved it, even. But another part of her wanted him to work for it.

Nicolai chuckled. "How about a little game of chase, then?"

Ali turned to face him, unsure if she'd heard him right. "Are you serious?"

Nicolai nodded toward the trail. "Go. I will count to ten and then follow you."

The thought both terrified and excited her, but would she play along with something like that? Did she even want to?

Nicolai shifted his weight, leaning close to her again. "One."

The single growling word sent a shiver racing through her entire body. But Ali hurried down the path, her heart in her throat as she rounded the first bend in the trail. She could no longer see Nicolai, but she heard his slow count-down in her mind.

Two.

Damn it. She hadn't thought this out. If she could hear him, he could hear her. And he would easily find her.

Three.

Trying to clear her mind, Ali forced her breaths to come in slow, controlled draws. She had to put up that mental barrier if she wanted to be able to hide and not give away her location.

Four.

"Concentrate, damn it," Ali whispered to herself.

Five.

That was the last number she heard from Nicolai. The second his counting faded out, Ali hurried toward the edge of the yard. With their connection severed, she had no way of knowing how much time she had. Would he rush through the rest or not even bother finishing?

Ali slipped into the shadows and crouched behind a massive oak tree. She couldn't see Nicolai yet, but she felt him getting closer. A low-level buzz spread throughout her body, and she knew it was because of Nicolai's proximity.

With her heart thundering with excitement, Ali peeked from behind the tree. Nicolai was nowhere in sight, but the buzzing awareness grew even stronger. Still, Ali let out a startled little squeak when Nicolai's arms snaked around her from behind.

"Got you," Nicolai laughed next to her ear.

"You cheated," Ali accused but still sank back into him, needing to feel his body against hers even if he wasn't playing fair. "No way you made it to ten."

"I may have skipped a few numbers." His arms tightened around her. "But I could not help myself. You are so tempting."

Ali struggled to catch her breath, but Nicolai didn't give her time to recover. He slid his hands up the back of her thighs, lifting her dress. But he was in for a little surprise.

The moment his rough hands touched her bare ass, he growled against her neck. "And very naughty."

Her breathless little laugh turned into a startled gasp when Nicolai spun her around without warning and pressed her back against the tree.

His bright eyes shone with hunger as he leaned in close. "You have no idea how bad I want you right now."

Oh, she knew. And between his throaty words and the ravenous look in his eyes, she felt emboldened. Ali let her head fall back against the wide trunk and held his gaze as her hand dropped to the front of his pants. Her palm rubbed against the undeniable bulge. "I think I have a clue."

Nicolai gripped her hands and pinned them against the tree above her head. His eyes bore into hers, his breaths ragged as if he struggled to control himself. With his mouth mere inches from hers, Nicolai whispered, "Stay still."

Ali nodded, the intensity in his eyes leaving her speechless. She knew he was on the verge of losing it. Though both terrified and excited, she happily obeyed. Even though the rough bark scratched against her skin, she held still, keeping her hands where Nicolai placed them. Whatever he had planned, she was more than ready for it.

Nicolai leaned closer, his nose brushing along her jaw as he drew a deep breath. He hummed with appreciation. "I love your scent."

Ali's eyes closed and she savored the feel of his lips on her skin. And a shiver raced through her when his rough tongue rasped over her pounding pulse.

A low rhythmic thrumming rose in his throat. "And your taste."

Ali wiggled restlessly, panting as his hands traveled down her arms. His fingertips brushed over her rigid nipples. The tight buds were so sensitive she felt it right through the fabric of her dress like the thin material wasn't even there.

It took every bit of Ali's self-control to not sink her fingers into his gorgeous hair and guide his mouth to the aching points.

Instead, she reined herself in and tilted her head to one side, allowing his mouth better access to the exposed flesh, giving him room to kiss and lick along her neck and collarbone.

His hands traveled down her sides, and his rough palms slipped beneath the hem of her dress again, and the feel of his warm hands gripping the backs of her thighs made her melt a little on the inside. And stole her breath when he effortlessly lifted her feet off the ground.

Ali clung to Nicolai's broad shoulders, hooking her legs around his hips. She felt vulnerable with her core bared to the cool night air. But the second Nicolai pressed closer and swiveled his hips against hers, she sucked in a ragged breath. The rock-hard bulge behind the zipper of his dress pants made her forget all about how exposed she felt.

Whatever shred of reluctance her mind clung to melted away. Screw waiting until they got home. And screw worrying about getting caught. The way Nicolai's mouth and hands felt on her skin. The way his powerful body moved against hers. She wanted him. And if everyone inside wanted to stand around and watch him rail her against the massive oak tree, that was on them. Ali only cared about Nicolai and him taking from her exactly what he needed. What they both desperately needed.

Knowing neither of them could stop even if they wanted to, Ali slipped a hand between them, going for his waistband. Thankfully, Nicolai eased back a fraction to give her room to work. With deft fingers, Ali popped the button loose and shoved her hand down the front of his boxer briefs.

Nicolai watched her, his expression darkening when she gripped his hot length. Ali followed his primal thoughts, bathing in the heat they so easily produced. She had a mind to tease him, but her own desperation didn't allow her more than two rough strokes before she freed him from the confines of his pants.

Ali's pulse pounded, and she felt it in every nerve ending in her body. She felt it strongest at her very center. She wanted him buried deep inside her. Needed him there more than she needed her next breath.

Reading her easily, Nicolai panted, "Then do not make us wait."

Ali's heart skipped a beat, but she held his gaze as she guided him to her slick entrance. His firm grip on her ass was the only thing keeping her aloft and stopping him from sliding into her aching body.

He didn't hold her there for long, though. The moment she had him lined up, he took a steadying breath and let her weight fall.

She took the full length of him, crying out at the sudden, delicious invasion. And Nicolai's knees nearly buckled.

They both stilled, except for their short, catching

breaths. And once he'd regained some semblance of control, Nicolai turned around and put his back against the tree for support.

Ali clenched her legs around him, she lifted herself until only his blunt tip was still wedged inside her. She held still for a heartbeat to gather her breath before she relaxed her legs and let gravity impale her on him again.

They both exhaled rough breaths, and Nicolai growled into her cloudy thoughts. *Keep that up, and this will be over sooner than either of us is ready for.*

Believe me. I'm more than ready. She argued.

Cupping her ass in his big hands, he held her tightly in place. She didn't know if he hoped to prolong the feeling of her wrapped around him, but she needed more. Nicolai nearly dropped her when she clenched her inner muscles. And had she not had such a tight grip on him, he would have.

Desperate for more, Ali begged him, *Lay me on the ground and take me hard. Now, Nico!*

"No, amor," he breathed, closing his eyes in an attempt to concentrate.

But Ali didn't want Nicolai to control himself. Instead, she gripped his hair, yanking his head back so he could see her face. "Do it. Nico, please."

She saw the war in his eyes, but he dropped to his knees, and he laid her on the ground.

Ali sucked in a sharp breath when her ass hit the cold leaves and then laughed happily at her victory over his control. Her satisfaction didn't last long though. Her next breath caught in her throat when Nicolai thrust hard, burying himself in her again.

And without giving her time to recover, he kept going, laughing devilishly at her suddenly struggling thoughts.

You wanted it, love.

Yes, I did…I do…harder!

He growled and slammed his hips into hers with so much force she slid across the leaves a few inches.

With a breathless laugh, she demanded. *Again!*

Nicolai obliged. Over and over and over again until they both shattered. He roared with his final thrust, his powerful release stealing the rest of his strength.

Ali lay shaking from the pleasure still pulsing through her core, and Nicolai lowered his head, placing a panting kiss to her parted lips.

"Ali? Nicolai?" a familiar male voice called from a distance, bursting their little bubble of bliss.

Nicolai stiffened above her. He lifted his head, searching the area beyond the tree line. *Shit.*

Ali stared up at him, panic ruining the moment between them.

Nicolai was on his feet so fast, she barely had time to process the feel of him pulling out of her. Shoving himself back into his underwear, Nicolai righted his pants and helped Ali to her feet as well.

All is well, love. Follow the path that way. He nodded to the trail leading in the opposite direction they'd come. *You can sneak back inside using the hall entrance and go clean yourself. I will distract him.*

"Okay," Ali whispered, giving him a quick kiss before she turned and headed back toward the house on unsteady legs.

Nicolai continued along the trail, in the opposite direction.

Ali moved as quickly as she could up the path and did as Nicolai suggested, entering the house through the back hallway. She kicked off her ruined heels and carried them inside to keep from tracking dirt onto Maggie's expensive carpet.

She hurried down the hall and peered around the corner, praying everyone was still socializing in the library. And when Ali saw no one lingering in the main hallway, she slipped into the bathroom near the base of the stairs. Locking the door behind her, she dropped her dirty shoes into the sink. She froze when she caught sight of her reflection in the giant, oval mirror hanging over the vanity. Ali clamped a hand over her mouth, staring at herself in disbelief.

She looked like a wild woman. Her dress was covered in the same dark dirt clinging to her shoes. Her eyes were wide and her face rosy with exertion or excitement, she couldn't tell which. Upon closer inspection, she found a few bits of leaves and twigs in her mussed hair.

With a little chuckle, Ali sent the mental image to Nicolai, and she could sense his amusement. She looked precisely like she'd been rode hard in the damp soil.

And after picking the bits from her hair, Ali brushed off her dress as best she could, but it didn't do much good. The dirt was pressed firmly into the fabric. There was no salvaging it so she could return to the party.

Not to worry, love. According to Greg, the party is winding down. People are beginning to trickle out. Take your time.

Great. But she would still have to face Maggie and explain what the hell happened to her. Or rather, them.

I told Greg we fell. And he has already relayed the message. Maggie is bringing you some clean clothes.

Great. Now she would have to face her friend and her twenty questions. With a heavy sigh, she stripped off her dress and tossed it in the sink with her heels before she cranked the shower on. At least she didn't have to worry about facing a room full of Maggie's friends and clients.

By the time she finished cleaning up, Ali heard a quiet discussion in the hallway just outside the bathroom. Maggie and Nicolai, to be exact. Though she couldn't hear their conversation, she recognized their voices instantly.

Just as she dried herself off and wrapped the towel around herself, Maggie knocked softly. "Hey girl. You decent?"

Ali opened the door, trying not to make direct eye contact with her friend, knowing she would be peppered with questions as soon as the door closed. Instead, she caught a glimpse of Nicolai in the hallway and had to smile. He looked every bit as messy as she had, minus the leaves in his hair. And she regretted nothing.

Maggie cleared her throat. "Can I come in?"

Ali stepped aside, giving her friend room to slip into the small bathroom with her, before shutting the door again. She nodded to the stack in her friend's hands. "Thanks for the clothes. You're a lifesaver."

Maggie sat them on the counter, eyeing the soiled dress and shoes in the sink. She arched a brow, casting Ali a skeptical look. "You fell?"

Ali chuckled, tossing the towel onto the counter. "You know me. I'm kind of a klutz."

Maggie snorted. "Looks like you two were rolling around in the mud like a couple of happy pigs."

Ali avoided her friend's eyes as she shimmied into her borrowed yoga pants.

"Can I ask you something? And you'll answer honestly?"

"Mm hmm," Ali hummed as she pulled the t-shirt on over her head.

"Were you having sex?"

Ali froze, Maggie's bluntness startling her. It shouldn't have. The woman wasn't exactly known for her subtlety. She always got straight to the point.

"You dirty little vixen. You were, weren't you."

The amusement dancing in Maggie's deep blue eyes made Ali smile. "Maybe."

Maggie burst out laughing. "Maybe, my ass. You were humping like bunnies, and I want every filthy detail."

15

Ali sprawled on her bed, listening to Nicolai's contented purr. Beside her, he lay propped on his elbow, drawing invisible designs on her naked back.

She'd always hated lazy days in bed because it allowed her time to get caught up in her rambling thoughts. But since Nicolai came into her life, she didn't mind them so much. His presence quieted the internal chaos and helped her enjoy simply lounging in bed.

The way his fingertips grazed over her skin; the slow, hypnotic motions drew every ounce of energy from her body.

"Alessandra?" Nicolai asked, his voice barely above a whisper.

"Hmm?" Ali hummed without bothering to open her eyes.

"I know it might seem too soon, and we have only known one another a brief time. But if I asked you, would you come with me to my home?"

Ali wasn't sure what she expected. But that was not it.

Rolling onto her side to face him, she searched Nicolai's tranquil expression. He appeared calm and carefree, but if Ali hadn't begun to learn how to read his expressive eyes, she might have missed his underlying nervousness. But why was he worried? Was he afraid she'd say no?

Honestly, she wasn't sure how to respond. It was one thing to venture out and go to Maggie's parties. Or spend a week in a cabin up in the mountains. But another country? The thought terrified her. Yet, something in her gut begged her to say yes.

This was her opportunity to visit the place where she was born. To learn more about where she came from. It may be a longshot, considering what Nicolai said about how few Jagara there were left these days. But even the tiniest chance she could connect with someone who might know something about her birth family made her want to go.

ALI PEERED out the small window as the plane began its descent. What would the jungle be like? Would it be everything she hoped? Everything she'd dreamed of? What would the air be like? Fresh and clean? Thick and damp? She wasn't sure what to expect. But she knew one thing. She couldn't wait to land.

Though small spaces didn't usually bother Ali, being stuck in such tight quarters for the last fifteen hours was getting to her. Back home, she could just open a window and get some fresh air. But knowing she couldn't do that on the plane only made her feel like she couldn't breathe.

Even with oxygen blowing in her face from the little nozzle above her head.

Once they sank beneath the thick clouds, a rolling carpet of deep green came into view. For a moment, she thought it was the ground. But as the plane drew nearer, she realized those spongy-looking hills were treetops. The trees crowded together, forming a continuous spread of green that stretched for as far as the eye could see.

Absolutely beautiful. And equally as terrifying. She'd never been anywhere outside of Missouri. Nowhere she remembered at least. This was all new to her. Not only was she traveling for the first time, but she did it with a man she'd barely known a month. She would meet his family. Be in his home, his personal space, just as he had been in hers.

She would soon stand in the middle of the rainforest where her birth family was from.

Nicolai took Ali's hand, drawing her attention. "You okay, love?"

Without taking her eyes off the quickly approaching rainforest, Ali shrugged. "I'm excited about potentially standing on the same ground my birth family stood. But I have no way of knowing if any of them are still alive. Or if they ever wanted me."

Unexpected tears flooded her vision. It had been years since the thought had crossed her mind.

"Of course they wanted you, Alessandra." Nicolai's firm tone drew her attention. His brows bunched as if he couldn't comprehend any other option.

"I don't know the details of how or why I was put up for adoption. Never even thought about it until I lost my mother. Even though she told me once that there was nothing in my records, I still contacted the woman who oversaw my adoption. She couldn't tell me anything. Because there was nothing. At all. So, what am I supposed to think?"

Nicolai cupped her cheek, his stare holding hers. "You are Jagara. There is no doubt in my mind that your family wanted you. Nothing short of death could separate a Jagara child from their family."

How could that one sentence be so comforting, yet so devastating? If what Nicolai said was true, Ali had no biological connection to anyone. But at least she had Maggie and Deanna. And now, Nicolai. Plus, even if her entire bloodline was gone, she could at least enjoy visiting their homeland.

Turning back to the narrow window, Ali silently watched as they dropped below the tree line. Seconds later, the wheels touched down, sending a shudder through the entire plane. Even though Nicolai had warned her, Ali sucked in a startled breath, her hold on his hand tightening.

They barreled down the runway, the scenery blurring past the window. But everything gradually came into focus as the plane slowed. With her heart pounding, Ali gazed out at the towering trees a short distance away from the runway. As many times as she'd dreamed of the jungle, watched documentaries, or obsessively researched it over the years, Ali never thought she'd see it with her own eyes.

Excitement quickly gave way to anxiety again.

"Talk to me, amor. I feel your discomfort."

She didn't know why the sudden shift again. Her entire body felt too warm, and a deep restlessness in the pit of her stomach made her feel almost nauseous.

"That is the calling. We feel it when our jaguar needs

to run." Nicolai explained. "It is strong when we are in the jungle. Even more intense when we go too long without shifting. Combine the two and it can be near impossible to ignore."

It had been over a week since Ali's first transformation. She hadn't felt the need arise since that night. Which made her wonder. "How often do you need to shift to keep that pull at bay?"

"There is no set amount of time. It is much like being hungry, I suppose. Any number of factors can determine how often your jaguar needs to emerge."

Her first time was scary and overwhelming. She wasn't in a hurry to do that again whether her body, or her jaguar, felt the need to do so. She didn't even know how to make it happen.

"It will come to you. Just as it did the first time. Only next time will be much easier," Nicolai promised. "When the time is right and you feel the need begin to burn in you, breathe deep and let your body take over. There is no need to fear the change. It is part of who you are."

Ali leaned her head against the seat and let his reassuring words wash over her.

When they were finally cleared to exit the plane, Ali happily followed Nicolai. She could smell the jungle before they even reached the door. And when she set foot on the top step, she closed her eyes and took a deep breath in. She filled her lungs with the thick, fragrant air and knew she was home.

Nicolai gave her hand a little tug. And Ali followed him, her eyes taking in everything as they descended the steps. Off to one side of the packed dirt landing strip sat several buildings. And beyond that, a towering weave of trees.

She wanted to go running into the jungle, but as Nicolai led her toward the smaller of the buildings, she knew she'd have to wait.

"Patience," Nicolai whispered next to her.

She smiled. *Okay. Okay.*

Once inside, Ali spotted two men talking at the rear of the hangar, standing next to an old beat-up truck. They both looked up when the door clicked shut behind Ali and Nicolai. The taller of the men stared for a moment before he turned away from his friend and approached them.

Ali watched Nicolai embrace the older man before they both turned to her.

"Alessandra, this is Grandi. He is a dear friend of the family."

Ali held out her hand. "It's nice to meet you, Grandi."

He took her offered hand, and with a slight bow, he pressed his forehead to her knuckles. When he straightened, his warm amber eyes met hers. And with a thick Portuguese accent, Grandi said, "I am so pleased you are finally here."

He turned to Nicolai and spoke so fast Ali couldn't quite catch everything he said.

"…lovely…happy for you…"

That was all she could make out, but she got the gist.

Switching back to English, Grandi motioned toward the truck. "Come, let us get you home. You must be exhausted from the trip."

After getting their bags loaded into the back, they settled in for the two-hour drive to Nicolai's home.

In awe of her surroundings, Ali leaned close to the

window, craning her neck to take it all in. It was nothing like what she'd expected. It was so much more...everything. More vibrant. More fragrant. The trees were enormous, their wide bases gnarled and covered in moss. Giant ferns lined the narrow dirt road, some crowding close enough she could reach out and touch them.

When they finally reached their destination, Ali stood next to the truck, staring up at the modest house. Much like all the others in the village, the two-story house was built on stilts. The rough, red-brown wood exterior and thatch roof blended into the surrounding jungle like it had been there for generations.

Nicolai offered her a hand. "Come, let me show you around. I will get the bags later."

"And I will make something to eat. You must be starving after all your traveling."

Ali opened her mouth to tell him he didn't have to, but Nicolai spoke first. "That would be much appreciated, Grandi. Thank you."

They stepped into a spacious entryway that surprised Ali. The same red-brown wood made up the interior walls, and despite the openness of the space, it felt quite cozy. Like home already and she'd barely stepped foot in the place.

Grandi disappeared through the door toward the back and Nicolai turned to her with a wide smile. "Would you like to take a tour?"

When she nodded, Nicolai pushed open the double doors to his right, revealing a good-sized living room. Four overstuffed couches surrounded a low table and the paintings on the walls held images of the jungle that echoed the scenery outside.

In the middle of the dining room sat a heavy wood table. Unlit candles and a vase of vibrant flowers in the center. More gorgeous paintings hung on the walls. And judging by the worn patches on the floor around the table, the room was a high-traffic area.

Frowning, Ali asked, "You live alone?"

"Mostly. But Grandi stays here and takes care of the place while I am away."

"That's nice of him." Ali nodded to the wear marks on the floor. "Someone do a lot of pacing?"

Nicolai laughed. "No. This is my family's home. My mother grew up here. As did her father and his father before him."

"Oh wow," she whispered, imagining all the memories the place held.

Nicolai led her through the kitchen, where Grandi stood washing potatoes in the large steel sink at the end of the long room. They climbed the back stairs, and Nicolai pointed to the first door on her right. "This is where Grandi sleeps when he stays here."

What Ali could see through the open door looked like it was well lived in. Not messy. Just lived in.

Across the hall was another bedroom. Next to that, a bathroom.

Nicolai hesitated at the end of the hall, his hand on the knob. "And this is *meu quarto*."

When he pushed the door open, Ali hesitated, surprised by the lack of space. And the lack of a bed. Strange.

Across from them was a bank of windows completely covered by thick curtains to block out the light. To the right was a closet with shelf after shelf of Nicolai's clothes. And to her left, an open archway that allowed an unobstructed view of the spacious bathroom. In the center sat a bathtub big enough to fit a small family.

"This is nice. Honestly, I look forward to spending some time in that tub," Ali turned to face Nicolai. "But I gotta ask. Where do you sleep?"

With a little smirk, Nicolai kicked off his shoes, and urged her to do the same. Then he drew her to the windows and swept back one of the curtain panels.

Ali's breath caught in her throat.

Whatever she expected the view to be, it was not the plush luxury that Nicolai revealed. There weren't windows at all. Instead, a massive pallet bed ran the full width of the room. Two king-sized mattresses could have fit in the space with room to spare. Why Nicolai needed such an expanse to sleep in was beyond her, but she hoped it wasn't because he shared his bed with others.

Nicolai's soft chuckle drew her attention. "I assure you, love. I am the only person who has slept in this bed."

A little embarrassed that he'd caught the stray thought, she cleared her throat and offered him a nervous smile. "Good to know."

"After my grandparents passed, there was no one to care for the house. And because I hated the thought of this place sitting empty, I moved in. The first thing I did was get rid of the bed. I didn't change anything else in the house, but I had to put something in a little more to my liking."

It was inviting. Ali gave him that much. She'd just never seen anything like it.

"Like a lot of Jagara, I've always preferred sleeping on the floor," he explained. "When I was a kid, I would drag my mattress over next to the window or out onto the balcony so I could be closer to nature. Eventually, my parents got rid of my bedframe and let me sleep on the floor."

Ali shook her head, amused by that bit of information.

Nicolai gave her hand a tug. "Come. Let me show you the view."

Leading her across the soft bedding, Nicolai pushed the fabric aside and stepped through the gap, drawing her outside. And what a view it was. They stood on a wide balcony overlooking a river that flowed through the back of his property. And just on the other side was a visible trail that led into the dense vegetation.

"It's so beautiful," Ali breathed. "Maggie would love it here."

Nicolai smiled.

Ali leaned against the railing. "I can't believe you live here. That you grew up here."

Nicolai slipped his arms around her and let her quietly take in her surroundings. "Would you like to bathe before dinner?"

Recalling the enormous bathtub in the other room, she leaned back against him with a heavy sigh. "That would be nice."

"Let me draw your bath and bring up our bags." Nicolai placed a gentle kiss against her temple. "Make yourself comfortable. I will be back shortly."

Ali watched him disappear inside and turned her gaze back to the river and the forest. It was so surreal being there. Her imagination, though wildly out of control at times, could never have conjured up this place. She was living in a dream. She had to be.

Closing her eyes, Ali enjoyed the thick, damp air

surrounding her. It felt much like the lingering humidity after a rainstorm in the middle of summer.

She'd always had a love for nature. But that calling Nicolai mentioned earlier grew stronger by the minute. She could feel that insistent tugging in her belly. The nearly uncontrollable urge to take off running through the jungle. To swim in the river and climb in the towering trees. To keep going until she could barely stand.

Knowing she needed to get control of herself, Ali took a slow, deep breath. With it came a riot of scents. Most prominent, flowers. Beneath the balcony, along the edges of the yard, and down by the river.

Beyond that, she could smell Nicolai's masculine scent. And even further, something downright mouthwatering. Potatoes, carrots, onions, and meat. Pork, to be exact. But how the hell did she know that?

Wild boar, specifically. Nicolai verified.

Ali smiled at the brush of his words in her mind. *This new sense of smell is amazing.*

"Yes. It is."

Ali jumped, startled by Nicolai's amused voice directly behind her. With her hand pressed to her chest, she spun to face him. "Don't do that. You scared the shit out of me."

He stood with his arms crossed over his chest and an amused little smirk on his face.

"Were you standing there long?"

Nicolai shook his head. "No, but I could hear you clearly the entire time. Your mind is strong today."

"And my senses feel amplified."

Nicolai stepped close to her, slipping his arms around her waist. "Being here in the homeland helps accelerate the process."

Ali snorted, tugging the hem of his t-shirt. "Obviously my hearing hasn't improved yet."

"It will. It just takes time." He placed a kiss to her forehead. "But for now, let me bathe you."

Ali grinned. "I think I can do that myself. But you can keep me company if you like."

"I would like very much."

Nicolai led her to the bathroom, and while he shut off the water, Ali stripped out of her clothes. She climbed into the oversized bathtub and sank into the steamy goodness. She groaned as she leaned against the tub's sloped back.

"Good?"

"Perfect." Ali looked up at him. "Only one thing could make it better."

Nicolai arched an eyebrow. "And what would that be?"

"If you joined me."

A spark of arousal lit his eyes, the mossy green color taking on that familiar iridescent sheen. Nicolai stood and stripped out of his clothes. With every inch of deep golden skin he revealed, Ali grew more excited.

The second Nicolai sank into the tub, he dragged her onto his lap. "Wrap your legs around me."

Without hesitation, Ali gripped his shoulders and straddled him.

Beneath her, Nicolai's hips flexed, his thick shaft pressing against her. No matter how many times they'd been intimate, that first touch always sent an electric thrill racing through her body.

Ali rocked her hips, her overheated core sliding along his rigid length. It felt incredible the way he slipped between her folds and his blunt tip rubbed against her clit. So, she repeated the motion, rocking her hips again.

Each lazy, deliberate movement drew primal sounds from Nicolai, and knowing how the contact affected him gave her such satisfaction. But as much as she enjoyed teasing him, Ali didn't know how long she could stand it before she put them both out of their misery.

Nicolai decided for her. He reached between them and notched his blunt tip at her entrance. With his eyes holding hers, he slowly dragged her down, burying himself to the hilt.

The delicious invasion stole her breath. And when Ali swiveled her hips, Nicolai gripped her tighter. *Hold still. I want to savor the feel of being inside you.*

His words alone would have made her melt, but the intensity in his voice and the hunger in his eyes sent a sharp zing of pleasure shooting straight to her center. It felt incredible having him buried deep inside her, but she needed more. She needed him to move.

"Patience, love."

Ali had zero patience, and with a desperate, pulsing need humming inside her, she couldn't stop herself. She leaned closer and traced her tongue along the shell of his ear.

Nicolai's control snapped in an instant. And when he plunged into her again, Ali's triumphant cry blended with his guttural growl. The sounds echoed around them, bouncing off the tiled walls.

They ground against each other, Nicolai's open mouth on her throat and his warm panting breaths dancing over her skin.

The intensity grew with every movement. And as Ali scraped her sharp teeth along the curve of Nicolai's shoulder, the sudden urge to bite him flooded her mind.

Nicolai wound his arms around her waist and held her tight against him. *Do it. Mark me while you ride me.*

Ali didn't hesitate. She struck hard, sinking her teeth into his skin. A rush of sensations flooded her senses. She could feel everything. Not only her own physical pleasure, but Nicolai's as well. The slide of their bodies. Him swelling inside her even more as her body contracted around him.

She held onto him as a mind-numbing release barreled through them both and her tastebuds flooded with his essence.

They both floated in a sea of bliss. Oblivious to the world around them as their bodies slowly calmed.

The first thing Ali became aware of was Nicolai's sturdy arms locked around her waist. Next, she heard the breath rushing in and out of their lungs. Him still buried deep inside her, and her mouth stretched wide with her teeth locked onto Nicolai's shoulder. The taste of his rich blood on her tongue did her in.

Panicked, she yanked away from him with a startled hiss, slamming into the opposite end of the tub. What had she done?

"Easy, love."

Nicolai's words barely registered. All she could focus on were the four bloody punctures marring his skin.

"Alessandra. Look at me."

Shaking her head, Ali squeezed her eyes shut, not wanting to see the damage she'd done to his perfect skin.

"Ali!"

His sharp tone got her attention, and her eyes snapped back to his.

"All is well, love," he assured her, his tone calm again. "I am not hurt. I promise you."

Ali glanced at the mark on his shoulder, and tears filled her eyes.

"Come to me, amor. Let me ease you."

Ali let him pull her back into the circle of his strong arms. She buried her face against his neck on the opposite side from the bite.

Nicolai held her, murmuring to her while he rubbed her back and kissed her softly wherever he could reach.

She could still smell fresh blood easing from the wound, but when she lifted her head and met his calm gaze, she felt a little better.

"I am sorry, love." Nicolai pushed her hair back and placed a gentle kiss to her forehead. "I should have warned you about how intense marking your mate can be."

"Was it like that for you when you marked me that first time? Could you feel everything I felt?"

With a ghost of a smile, Nicolai nodded. "Yes, and I loved every second. But if I am honest, it pales in comparison to the pleasure I felt when you sank your sexy little teeth into me."

When she still felt skeptical, Nicolai pushed the memory into her mind, and the intense pleasure that coursed through her left her panting.

"See. There is no reason to be sorry."

Ali nodded. She finally understood.

"Good." Nicolai smiled. "Now, let us finish this bath so we can go get some food. I am starving."

16

Ali followed Nicolai back downstairs, her mind still reeling from their encounter in the bath. But the mouthwatering scents permeating the air quickly drew her attention. Her stomach let out an impatient growl and Nicolai shot her an amused look over his shoulder.

Ali stopped at the base of the stairs, surprised to see another man leaned against the counter beside Grandi. They chatted quietly, their deep voices mingling together like a soothing song. But that wasn't what had her attention.

The newcomer had wavy blue-black hair spilling halfway down his back, and he was built with long, heavy muscles like Nicolai. And when he turned to watch them come into the room, Ali choked back a gasp.

In utter shock, all she could do was stare. Sure, Nicolai had mentioned his brother was his twin. Ali assumed they looked alike, but she hadn't expected them to be identical. The only visible difference she could see, other than the length of their hair, was the shadow of a beard sprinkled along his chiseled jaw.

"My brother," Nicolai's twin said in an accent even thicker than Grandi's. "Introduce me to your beautiful mate."

Both men turned to her, and Nicolai beamed. "D'mitri, this is my Alessandra."

She offered her hand. "Just Ali. Nico is the only person that calls me Alessandra."

D'mitri smirked, shooting Nicolai an amused look before lightly gripping her fingers and pressing his forehead to the back of her hand. When he straightened, D'mitri's pale green eyes met hers. "These are joyous times. My brother has his mate. And I a new sister."

Ali didn't know how to respond to his excitement. She didn't know what it was like to have a sibling. Maggie was the closest thing to a sister she'd ever had. And a brother? She could only imagine what that was like.

It was strange though. As terrifying as it was to meet new people, something about D'mitri felt different. Maybe it was the familiarity of his face because she'd grown so comfortable with Nicolai. Or maybe it was something more. Something deeper. His presence felt incredibly soothing, and though he put off a slightly feral aura, D'mitri seemed a bit more laid back than Nicolai.

"Come. Let us have a drink to celebrate." He motioned toward the counter, where Grandi had sat out a dark burgundy bottle and four glasses.

Ali didn't usually drink, but she couldn't deny him. His excitement was too contagious. One drink couldn't hurt.

AFTER DINNER, Ali helped Grandi in the kitchen while the brothers had a private conversation by the river. Ali glanced out occasionally, fascinated by how they interacted. It was interesting to her that not only did they look so eerily alike, but they moved the same.

"Miss Ali?" Grandi said, drawing her attention.

"Yes?"

"I believe that dish is more than sufficiently clean."

Confused, Ali looked down at the plate in her hands. Who knew how long she'd been scrubbing the thing.

Grandi's side of the sink stood empty. He'd already rinsed the rest of the dishes and put them in the drying rack.

"Sorry. I was distracted."

He smiled down at her. "I see that."

Ali handed him the plate to rinse. "Can I ask you a personal question?"

"Yes, of course."

"Nicolai said you stay here when he's away."

Grandi nodded.

"What about your family?"

Grandi shut off the water, his expression difficult to read. "Most of my family is gone. My only living blood relative is my niece, Kaela. But I am the last of my tribe."

"Oh." Wait. What? How was that possible?

Seeing her confusion, Grandi explained. "Kaela is my sister's daughter. She is of her father's tribe, the Loeb. She has no close relatives among them. Only very distant second cousins. So, when her parents passed, she came to live with me."

How sad. "I'm sorry. That must have been hard for you both. At least you had each other."

"Yes. And the Montez." He nodded toward the twins. "Those boys out there are as much family to us as our blood kin. So is their father."

"What about your mate?"

Grandi's gaze grew distant, and the sorrow in his eyes made Ali wish she hadn't asked.

Feeling bad, she rushed to say, "You don't have to answer that."

His deep amber eyes searched her face, but then he spoke anyhow. "My Gianna and our youngling were both taken from me shortly after the little one's birth. I felt as if I turned the entire jungle upside down looking for them, but I never found anything except the babe's swaddling cloth."

Tears stung Ali's eyes as Grandi talked about his lost loved ones. Her heart ached for him. It was bad enough Ali losing her mother, the only family she'd ever really known. She couldn't imagine the kind of devastation he must have suffered.

"It took me many years to heal my heart. I still feel their absence every day, and I miss them terribly. But as tragic as it is, life works the way it is meant to."

Ali didn't know what to say to that. How could the man be so accepting of the hand fate had dealt him? Not that he had a choice, really.

"Though they can never replace those I lost, Kaela and the Montez tribe have been my only family for the last twenty-three years." Grandi offered her a warm smile and rested his hand on her shoulder. "And now, you are a part of it."

Overwhelmed with emotions, Ali fought to keep the tears from falling. The man beside her was all but a stranger to her and there he was, welcoming her into his little family circle with such wholehearted acceptance.

Ali cleared her throat. "Nicolai said you and his father are close."

Turning around, Grandi leaned back against the counter and crossed his arms over his chest. "I have known Burian since we were young cubs. We grew up friends because our parents were close. And when I lost my mated family, he and Dalah took me into their home. A year later, when Kaela came into the picture, they happily took her in as well."

"They sound amazing. I'm glad you had them."

Grandi shifted his gaze back out to Nicolai and D'mitri. "As am I."

17

Ali woke the next morning, the muted light of dawn greeting her when she opened her eyes. The heavy drapes leading outside were drawn back, and through the sheer curtains swaying in the light breeze, she saw Nicolai standing on the balcony.

His naked body was on full display and Ali smiled to herself, taking in the beauty of his muscular form. Though she understood that nudity wasn't that big a deal to Nicolai, it would take her a while to grow accustomed to it herself.

In private, it was mostly a non-issue. Mostly. She still clung to a bit of shyness with Nicolai. But being outside where the neighbors might see her? Ali didn't know if she could do that just yet. It shouldn't bother her. They were strangers. What did she care what they thought? Especially if they were accustomed to seeing Nicolai running around naked.

Still, Ali found the shirt Nicolai had stripped out of the night before and she pulled it on. His scent clung to the soft fabric, and Ali couldn't resist bringing the collar to her nose. The man overwhelmed her senses. Did he have to smell so damn good all the time?

Ali quietly slipped outside, hesitating a moment to appreciate the view. Nicolai was a gorgeous man. He stood staring out at the river and the thick foliage beyond it. And despite his distracted expression, Ali knew he was fully aware of her presence. He always knew when she was near. His heightened senses made sure of that.

"Good morning, love," Nicolai said without looking her direction.

Ali wrapped her arms around his waist and rested her head against his back. "Morning."

Nicolai released a contented sigh, covering her arms with his and giving them a gentle squeeze.

Despite how humid it felt already, Ali burrowed closer, loving the feel of his warm skin pressed against her cheek.

"Sleep well?"

Ali nodded. In the month she'd known Nicolai, she'd slept better than she had her entire life.

"Good. It will likely be a busy day today."

Ali tensed a little. "Why? What do you have planned?"

Nicolai chuckled and turned in her arms to face her. "No need to worry, love. I only want to take you down some of my favorite trails. And later, to meet my father and Kaela."

Nicolai pressed a kiss to her forehead.

"But I imagine my friend Marius will find us at some point."

Great.

"Come. Let us get dressed. We can go on a little adventure before we make our way over to my father's place."

Nicolai led her inside and dragged her suitcase onto the chair next to the closet.

"I suggest something lightweight. Something easy to get out of."

Ali hesitated, watching him draw on a thin pair of gym shorts. "Are you planning to get me naked out there?"

"No, but you may feel the need to let your jaguar out. And you will want as little resistance as possible."

It made sense. And she was glad she packed her favorite yoga pants. They were perfect. Light. Airy. Easy to slip off. She thought about leaving Nicolai's shirt on, but figured a soft, cotton camisole might be a better choice.

Ali quickly dressed, admiring how good Nicolai looked in his shorts. Her eyes were drawn to the way the thin fabric draped over him, and her mind started down a track that wasn't good if she really wanted to go for that walk.

Nicolai cleared his throat, and Ali looked up at him.

"We have time for that later, love. For now, we walk." He reached into the closet and snagged something else from a box in the corner. "You want one of these before we go?"

A blueberry granola bar. Her favorite. She took what he offered and tore open the wrapper. "Thank you."

They both scarfed down the easy breakfast before descending the steep stairs to the back yard. A large circular close-cropped lawn separated the house and the lazy river. A well-traveled path ran alongside the shimmering water, through oversized ferns, and to a thick tree lying across a narrower section of the river.

Nicolai hopped onto the wide log, offering Ali a

helpful hand up. But she didn't take it. She simply leapt, landing next to him with little effort, surprising them both. Clearly, her strength and agility were the latest to surface.

Nicolai dropped a kiss to her upturned mouth. "Impressive."

Ali agreed. She considered herself to be in decent shape, but she'd never been able to jump like that so easily. Or at all, honestly.

She noticed a pattern, subtle changes within herself. She felt an unusual stirring in her belly and a faint buzzing in her head just before her new senses and abilities surfaced. She couldn't help wondering if it would always be like that or if those sensations would eventually fade into the background. Was she noticing them because they were so new? Or was that just her body's warning system of sorts, letting her know that her jaguar senses were kicking in?

"Come on." Nicolai crossed to the opposite side of the river and Ali followed him onto the narrow path.

They walked for a while, Ali taking in her surroundings with pure awe while Nicolai led the way. The jungle was everything Ali dreamed of and so much more.

She hadn't realized just how much wildlife they would come across. Or how loud the animals and insects would be. Ali found the constant drone of noises strangely peaceful, but the farther they traveled down the path, the more the urge to run grew in her belly.

Easily reading her, Nicolai jogged along the path. He gradually increased his speed until he ran flat out, barreling down the trails. *Are you keeping up, amor?*

Yes, Nico. She was right behind him. *And if you don't speed up, I'm going to pass you.*

Without slowing or missing a single stride, Nicolai stripped out of his shorts and kept going.

Ali stumbled, nearly lost her footing, but quickly righted herself. She hardly believed her eyes. She'd never seen anybody get out of their clothes so fast.

Though a little stunned, she didn't mind so much that he was faster. She happily followed a short distance behind him, taking in the glorious view of his muscular ass and thighs as he ran.

In a blink, the man was gone. And running in his place was his beautiful, black jaguar.

Astonished by his quick, efficient transformation, Ali could only hope to be able to do the same one day.

Come, love. Keep up with me if you can, Nicolai teased.

Ali took a deep breath and kicked her ass into gear, tearing through the jungle after him. She could hear his laughter through their mate bond and felt his happiness as if it were her own. He loved to run in this form, and she loved to watch him and feel his joy.

Who knew she'd ever enjoy running? And stranger yet, she raced through the middle of the rainforest, chasing after a jaguar. She almost laughed out loud just thinking about the absurdity of the situation. And how completely happy she was despite the utter insanity.

That restlessness she'd felt in the pit of her stomach when they first arrived was back with a vengeance.

Ali slowed, recalling what Nicolai had said. It was the jungle drawing her in, calling for her to let her jaguar emerge.

Coming to a stop in the middle of the well-traveled path, Ali forced herself to take slow, deep breaths. Heat rushed to the surface and when the trembling began, a familiar panicky feeling bubbled up from deep inside.

Easy, amor. Nicolai padded over to her. *Your body wants to change. Allow yourself to relax and embrace it.*

Ali closed her eyes, panting as she tried to do as he said. But it was hard to relax when her body felt so out of control. Like that first time the transformation overtook her. All she could think about was the pain and the lack of control.

I am right here with you. Nicolai rubbed against her side. *You are doing well.*

The press of his massive body helped to soothe her, even if only for a moment before the intense shifting inside grew stronger.

Ali forced herself to take slow, deep breaths. But breathing didn't help much when the trembling took over and the desperate need to get out of her clothes over-whelmed her.

With unsteady hands, Ali yanked off her shirt. She fumbled with her yoga pants, but when she finally managed to get out of them, she dropped to her knees. An intense, tingling heat spread throughout her body. It felt much like the aftermath of when a foot falls asleep. That achy, pins and needles feeling that takes over. Except this wasn't just her foot. It started in her gut and then spread through her entire body, every nerve on fire as it woke with a vengeance.

Nicolai talked her through it all, giving her words of encouragement. Nuzzling her.

Muscle and bone stretched, twisted, and reformed. And just when she thought she couldn't take any more, the pain dissipated.

Panting, Ali opened her eyes again and the world around her had transformed right along with her. It had gone from deep, rich colors to unbelievable brilliance and vibrance. The air didn't feel quite so heavy anymore, and she could see farther than humanly possible.

Ali climbed to her feet, her legs giving a little wobble before holding strong. She still felt a low-level ache radiating through her, but it was nothing like that first time. She didn't have that same exhaustion. Or the waves of shuddering. Her body felt stronger than before. And her mind clearer. Nicolai was right. It still wasn't a walk in the park by any means. And not necessarily easier than the first time, but it hadn't lasted nearly as long. And the recovery time drastically shorter.

Ali turned to Nicolai, a giddiness bubbling up when their eyes met. She thought his jaguar was beautiful before. But with her enhanced senses, she could see every detail of his features. The tiny flecks of amber in his sage-green, iridescent eyes and the emerald ring around the outer edge of the pupils. The spots and rosettes covering his body, from his blocky head to the tip of his bulbous tail. She could even see the individual hairs with stark clarity.

He nudged her with his nose. *Let us run, Alessandra.*

She turned, awkwardly padding back and forth. And once she got the hang of moving all four legs, she circled Nicolai and then trotted a little way down the path. She had a hard time concentrating on where she was going, though, because she kept seeing her paws as she ran.

Alessandra, if you do not run, I will run over you, Nicolai teased her.

With that, Ali got a burst of energy and hunkered

down, picking up speed as she barreled through the thick ferns. The way her muscles moved beneath her skin and the air shooting in and out of her lungs felt incredible. She'd never felt so alive. And in her jaguar form, she was free. Completely free. No worries. No troubling thoughts. Simple, exhilarating freedom.

Ali ran until her legs grew tired, the muscles trembling with need for a moment of rest. Slowing, she turned just in time to see Nicolai leap at her. He took her to the ground, and they rolled a couple times before they came to rest with her pinned beneath his heavier body.

Without conscious thought, she shifted back to human form. Nicolai's massive feline body caged her in. His wide, jet-black face hovering mere inches from hers. The heat from his panting breaths feathered over her skin, and those shimmering sage-green eyes watched her carefully.

How was that?

Breathless, she smiled up at him. "Amazing."

18

On the way back home, Nicolai watched Ali as she sped through the underbrush in front of him. He had a hard time keeping up with her. She was fast, and her reflexes were amazing as she darted around some obstacles and hopped others. The way she moved was beautiful. Everything about her was beautiful.

As they neared the river, Ali skidded to a stop.

What is it?

The big golden cat tilted her head back, and Nicolai could see her nostrils flare. On instinct, he sniffed the air as well.

Is it the food? he asked hopefully.

Yes. It smells amazing.

Let us go for a swim to cool down before we go and raid the feast that Grandi is preparing.

Ali took off down the trail, and Nicolai followed, this time keeping up with her easily. He had the strangest feeling that she was letting him.

As the trees thinned, Nicolai could see a small section

of the house through the brush. Ali didn't run toward the house. She veered off the trail, racing full speed to the river.

The pure joy in her usually chaotic thoughts filled him with so much satisfaction. He could feel her excitement. Her overwhelming sense of freedom and belonging. She loved the jungle.

When Ali reached the water's edge, she launched herself into the air and landed in the middle of the river with a great splash.

Nicolai slowed, trotting to the center of the natural bridge. And when Ali surfaced in her human form, she looked like a river goddess rising from the deep. The water droplets glistening on her skin. The color in her cheeks. The absolute happiness shining in her amber eyes.

Shifting to his human form, Nicolai settled into a relaxed crouch. He watched her toss her head back and laugh. "That was so incredible!"

He couldn't stop his own smile from spreading. It made him happy beyond words to see his mate so jubilant.

Ali swam toward him. "Are you not coming in?"

He wanted to keep watching her enjoy herself but couldn't pass up the invitation to join her. Rising to his full height, Nicolai watched something in her eyes shift as they raked over his naked form. The appreciation shining in her amber eyes looked the same as what he felt when he admired her beauty.

Nicolai dove in, the balmy water enveloping him like a warm embrace.

When he surfaced, Ali swam closer, slipping her arms around his neck. "Thank you."

"What for?"

"For bringing me here. For showing me all this." Ali indicated their surroundings. "I've always wanted to visit the jungle, but I never would have been able to if not for you."

Nicolai wrapped his arms around her waist and pulled her close. "I am glad you are here. It makes me happy to share this place with you."

Ali wrapped her legs around him and gave him a squeeze. "You know what I want to share with you right now?"

Nicolai arched a brow. "What's that?"

"Some of that mouthwatering food I can smell all the way out here."

Nicolai chuckled. "We should get cleaned up before we head to the kitchen. Grandi would murder us both if we walked in there like this."

AFTER A QUICK BATH, they joined Grandi for an early lunch.

Open-faced sandwiches. Choice cuts of seasoned, tender meat on toasted slices of homemade bread. Smothered in onions and rich brown mushroom gravy. Ali stuffed herself, but it was worth it.

Fortunately, it was a long drive to Nicolai's father's home. She had plenty of time for her food to settle before they arrived.

Kaela greeted them at the door, a wide smile on her pretty face. She pulled Ali in for a quick hug. "It is so good to finally have another female around. Do not get me wrong. I love these hardheaded men, but I am sick of being the only girl around here."

Nicolai snorted. "Do not lie. You like being the center of attention."

Kaela made a face at him before turning back to Ali. "He's just jealous because his father loves me more."

"I thought I was the favorite."

Ali turned to see D'mitri leaning against the doorframe behind Kaela. His wounded tone sounded genuine enough, but the hint of a smirk tugging at his lips said otherwise.

Kaela rolled her eyes and turned back to Ali. "I will go get *Pai*. He has been climbing the walls all day waiting for you to get here. It surprises me that he did not beat me to the door."

As Kaela moved by D'mitri, she reached out and flicked the tip of his nose.

D'mitri's ghost of a smirk turned into a full-blown smile. He didn't watch Kaela leave though. He turned his focus back to his brother and Ali. Straightening to his full height, D'mitri motioned toward the room behind him. "Come sit."

The brothers fell into conversation, Nicolai asking D'mitri about his latest woodworking project. While it was interesting, Ali's nerves wouldn't let her sit still and pay attention.

To say she was nervous about meeting their father was an understatement. She'd never been around anyone with dementia before. And though Nicolai assured her everything would be fine, she still couldn't help wondering what Burian would be like.

Looking around the room, her gaze fell on something that drew her attention. She had seen many times on TV and in movies where people had a portion of a wall decorated with photos of their loved ones. But she'd never seen anything like it in person. Especially nothing like the cluttering of frames covering the long wall to her left.

Moving closer, Ali scanned over the pictures. Happy faces stared back at her. Some young. Some old. And some vaguely familiar. She smiled when she spotted the twins in one. They sat side by side on the top step of that very house. Both with an arm around the other's shoulders, and identical wide grins on their young faces. They couldn't have been more than ten or eleven. But there was no denying it was them. Those matching, pale green eyes practically glowed as they stared up at the camera.

Beside that picture was another of the boys. A few years older. They sat on a stone bench in the middle of a gorgeous flower garden with a dark-haired girl tucked between them. Kaela, maybe? The girl had the same raven hair and deep-set chestnut eyes.

They all looked so happy. So close. Ali envied them that. Growing up, she'd had no siblings or cousins, or even friends, to share that kind of bond with. She couldn't even imagine how different her life might have been if she had.

"Well, this is quite a sight."

The man's deep, almost rumbling voice filled the room. Not loud. Simply…full. Of warmth and strength. Like a big mug of rich hot chocolate. In a matter of seconds, Ali could see why Grandi spoke so fondly of the man. Burian's very presence exuded acceptance and comfort. She could see where the twins got that particular trait from.

Approaching the brothers, Burian clasped a wide palm to the backs of each of their necks and pulled them close.

With the trio's foreheads pressed together, he said, "It is good to have both my sons in one place again. It has been too long."

Nicolai chuckled. "*Pai*, it has barely been a month."

Burian straightened, meeting Nicolai's gaze. "As I said. Too long."

He released the brothers, patting them both on the shoulder before turning to Ali. He hesitated, staring for a moment.

"And who is this lovely creature?"

Ali's face warmed, still a little unaccustomed to being the focus of someone's attention. Nicolai must have sensed her awkwardness, because he cleared his throat and introduced her. "This is Alessandra. My mate."

Burian's handsome face lit up. "In that case, I forgive you."

Ali offered him a smile as he approached. "It's nice to meet you."

"And you as well, my dear."

She didn't know what she expected by way of greeting, but it wasn't for him to pull her into his arms and give her a firm squeeze.

Ordinarily, she didn't much care for people touching her or taking up space in her bubble. But with Burian, she didn't get that overwhelming sense of being smothered. Instead, his strong embrace was more like a haven, and Ali didn't know how to feel about that.

By all logic, the man should have frightened her. His size alone should make her uneasy. Burian was built like a Mack Truck. Just a hair shorter than the twins, but sturdier.

When he put her at arm's length, Burian beamed at her. "I welcome you into our family with great joy."

Unexpected tears welled in her eyes, and she managed to choke out a weak "Thank you."

Taking Ali's hand, he tucked it into the crook of his elbow and led her to the couch. He settled next to her with his big body angled toward her. "So, tell me about yourself, lovely. Who are your people?"

"Pai." Nicolai spoke up. "She was adopted. She was not raised in the Jagara way."

A hint of sympathy flashed in his eyes. "Well. Then we will have to show you our ways and what it means to be part of a tribe. You are family now. And we take care of our own."

Ali opened her mouth to thank him, but the words got stuck in her throat. It had been a long time since she felt like she truly belonged anywhere. Sure, she had a couple great friends in Maggie and Victoria. But no matter how much they had torn down her walls, there had always been a barrier between them and her. Like she never fully belonged. And how could she when she never fully knew who she was?

As if he understood her inner turmoil, Burian patted her hand and offered her a warm smile. "I can start by telling you stories about my boys."

Both brothers groaned in unison, making Ali laugh. Their response made her even more curious.

Ali loved the stories. And the more Burian talked, the more she liked him. There was a warmth he gave off that made her feel loved. Even if they had only just met. Something told her that he was the backbone and heart of the family.

Burian's attention drifted to the window, a faraway look in his eyes. "The flowers are blooming again."

Ali frowned, confused by the abrupt shift in the conversation.

"You know, my Dalah is a wonderful gardener. She can take even the saddest, sickest plants and give them new life." He swung his focus back to Ali. "Would you like to join me for a walk in the garden?"

She didn't miss the worried look Nicolai and D'mitri exchanged. Or the present tense Burian used when mentioning his wife. Ali knew Nicolai had lost his mother years ago, so the direction the conversation had drifted made Ali all too aware that Burian was slipping into one of the episodes Nicolai had warned her about.

"*Pai*," D'mitri spoke up. "Maybe another time."

Burian looked to his sons, a contemplative expression on his handsome face. "I suppose."

Following the twins' lead, Ali gave Burian a small smile. "You can show me next time."

His eyes lit up. "I look forward to it. If you are anything like the rest of us, you will love it."

"I'm sure I will. My friend Maggie has a massive flower garden in her back yard. I could spend hours out there. And I have. Something about being surrounded by nature soothes me."

Burian nodded. "That is a Jagara trait. We need to feel connected to the wild. We were born of the jungle. We thrive in the jungle. We can survive in the city, but nature always calls us back to the homeland eventually."

Nicolai had said as much. And in a way, she'd always known that on some level. Any time she went to Maggie's, she felt recharged once she'd spent time outside. Especially, when she kicked off her shoes and walked around on the grass or buried her hands in the soil.

Burian reached out, his knuckles brushing against her cheek. "You know, you have your father's eyes."

Startled by his words, Ali could only stare at him. How could he know such a thing? Nobody knew anything about her family.

"He must be so pleased that you and my Nicolai are mated."

She had no clue what to say to that. Lucky for her, Kaela chose that moment to walk into the room. She exchanged a look with the brothers and offered their father a hand. "Come, Burian. It is time for your medicine."

With a heavy sigh, he got to his feet. "Yes, we must keep me clear of mind."

His joking tone made Ali smile. But sadness bubbled up inside her as she watched him tuck Kaela's hand into the crook of his arm and let the petite brunette lead him from the room.

She met Nicolai's stare from across the room. *Should we go?*

Before he could respond, D'mitri spoke up. "Are you staying for dinner?"

19

Ali woke the next morning, Nicolai's words a low echo in her mind. *Spin. Kick. Thrust.*

Confused but mildly amused, she laughed. *What are you doing?*

Ali heard a muffled grunt outside, followed by Nicolai's frustrated swearing and deep, unfamiliar laughter. Curious, Ali eased closer to the balcony, trying to see what the hell was going on out there.

In the yard below, Nicolai lay flat on his back and a freakishly tall sandy-haired man stood over him. Ali's heart did a funny little flip. Instincts demanded she go defend her mate, but logic and quick observation made her realize the man was a friend.

The guy offered Nicolai a hand and helped her frustrated mate to his feet with ease. He slapped Nicolai's shoulder, his rich laughter carrying easily across the cropped lawn.

Without so much as a glance in her direction, Nicolai

reached out to her through their mate bond. *Get dressed, love. Then I will introduce you to Marius.*

Ali didn't waste time. She made a quick trip to the bathroom and then threw on some fresh clothes. Both men looked up at her when she stepped onto the balcony. The way Nicolai's face lit up made her smile. "Good morning."

"Good morning, love. Did you sleep well?"

She nodded. *Better than I thought, I guess. I don't even remember you getting out of bed.*

I did not want to wake you. You looked so peaceful.

Ali's gaze flickered to the massive guy standing next to Nicolai. Though she still felt awkward around new people, Ali forced herself to be polite. "Good morning, Marius."

He returned the greeting. "You must be Ali. Nicolai warned me of your beauty."

She felt her face begin to heat but pushed away the awkwardness and offered him a shy smile. "Nico is slightly biased."

He spoke up. "Does not make me wrong."

"For once." Marius smirked his focus remaining on Ali. "It is nice to finally meet you. My friend has not shut up about you all morning. I figured he needed a good sparring session to bring him back down to earth with the rest of us for a bit."

Ali couldn't stop her smile from spreading. "Well, by all means. Don't let me interrupt."

Nicolai shook his head, disbelief on his handsome face. "I see how it is. My best friend and my mate. Plotting against me."

Without warning, Marius swung at Nicolai, barely clipping his shoulder as Nicolai dodged the punch.

"Good. Do not let your female distract you."

As they both fell into a defensive stance, Ali hopped onto the railing to watch them spar. It was a martial art she'd never seen before. Their movements were beautiful and fluid. Much like a graceful dance, but with bursts of aggression.

Despite their size difference, they were closely matched in skill. One moment Nicolai had the upper hand, the next, Marius did.

Marius caught Nicolai from behind. Ali held her breath as Nicolai flipped the bigger male onto his back and pinned him to the ground with his knee in the guy's throat.

"I thought you were faster than me." Nicolai teased.

Marius laughed. "I am. I just thought I'd let you look good in front of your mate."

Marius looked up at Ali, but the second he saw her watching them, his amused expression faltered. He stared for a moment, his gaze slowly shifting back to Nicolai. A sense of dread settled in the pit of her stomach, and whatever Marius said to Nicolai hit him like a punch to the gut.

Nicolai's wide eyes snapped up to her, and Ali tensed. Something was wrong. And she was afraid of what that stunned look on his face meant.

On instinct, she tried to connect with him through their mate bond, but all she encountered was a wall.

Paranoia made Ali look behind her. No one. Nothing. Only the sheer curtains hanging over the open doorway. Nervous, she turned back to find Nicolai on his feet and a faraway look in his bright eyes.

"What's wrong?"

Neither man responded. But Marius placed his hand on Nicolai's arm and whispered something to him. They exchanged a long look before Nicolai nodded and turned away, walking on unsteady legs toward the river.

With her heart in her throat, Ali demanded an answer. "Nico. What's wrong?"

When he didn't respond, she hopped off the railing and hurried down the steps.

Marius met her at the bottom, stopping her from going after Nicolai. "Leave him."

She tried to step around him, but again, he blocked her path. Ali looked up at him like he'd lost his mind. "What are you doing? Get out of my way."

Marius shook his head. "Nicolai needs a minute. Let him gather his thoughts."

She peered around his massive frame at her mate. "Why? What happened?"

"Destiny, sweet female."

She looked back up at him and when she saw the soft smile on his face, she frowned. "What?"

Marius laid a gentle hand on her shoulder. "Come inside. We can have a drink and let your man calm down."

The building panic demanded she go to Nicolai, but something in Marius's kind eyes told her she could trust him. Still, it felt wrong to leave Nicolai alone.

Ali peered around Marius again. Nicolai stood with his back to them, staring out across the river with his hands buried in his hair. She still felt the overwhelming urge to go to him. To comfort him, whatever was wrong.

Go with him, love, Nicolai whispered into her mind. *I will be in shortly.*

Are you okay?

Yes, amor. I only need a minute.

Are you sure?

Just go with Marius.

Ali looked up at the man blocking her way and reluctantly let him lead her in the side door and through the kitchen. Once they made their way into the sitting room, Ali couldn't sit still. She paced back and forth, her thoughts utter chaos. What the hell was going on? What had caused Nicolai to have such a reaction? Why the hell did he need some time alone if he was okay?

She glanced at Marius and felt frustrated by his utter calm. He didn't say a word, only watched her pace while he sat still with his hands clasped loosely in his lap.

She wasn't sure how much time passed, but it felt like an eternity before Nicolai finally came into the room. He barely glanced at her before he asked Marius, "Where is Grandi?"

"I have not seen him."

"Can you go find him please?"

Marius nodded, clasping Nicolai's shoulder for a heartbeat before disappearing into the hallway.

Nicolai finally looked at Ali. Really looked at her as if seeing her for the first time. Then he closed the distance between them and pulled her into his arms.

Ali could feel a strange blend of emotions rolling off him but couldn't quite get a hold on any of them. Worried, she wrapped her arms around him too. "Nico, talk to me. What the hell is going on?"

When he didn't reply, she gave him a squeeze.

"Tell me what's wrong."

"Nothing," he whispered against her hair. "Absolutely nothing."

"Don't lie to me."

When Nicolai finally released her, his gentle fingers

stroked over her cheek. The unexpected awe on his face confused her, but she let him guide her over to the couch and sat where he indicated.

Nicolai settled on the low table in front of her and took both her hands in his. "Alessandra, there is something I need to explain to you. It is something I should have thought about, but I completely let it slip my mind. I do not know what is wrong with me. Why I did not think of it before..."

"Nico, please. Just tell me." She begged. "I'm kind of freaking out here."

"A few generations back, there were a total of ten tribes. Today, only three are active. The Dekova. The Parmali. And the Montez. Remnants of other tribes remain, but only a single surviving member here and there. Like Kaela. She is the last of the Loeb tribe."

"Like Grandi. He said he was the last of his tribe."

Nicolai nodded. "And my cousin's housekeeper, Henrik, is the last of his."

"Okay, but what does that have to do with why you were so upset?"

He took a breath and said without breaking eye contact. "Each tribe has a unique symbol that represents their people. Long ago, every new member born into the tribe received this mark during their naming ceremony."

The bottom dropped out of Ali's stomach. She had an eerie feeling she knew where this conversation headed. The tattoo on the bottom of her foot. Marius had spotted it and pointed it out to Nicolai. That's why he'd needed a moment. He recognized the symbol for what it was: a tribe mark. And judging by his reaction, he knew exactly which tribe the mark belonged to. Which tribe she belonged to.

Nicolai nodded, easily reading her thoughts. "Tribal marking is one of the traditions we have all but lost in recent generations. Two families, that I am aware of, still cling to it. The first is the Dekova tribe. Marius's family." He paused, giving her hands a gentle squeeze before continuing. "And the other, the Zendori tribe."

"Wh…" Ali swallowed hard against the lump rising in her throat. "Which tribe?"

Holding her anxious gaze, Nicolai cleared his throat as if fighting intense emotion. "You are Zendori."

Ali's heart pounded with excitement, relief, and dread all at the same time. Finally knowing where she came from, knowing the name of her birth family was a relief. But one thought rushed to the forefront. What if she was the only one left? How devastating would that be to learn what tribe she was born into, only to find out that she was the last one left? Though terrified of the answer, Ali had to know. "Are there more?"

"Just one," Nicolai whispered, his eyes shifting to something over her shoulder.

Ali turned, following his gaze. And her breath left her in a rush. Grandi stood in the doorway, an unfathomable expression on his handsome, weathered face. With a trembling voice he said, "I should have known."

Ali looked to Nicolai for an answer, but his gaze was cast downward. She could feel the flood of his emotions.

"I thought I was the last of my tribe," Grandi continued. "Yet here you are."

"Zendori," she said in disbelief. "You are Zendori?"

"Yes."

Ali stared at the older man as tears streaked his handsome face. She'd wondered about her birth family all her life and standing in front of her was the only living relative she had. As tears flooded her own eyes, she forced a breath and whispered, "I have family?"

"Yes." Grandi's voice broke.

"Not just family," Nicolai interrupted gently. "A father."

Ali's head whipped back to him, her heart hammering in her chest. "How could you know that?"

"You are the same age as the youngling he lost. And there is no other explanation for the tribe mark on your foot."

Ali turned back to Grandi, searching his features carefully. The hard angles were masculine, but his eyes held an unmistakable softness. She'd noticed it the first time she'd seen him. Eyes that had seen too much sorrow now held utter relief and joy. Eyes the same shade and shape as the ones she'd seen in the mirror for the past twenty-three years.

Burian hadn't been slipping into confusion after all. He was right. She really did have eyes like her father. How had no one but Burian seen it before? And why didn't he tell her about Grandi if he knew?

Tears flooded her vision. She finally knew where she came from. *Who* she came from. Grandi was the piece of her that she knew had been missing her entire life. Blinking quickly to keep the tears from spilling, she closed the distance between them and wrapped her arms around him.

The moment Grandi's strong arms engulfed her, Ali completely broke down, sobbing against his warm chest.

Three days ago, the man had been a stranger. Two days ago, he'd opened up to her about the tragic loss of his loved ones. Today, they both found something neither of them thought they'd ever find. Each other.

———————

WHEN THE EMOTIONS DIED DOWN, Nicolai and Marius left the two of them alone to get more acquainted.

Settling on the couch, Grandi and Ali traded stories about their lives. She told him all about what it was like growing up. About her mother and how amazing she was despite all of Ali's issues. And then the downward spiral she fell into after her mom's death.

Grandi took her hand, holding it tight as he let her talk through it all.

"But it's all been fading away since Nico came into my life. I didn't understand it at first, and I'm still struggling with aspects of it, but it's getting better every day."

Grandi gave her hand a gentle squeeze. "It makes my heart happy knowing that fate paired you two together."

Ali turned to face him, one leg tucked beneath her, and her arm propped on the back of the couch. "Maybe I'm a little skeptical still, but can you explain to me how you are so certain I'm the daughter you lost?"

Grandi leaned back against the couch, angling himself more toward her. "Like many of our tribes, our numbers have decreased over time. My family was always small though. My grandparents passed when my father was young. For a long time, it was just him and his little sister. Sadly, she had a terrible accident and died before her Awakening."

How awful.

"My father was alone for nearly ten years before my

mother came into the picture. Then a year later, my sister was born. Four years after that, they had me. Together, they were reviving the tribe. Then my sister mated to a Loeb. And since my mother couldn't have any more children, I knew it would be up to me to grow the tribe one day. I looked forward to it. But I was so over the moon when I mated to my Gianna, increasing tribe numbers was the last thing I cared about. I only wanted her and whatever family we created together." Sadness flickered over his features. "But you know how that ended."

Yes. She did. And her heart broke for him all over again. She couldn't imagine what he must have been through. He'd lost so much. His parents, his sister, his mate, and his newborn daughter. His tribe was long gone, and his niece was the only biological family he had left. Until Ali came back into the picture.

Grandi stared off into space, his thoughts clearly not focused on the present. And Ali took a moment to study his weathered features. She wondered what he was like at her age. What her mother was like. Did they have a connection like the one she had with Nicolai? How long were they together?

Ali didn't want to pick at an old wound, but her curiosity was too much to tamp down. "Will you tell me about my mother?"

Grandi shifted his attention back to her and gave a sad smile. "My Gianna was a beautiful, delightful female. So vibrant and caring. She loved going on adventures deep into the forest, and she was a gifted storyteller."

Ali gasped. "Really? Was she an author?"

Grandi chuckled. "No. She never wrote any of it down."

"Oh." What a shame. Ali would have loved to read her stories.

"Gianna had quite the imagination. I could sit for hours listening to her weave the most elaborate tales."

Though she had no memory of her, it warmed Ali's heart knowing that she shared something with the woman aside from DNA.

Grandi gave her hand another squeeze. "I wish she could see you now. She would be so happy you mated to a Montez. Especially Nicolai. He is a strong male with the integrity of his father and the kindness of his mother. He is a worthy mate, one that I am proud to have my daughter spend her life with."

Ali smiled. "He is pretty great."

Taking a deep breath, Grandi looked up at the clock. "Come, now. Sit with me while I prepare some lunch for you and the boys."

Ali followed him into the kitchen. And out back, she spotted Nicolai and his friend, Marius. They'd gotten back to the sparring session Ali had interrupted earlier.

She stood for a moment, watching them. Amazed by their agility and flexibility. It, for sure, was a thing of beauty. An artform, really. Something Ali wouldn't mind learning one day.

She'd have to ask Nicolai to teach her. Marius was clearly a great instructor, but somehow, she didn't think she'd much enjoy sparring with such a massive man. She wouldn't stand a chance at matching his skill or strength.

Grandi opened the fridge, drawing her attention. As he took things out and placed them on the counter, Ali offered to help.

Without a word, Grandi handed her a knife, and they

stood quietly chopping vegetables. She still couldn't believe how things had turned out, and she kept catching herself staring across the little kitchen island at Grandi as they prepared the meal together. Father and daughter.

Funny. It felt strange to call him by his first name now that she knew he was her dad.

When he caught her staring, he hesitated, his brows drawing together in concern. "What is it?"

Ali shrugged one shoulder. "I don't know what to call you."

His frown deepened. "What do you mean?"

"I can't exactly call you Grandi anymore, can I?"

"Why not? You can call me anything you like."

She searched his face for a moment before she asked softly, "Is *pai* okay?"

He hesitated, a sudden shimmer of tears lighting his amber eyes before he nodded. "If that is what you prefer."

Hearing the slight hitch in his voice had Ali fighting another wave of emotions. But she cleared her throat and smiled. "*Pai* it is."

20

For the next week, Nicolai took her for morning runs and showed her all his favorite places to go when he needed to get away for a while. She met some of the locals. Visited with Burian and D'mitri several more times. Even spent some time in the garden with her new cousin, Kaela. They didn't have much in common, but it was nice to know she had actual blood family.

When not visiting with someone or out exploring the wilds, Ali spent a lot of time down by the river. It was her new favorite spot. The sound of the flowing water and the scent of the surrounding forest soothed her to her very core.

Thanks to their mate bond, Nicolai knew when she needed time alone, but he was never far away. While she swam, he sat on the balcony, his feet propped on the railing with a book in his lap. He never intruded into her thoughts, but she felt him there, always connected just enough to know when she needed him. Strangely, that comforted her on a level she couldn't quite understand.

Just before dinner, she crossed to the far side of the river. *I'm gonna go for a run,* she informed Nicolai. Before he could respond, Ali took off down the trail. Aside from her private time with Nicolai, running had become her new favorite activity to ease her when anxiety began to creep in.

She ran for a while before she shifted and then crouched low so she could go faster. She ran for a long time, and when she reached another river, she splashed in the shallow water to cool off.

She sprawled on the bank to relax in the soft grass for a while. The massive, towering trees formed a canopy above her, and she lay for a long time, taking in the sights, scents, and sounds of the jungle around her. She loved it, and though she was content to never go home, she knew she'd miss it. She knew she would miss Maggie too, but she couldn't ignore the feeling that the jungle was her true home.

Ali sat up, resting her arms on her knees while she stared across the river. So much had changed in her life already, but there were bigger changes still to come. Like breaking the news to Maggie. And Deanna.

When she felt rested enough, Ali dragged herself off the bank and began her journey back to Nicolai. Halfway there, he broke the silence and warned her. *We have company, love. Be sure to shift back before you are within sight of the house.*

She agreed, wondering who it could be. Did he have friends that didn't know about their Jagara side?

Do not rush. Take your time and come join us in the front room when you are ready.

Though she'd liked everyone she'd met so far, Ali

wasn't sure she felt ready to socialize just yet. She wanted to stay gone longer, but curiosity drew her back to the house anyway.

Ali slowed her pace when she got close, and she shifted back to her human form about two hundred yards out. And as she approached the river, she caught a vaguely familiar scent. Like jasmine and oranges.

Intrigued, but desperate for a quick dip in the river, Ali dove in. The water felt balmy and soothing like before, taking that last little bit of remaining tension out of her shoulders.

When she finally swam her fill, Ali climbed onto the grassy bank and smiled. Someone, likely Nicolai, had gathered her forgotten clothes and stacked them neatly at the bottom of the stairs. Along with a clean, fluffy towel.

Once she'd dried off and dressed, Ali went in through the kitchen door. Grandi stood in front of the sink, washing vegetables. He looked up from his task when the screen door closed behind her. "Feeling better?"

She nodded. "I never thought going for a run would ever be my happy place."

Grandi just grinned, his eyes crinkling at the corners as he sat a glass of juice on the counter beside her.

Ali didn't even realize how thirsty she was until she'd downed half the glass. The cool, sweet liquid quenched her thirst so much better than water would have. "Thank you, *pai*."

"You are most welcome." He turned back to his task and added, "Everyone is waiting for you in the front room."

Ali made her way through the dining room, hesitating

when she spotted the two people sitting opposite Nicolai in the den. The last two people she expected to see.

When Nicolai shifted his attention to her, Greg and Maggie both turned and followed his gaze. Maggie shot off the couch, a wide grin on her face as she rushed across the room. "Hey!"

"Hey!" Ali said in shock as she hugged her best friend. "What are you doing here?"

Maggie gave her a squeeze and then put her at arm's length. "Just thought I'd come see the tropical paradise keeping my bestie away for so long."

Ali stared at her friend, unsure how to respond. It had barely been a week.

"Actually," she whispered. "Nicolai called. Said he thought you might be missing me."

Ali looked over Maggie's shoulder. *You did this? For me?*

Nicolai nodded.

Thank you.

Anything for you, my love.

Ali fought back a wave of emotions and shifted her focus back to Maggie. "So." She cleared her throat. "What do you think so far? About being in the wild, I mean."

"A little warmer than I expected, but Nicolai was right. Pictures don't even come close to doing it justice. It's so beautiful here."

"Just wait until I show you the river. Or the swimming hole Nico took me to the other day. It's so pretty. The water is the most incredible teal color I've ever seen. Like something out of a dream. We have got to take you to see it. You'll love it."

Maggie's eyes sparkled with amusement. "We'll have

plenty of time for that. Greg convinced me to take a few weeks off. Insisted that I needed a break. Apparently, I've been working too hard lately."

The quick look she tossed over her shoulder at him said she didn't agree. But Ali knew her friend well enough to know that Greg was right.

Besides, no matter how much Maggie had dreamed of taking a trip to South America, she probably never would have gone if it'd been left up to her. She was too much of a workaholic. And when she wasn't working, she spent all her free time doing things for others. Whether it was helping her elderly neighbor with something around the house or volunteering at the local shelter, she seemed to be always giving to others and rarely took time for herself. The only time she ever truly relaxed was when she and Ali had the occasional sleepover.

"Well, I'm glad you're here. So much has happened since we got here. I have so much I want to show you and tell you. I don't even know where to start."

Nicolai cut in. "That can come later, love. Let them get settled and we can all chat over dinner."

Maggie agreed. "I could go for a shower, for sure. And get into some fresh clothes."

"Come." Nicolai motioned toward the hallway. "I will show you to your room."

After another hug from her friend and a warm smile from Greg, Ali made her way back to the kitchen to see if Grandi needed help with anything.

"I HAVE SOME NEWS."

She knew by her friend's suddenly anxious expression, Maggie thought she was going to say she was pregnant, getting married, or something equally dramatic. Ali had to remind herself that marriage was likely in her near future, but Maggie didn't need to know all that just yet.

Not wanting to keep her friend in suspense, Ali got right to the point. "The last week has been eye-opening for me. I've discovered a lot about myself and learned a lot about my heritage. And my lineage."

Maggie sat forward, grabbing Ali's hand. "Sweetie, that's so great."

"I also found out what the mark on my foot is and what it means. It's a tribe symbol, something my people give their children just after birth. Each tribe has a unique symbol, so I know which tribe I was born into."

Her brows shot up. "Oh wow."

"I am Zendori, just like Grandi, and we are the last of our tribe."

A strange mix of relief, sadness, and happiness danced over Maggie's features. But she hadn't heard the one little detail that made all the difference.

With tears suddenly stinging her eyes, Ali cleared her throat and managed to choke out, "Maggie, Grandi is my father."

Her friend's gaze jumped to his end of the table. Her eyes wide with surprise, she stared at the man in question. Speechless, Maggie blinked a few times before turning her focus back to Ali. "You're serious? How…" Her words trailed off again.

Maggie's shocked expression said it all. And Ali understood the feeling. "It's crazy, right? It took a bit for the news to settle in for me too." Ali scoffed. "If I'm honest, I think I'm still trying to wrap my head around it."

Maggie's eyes flicked between father and daughter as if searching for similarities.

"I came here hoping to learn something about my past, but I never even dreamed I might somehow find a living relative. Much less one of my parents."

Tears filled Maggie's eyes and she dragged Ali close. Her voice quavered when she whispered, "Oh, sweetie. I'm so happy for you."

AFTER DINNER, Ali and Maggie went for a walk out back. They strolled through the spacious back yard and down by the river. Maggie had much the same reaction Ali did the first time she'd seen it all. Pure awe and joy.

As much as Maggie loved interior design, she'd always had a soft spot for nature. Her massive flower garden was proof of that. Ali still didn't understand how the woman had time to take care of both, but somehow, she managed just fine.

"It's so beautiful here. I can see why you love it so much."

"Yeah." Ali let her gaze drift over the yard again, taking everything in. Though it'd only been a little more than a handful of days, it already felt like home. "If I'm honest, I could see myself living here."

Maggie turned, studying her profile for a long moment. "You do seem surprisingly comfortable here. But I suspect a lot of that is because of Nicolai."

True, but there was so much more to it than that, so much more that Ali couldn't tell her friend.

"Well." Maggie cleared her throat. "If you decide to stay, you know I'll miss you like crazy. But I'm happy for you. I really am."

Ali searched Maggie's watery eyes. "I'll miss you too."

Maggie cleared her throat again. "It won't be too bad though. I can come visit any time. And look at all the frequent flyer miles I'll accumulate."

Ali smiled.

Maggie glanced back at the house, shaking her head. "I still can't believe you found your father."

"I know. I think we were all a little shocked."

Maggie hesitated, her eyes growing cautiously curious. "What about your mother?"

Ali didn't know how to answer that. Grandi said she'd gone missing. But like Nicolai has said about his friend's sister, there would be no way for her to sever their mate bond. Death was the only way to permanently break that connection. "Grandi said she died when I was a baby."

Maggie made a soft, sympathetic sound in the back of her throat. "I'm so sorry, Ali."

"It's alright. At least I have him. It's more than what I had before. Besides, at least I know where I came from."

They walked along the river's edge, following the path to the massive fallen tree. Maggie asked quietly, "How are you with everything else? The panic attacks, I mean."

"Good. Surprisingly good." Ali bumped her friend's shoulder with her own. "What about you? Tell me how things are going with you and Greg. It must be good if you're willing to take a trip to Brazil together."

Maggie stopped and faced her. "I'm falling hard for him."

That much was obvious. "You two have been friends for so long. Have you seriously never thought of him as anything more?"

"Not really. I mean, he's obviously an attractive guy. I've always thought so, but I never considered being more than just friends with him. And then one day, it just kind of happened." With a faraway expression, Maggie added, "A couple days after that first party, I had lunch with him. We'd just finished dessert. I was rambling about one of my projects. And out of nowhere, he just leaned in and kissed me. I was in such shock I didn't know how to respond at first."

Ali's eyes widened with surprise. "Was it awkward?"

Maggie shook her head, a secret little smile on her face. "It was perfect. The whole thing gave me butterflies, and I've never in my life had that happen before."

Ali smiled. She knew the feeling.

"We sank into the kiss like we'd done it a million times. We were so into the moment that we forgot where we were. Until a man at the next table cleared his throat. I was so embarrassed that we lost all sense of our surroundings that I dragged him out of there. Of course, he thought it was hilarious."

"I thought I noticed some tension between you two after that."

"Yeah. I wasn't sure where things were going. And besides, I was more focused on worrying about you and this newness with Nicolai."

Ali scoffed. "Please. I would have welcomed the

distraction. And the juicy details. It's not like you date often."

"Yeah. Well, I'm telling you now." She hesitated, and to Ali's surprise, Maggie's cheeks flushed a subtle shade of pink. "And I will say that he rocked my world that night. For hours. I don't think I walked straight for a week."

Though a bit taken aback by her friend's bluntness, Ali laughed. "Yeah, I know the feeling. Nico can be a little intense sometimes."

Maggie smirked. "I'm not surprised. He looks like a gentleman, but he has an underlying wild-man energy."

Ali burst out laughing. "Girl, you have no idea."

"Well, there's nothing wrong with a man getting a little animalistic in bed. As long as he's treating you right."

Ali snorted, finding it funny that her friend used the word "animalistic." Maggie would flip if she knew just how right she was.

Greg and Nicolai joined them a short time later.

"You ladies up for going on a little adventure? Nicolai was telling me about this spot I wouldn't mind seeing."

"Isn't it getting dark soon?" Maggie turned to Nicolai. "Is it safe to be out in the jungle at night? Isn't that when some of the bigger predators come out?"

"Most wild animals out here tend to steer clear of people. It is the little poisonous ones and the toxic plant life that should worry you more. But if you do not stray from the path, you will be fine."

Maggie gave a nervous laugh. "That's not helping to sell me on going. The more you talk, the more I want to stay here and spend time with Grandi. And don't think I didn't notice the most-of-the-animals-avoid-people part."

Ali caught Nicolai's faint smirk, but he schooled his

expression and assured her friend. "The monkeys get curious sometimes, but they keep their distance. Being in a group helps. Like I said, stay on the path and you will be perfectly safe. I promise."

Ali could see her friend's lingering doubt, but Maggie let out a harsh breath. "Okay. I'm trusting you."

Ali linked arms with Maggie and led her across the river. Greg and Nicolai fell in behind them as they strolled down the path.

Maggie took in all the sights and sounds of the jungle, seemingly unbothered by the heat and humidity. Ali was glad. She knew what it was like to be in an environment and feel like she couldn't breathe, but Maggie seemed to relax, little by little. Until an enormous, brightly colored bird swooped down just over their heads, nearly touching them.

Maggie squealed and covered her head, but the bird was already gone. Seeing her reaction was so comical, Ali couldn't keep the giggle contained as she asked Maggie if she was okay.

"No, I'm not okay! A pterodactyl almost took my damn head off!"

Behind them, the guys joined in, their laughter ringing clear in the heavy evening air. Maggie didn't share their amusement. She threw an angry look over her shoulder, and Greg held up his hands as if warding off an invisible attack. But the second Maggie faced forward again, Ali caught the little smirk he threw in Nicolai's direction.

"Fucking birds," Maggie muttered under her breath as she continued down the trail.

Ali caught back up with her and hooked their arms together again. They'd only made it twenty or thirty more feet when behind them, Greg asked, "What kind of track is this?"

Ali looked back at the two men to find Greg crouched, pointing at a mark near the center of the trail. Nicolai glanced up at Ali before he gave a calm answer. "Jaguar."

Greg's head snapped up and he stared at Nicolai with wide eyes. "A jaguar? Are you serious?"

Nicolai nodded. "By the looks of the track, it came through here less than two hours ago."

Maggie's hand tightened on Ali's bicep. "Do you think it's still close?"

"Yes, but it is nothing to worry about," he said, throwing Ali an amused look.

Maggie laughed with a hint of hysteria. "Nothing to worry about? From the looks of that print, the thing is massive."

Ali patted her friend's arm. "We'll be okay. Like Nico said, they won't bother us."

"Well, I think we should head back to the house. It's getting dark, and I don't think I want to be out here with that thing."

Greg took Maggie's hand. "Come on. We can come back tomorrow when there's more light."

Ali fell into step beside Nicolai, a little smile on her face as they followed Greg and Maggie back toward the house at a slightly quicker pace.

The nervous couple scanned the forest around them, searching for the jaguar that had made those tracks, not knowing just how close it really was.

21

Ali woke with a start, disoriented and her heart racing. Panting hard, she searched the darkness, looking for what might've woken her. She didn't see anything. And outside, the symphony of nocturnal animals still howled and screeched like nothing had disturbed them.

Detecting no outward cause, Ali blamed her sudden wave of anxiety on her dream. She didn't recall anything about it, and judging by the way she felt, she was glad she couldn't remember.

Forcing herself to take a deep breath, Ali turned her focus to Nicolai and smiled. He lay with his head resting on her belly, his arm tucked tight around her hip like he thought she might sneak away while he slept.

Needing to feel more connected with him, but not wanting to disturb his sleep, Ali slipped her fingers into Nicolai's silky hair. He stirred, snuggling closer. A contented purr instantly sprang to life in his throat, vibrating through her. Ordinarily, it would have calmed her, but with every heartbeat that passed, the more her unease grew.

Strange. She hadn't had one of her episodes since the first time her jaguar emerged. Unless she counted when she and Nicolai had gone for that first run together. But that was nothing compared to the usual intensity she felt when her body was out of control.

Unable to lie still any longer, Ali gently extracted herself from Nicolai's hold and stepped onto the small balcony. The thick air clung to her like a second skin, hugging her gently. But despite taking deep, controlled breaths, her entire body flushed, and a low-level vibration began in the pit of her stomach.

She leaned against the railing and closed her eyes. *Please, not now,* she said to herself, but her body didn't listen. The panic attack hit her faster and harder than ever before. Something was wrong. She couldn't force herself to take slow even breaths the way she needed. And the hair on the back of her neck stood on end.

That's when she caught the strange scent. It was like nothing she'd ever come across, but something about it was oddly familiar.

Behind her, Nicolai's sleepy voice rasped. "Alessandra."

Startled, she spun around to face him. With her internal chaos and everything else overwhelming her senses, she hadn't heard him join her on the balcony.

Instantly, Nicolai's brows drew together with concern. "Are you well, love?"

Not wanting to worry him, she forced a smile. "Yeah. Just woke and couldn't go back to sleep."

He stepped close and pressed the back of his hand

against her forehead. "You feel fevered. And you are trembling."

"I'm fine." She tried assuring him. "I think I just need something to drink."

"Come. Sit." He steered her back to the bed. He fussed over her, tugging his shirt over her head and rubbing her arms as if to soothe her.

Ali placed her hand on his, stilling his movements. "It's just a panic attack. I'll be fine."

Nicolai's entire body stiffened.

"Nico, it's fine. I…"

"Shh," he hissed, closing his eyes.

Ali understood something was wrong when he tilted his head, and his dark brows drew together with intense concentration. Worried, she whispered through their mate bond. *What are you hearing?*

Quiet, love. Listen.

Ali focused, but she heard nothing. Absolutely nothing. All the forest creatures had gone quiet. Nico's nostrils twitched, and Ali followed his lead, testing her new sense of smell.

That strange, intriguing scent from before was even stronger. It smelled incredible. She wanted to find it and rub herself all over it.

Alessandra, Nicolai snapped, giving her a small shake. *Look at me.*

Her eyes flew open, his worried tone making her heart skip a beat. *What's wrong?*

That scent is Naymati.

She stared up at him. *What the hell is a Naymati?*

The Jagara people's oldest enemies. They usually steer

clear of our territory, but on occasion they wander onto our lands. *Never this far east, though.*

Feeling Nicolai's unease, Ali got to her feet and followed him as he moved to the closet. *What are you doing?*

He handed her a pair of pants. *I am getting you some place safe. I do not want you anywhere near the house when he comes.*

Maybe he's just passing through.

Nicolai turned to face her. *I assure you, if the Naymati caught your scent on one of our trails, he is coming, and he will stop at nothing to have you.*

My scent? You're serious?

I would never joke about your safety, love. My friend lost his mate. I will not lose you. Especially to one of those vile creatures.

Ali caught a glimpse of a man in Nicolai's thoughts that looked eerily familiar, and her heart sank. He looked too much like the frightening, pale-skinned male that had haunted her dreams.

The one that stalked her and chased her through the dark forest had to be Naymati. And knowing one of his kind was out there skulking around in the darkness terrified her.

Nicolai slowly turned to face her. *You dreamed of them.*

Ali nodded. *I hoped they weren't real.*

They are very real. And their presence in our territory is not to be taken lightly. In the past, Jagara females disappeared. Some of the elders believe the Naymati were responsible, but they had no proof.

Nicolai's attention shifted to the bedroom door. He only hesitated a heartbeat before taking the two long strides and yanked the door open just as Grandi lifted his hand to knock.

"I know. I smell him."

As Nicolai went back to the closet, Grandi stepped into the room, tossing a worried look at Ali before responding in a low voice. "I woke the others. They are getting dressed."

"Good." Nicolai turned back to Ali. *Go with Grandi. He will take you and your friends to Marius. You will be safer there.*

And where are you going? Ali demanded.

I need to make sure the Naymati does not come after you.

She grabbed onto his arm. *What? No!* She didn't want him anywhere near that terrifying male.

Nicolai cupped her cheek. *Please try not to worry. I will take care of it.*

Tears filled her eyes. *What if something happens to you?*

I can take care of myself. I was trained for this.

Ali stared up at him, her heart racing. *I still don't want you to go.*

Nicolai took her face in his hands. *Alessandra, we do not have time to argue. I must go.*

Though her every instinct screamed that they needed to stay together, Ali trusted Nicolai. She didn't want him out of her sight, but she knew she had to let him go.

When she finally agreed, Nicolai placed a lingering kiss to her forehead. *I will see you soon.*

Ali nodded. *Be careful.*

Grandi laid a comforting hand on her shoulder as

Nicolai turned to leave. Just before he disappeared through the hanging fabric, she called out to him.

When he turned, she drew a shuddering breath and whispered, "I love you."

Nicolai smiled, his vibrant green eyes sparkling with happiness. "I know, love. I love you too."

NICOLAI SHIFTED to his jaguar form and crossed the river, quickly taking to the trees. He could have stayed with Ali and protected her if the enemy came closer. But the primal need to eliminate the threat to his mate demanded he pursue the trespasser.

Nicolai raced through the forest, leaping from tree to tree as he followed the earthy scent of the Naymati. And when it grew to near unbearable heights, Nicolai stopped, settling on the limb to take in his surroundings.

He immediately spotted the pale, lean form crouched in the underbrush. The male's dark eyes scanned the immediate area. His head tilted back, his eyes closing as his nostrils flared. The raw, inhuman sound that escaped the male sent pure fury zinging through every cell in Nicolai's body.

He barely held back a growl, his muscles trembling with the need to attack. No one had the right to react with such blatant hunger to his mate's essence. Especially not some vile creature who wanted to do unspeakable things to her.

Nicolai crept silently down through the limbs, stalking closer to his target. But just as he prepared to spring from the branch above the Naymati, the bastard took off through the brush, headed straight for Nicolai's home.

Leaping onto the ground, Nicolai gave chase, fighting the panic that threatened to swallow him. As quick as the Naymati moved, Nicolai couldn't be sure he'd catch him before he reached the village.

With terror building in the pit of his stomach, he reached out to Ali through their mate bond. *Please tell me you are in the truck heading away from the house.*

Yes. Ali immediately replied, sharing her view from the back seat of Grandi's beat-up old truck. The male took the rutted road as fast as he could, jarring himself and the three passengers as he made his way toward Marius's village.

In front of Nicolai, the Naymati ducked and weaved through the underbrush, dodging trees and trying to lose the jaguar tight on his heels. Fortunately, Nicolai was equally as agile. When the male hopped a fallen tree, the big cat went under. He slammed into the stunned male and they both went tumbling across the forest floor.

As they rolled, the Naymati kicked hard with his feet, flinging Nicolai off him. The quick move launched Nicolai into a nearby tree and knocked the breath from his lungs.

The male drew a blade from the folds of his robing as he rolled into a crouch. Thin, pale lips peeled back from his jagged teeth, and he let out a vicious hiss.

Nicolai's jaguar quickly righted himself, rage scrunching his face into a ferocious snarl.

With a breathless laugh, the Naymati taunted Nicolai. "Of course, you would need the aid of your beast. I should have known your kind would never fight like a true male."

Nicolai popped his teeth together as he circled his prey.

He didn't give a shit what the bastard thought of him. All he cared about was protecting his mate by delaying the enemy. He would do anything he could to allow Grandi time enough to get Ali and the others to the safety of Marius's home.

The Naymati drew a deep breath in, a wicked smile on his pale face. "Your female smells of wild nectar. Tell me. Does she taste as sweet?"

Nicolai didn't move. He forced himself to remain in control of his temper.

"I think I will have to see for myself. And once your female has a taste of me, she will be begging for more."

Nicolai's anger skyrocketed, but he held on to his control. Reminded himself that they were only words. Let the male talk. The fucker could say whatever he wanted so long as he wasn't anywhere near Ali.

Seeing that Nicolai wasn't falling for the bait, the Naymati grinned, displaying those jagged teeth again. "I will have your female. She will be mine to touch. To taste. And to mate."

Though the thought of the vile male anywhere near his Alessandra infuriated him, Nicolai didn't react.

That only infuriated the Naymati. With a glinting blade in hand, he lunged forward, narrowly missing Nicolai. Angry that he'd missed, the male spun around, ready to attack again. And before he could right himself, Nicolai knocked the weapon from the male's hand with a quick swipe of his paw.

The Naymati stumbled, a look of sheer disbelief on his pale face when he saw the stripes of blood welling on his forearm. He turned furious eyes back to Nicolai. But before the male could come at him again, something slammed into Nicolai, sending him rolling into the underbrush.

He righted himself just in time to see the Naymati snatch his knife off the ground and disappear down the trail leading back toward Nicolai's home. With a second Naymati male right behind him.

ALI WAS A BUNDLE OF NERVES. She'd seen Nicolai sparring with Marius and trusted that he could take care of himself. Still, the vivid memory of her Naymati nightmares terrified her.

"What exactly is going on?" Greg asked, staring across the front seat at Grandi.

Grandi glanced at Ali in the rearview before offering a vague explanation. "There is a rival tribe that, on occasion, does not respect our borders and wanders into Jagara territory. They are a vicious tribe who tend to take what they want. Our women being one of the things they covet most. As a precaution, we are taking Ali somewhere safer. Somewhere we will all be safer."

Maggie exchanged a look with Greg. "And where are we going?"

Grandi kept his eyes on the bumpy, rutted road. "Marius is the nearest of our people. He is a skilled fighter. Fiercely protective."

"Good to know," Greg muttered.

Staring out into the darkness, Ali watched the trees and underbrush speed by her window. She thought she caught a movement at the edge of the trees. A figure keeping up with the car. She wasn't sure if it was her imagination, but as she opened her mouth to warn Grandi anyway, he slammed on the brakes, flinging her and Maggie against the back of the front seat.

"No," Grandi breathed.

"Oh shit." Greg whispered.

Ali lifted her head to see why they'd stopped so suddenly. Her heart sank. Across the road in front of them lay a massive tree.

Grandi looked back at her. "We must get out and run. The village is no more than a mile away."

Ali met her father's eyes, switching to their native language. "*We will never make it.*"

He ignored her, reaching for the door handle. "We are wasting time. We need to move."

Ali closed her eyes and reached out to Nicolai. *Where are you?*

About two miles past the house. Are you with Marius?

No. We were stopped about a mile from the village.

What happened?

There is a tree across the road. We can't go around. Grandi says we need to run, but there's no way Maggie and Greg will make it.

Then go. Now. I am on the trail of a Naymati male, and he is headed your direction. I have no idea how far ahead of me he is. Do not worry for Maggie and Greg. They will be safe with Grandi.

Ali looked over at Maggie and then at Grandi. "*Nico said for me to run. Which direction? How will I know which house belongs to Marius?*"

Grandi pointed. "*Northwest. His home is farthest east on the outskirts of the village.*"

"Let's go," Ali snapped, jumping from the truck.

The others followed quickly and Grandi handed Greg a handgun. "You two get in the middle and follow Ali. I will take the rear."

Without hesitation, they took off through the jungle, running toward Marius's house. They were quick, but Ali itched to pick up the speed. No matter what Nico said or how much her instincts demanded she go, Ali couldn't force herself to leave them behind just to get herself to safety.

She felt the familiar stirring beneath her skin, her jaguar rising, trying to emerge. Her need to shift had never been so demanding, and with every passing second, it intensified even more. She fought it, pushing it down as she ran. But soon, her jaguar leapt to the surface, clawing to get out.

The feeling was so strong Ali stumbled, barely catching herself on the nearest tree. Looking back at the others, she felt a miniscule bit of relief that they were only a few yards behind her. Before they could catch up, she took off again.

She hopped a log on the trail in front of her and landed in a crouch. He was close. She could smell him. Closing her eyes, Ali inhaled deeply, her body stirring from the potent male scent.

"Keep moving!" Grandi called out to her. *"He is too close!"*

"What the fuck was that?"

Greg's startled words brought Ali out of her bizarre trance, and she glanced back at him. Following his gaze and caught a glimpse of something ducking into the thick underbrush.

Nico, please hurry. He's close.

Run. He is after you. Not them.

I can't leave them.

A menacing growl echoed through her mind.

"You cannot have her!" Grandi yelled.

Ali spun around and searched the jungle where Grandi focused. She saw nothing, but she felt eyes on her.

"Ali," Maggie whispered, her breathing ragged. "I can't see anything."

Ali scanned the area, trying to spot her stalker.

"Can I shoot him?" Greg asked angrily.

Grandi still stared into the same place. "Go, Ali. Keep moving."

She grabbed Maggie's arm and took off again. They were only about a hundred yards away when a gunshot rang out. Maggie yelped, but Ali kept going, dragging her friend behind her. "Move it, Maggie!" Maggie sped up, and when Ali could see a faint flicker of light through the trees ahead, she said, "We're almost there. Run faster."

"I can't!" Maggie panted.

"Yes, you can! Run!"

She heard running behind them and knew it was Greg. As the trail widened, Ali spotted movement ahead of her and skidded to a stop.

"What?" Greg called from behind her.

"Someone is there, and it's not a friend of ours."

Greg pushed past her, standing protectively in front of them. "Do we keep going?"

"Yeah," she breathed.

They moved forward until they came into a small clearing. The second Ali spotted him, the air left her lungs. Crouched on a fallen tree just off the trail was a man with long, pale blond hair.

"I'll distract him," Greg whispered. "You two run."

Ali watched with wide eyes as the Naymati dropped to the ground, striding forward with a catlike grace. Ali's body came alive. His scent hit her like a wave, crashing into her and making her temperature rise.

He spoke with a strange accent, his focus solely on Ali. "I will have you, female."

"I don't fucking think so," Greg snapped.

The moment he took an aggressive step forward, the Naymati snarled, baring a row of jagged, pointed teeth.

Greg paused. "Oh, shit."

When the Naymati male advanced on him, Greg didn't hesitate to pull the trigger. Unfortunately, the bullet didn't reach its intended target. The Naymati darted out of the way and rushed Greg. He slammed into him so hard he knocked Greg clean off his feet and sent the gun tumbling away into the darkness.

The second they hit the ground Greg wrapped his legs around the frightening male. The Naymati hissed, struggling to free himself, but Greg hung on for dear life. He grunted, "Get the fuck out of here!"

22

Nicolai tore down the trail, following the path Grandi had taken Ali and her friends. He hated that they'd had to flee on foot, but they'd had no other option. Throughout the entire ordeal, he caught disjointed images from Ali. So, when Nicolai was suddenly alone in his head, he panicked and called out to her. *Alessandra?*

No answer.

Ali! he snapped.

Still nothing.

Both furious and terrified something had happened to his mate, Nicolai kept racing down the trail he knew she'd taken. He knew something had happened. Trying not to think the worst, he kept running, knowing in his gut that something wasn't right.

As he approached a clearing, he spotted Grandi crouched over someone who sat on the ground, leaning back against a tree. Nicolai shifted quickly and skidded to a stop next to them. Maggie had her eyes squeezed shut, clutching her side as tears streamed down her unusually pale cheeks.

"What happened?" Nicolai demanded.

Grandi looked up at him. "I do not know. I just got here. I was following the Naymati's scent, and when I circled back, I found her like this."

"A man attacked us," Maggie informed him, her eyes wide with fear. "I tried to stop him, but he threw me against the tree. He was so strong. I tried. I really did, but he took her. He took Ali."

Nicolai growled.

"Why did you bring her here?" Maggie sobbed.

He ignored her question and asked, "Where is Greg?"

"Why, Nicolai? If you knew it was dangerous for her here, why did you bring her?"

"I did not know."

Maggie swallowed hard, clearly in a lot of pain.

"Where is Greg?" he asked again.

"He went after them." Maggie pointed with her free hand toward the north.

Nicolai shifted his gaze to Grandi. "Please get her to Marius and tell him what happened."

Grandi nodded, and Nicolai sprinted toward the thick grouping of trees where Maggie had pointed. He immediately caught the mix of scents on a new trail, and the moment he was out of Maggie's line of sight, he shifted again. He needed his jaguar's speed to catch up to them.

ALI WOKE with her cheek pressed against a cool, hard surface. For a moment, she felt disoriented. But then everything came flooding back. Running. Seeking shelter. Eerie, inky eyes in the darkness. The attack. The chaos.

Uncertain of her current location, Ali cautiously opened her eyes. Just out of arm's reach, a pair of pale bare feet came into focus. She didn't have a clue where she was. Not in the jungle anymore, that was for sure. But she did know she wasn't with friends anymore.

Pushing herself into a seated position, Ali's head spun as she slowly let her gaze rise. Past a lean, muscled body. To a frighteningly handsome face. Sure, he looked good, but considering how she'd ended up in her current situation, she was pretty sure he was psychotic.

Ali's heart skipped a beat when he eased closer, but she kept a close eye on him. She didn't trust the deceivingly reassuring smile he gave her. He had abducted her. His intentions were not good ones.

Ali slowly backed away until her back hit a wall, but he kept coming. When he crouched in front of her, Ali held her breath, staring up at him and waiting to see what he planned to do. If he touched her again, she wouldn't hesitate to fight him. He may be stronger, but whatever his plans were with her, she wouldn't make it easy for him.

Lowering his head, he brought his eyes almost level with hers. And as Ali stared into the depths of his black eyes, a strange calming sensation came over her. Everything in her knew she couldn't trust the guy. Still, when he eased even closer, her head dropped back against the wall, and she felt herself relax further.

"You want to stay here with me and be mine. I see it in your eyes."

Even though Ali's brain told her that she didn't belong

there with him, she couldn't stop herself from agreeing with him.

"Good. That is very good." He smiled, showing her a hint of his unusual teeth. She knew she should be terrified, but she felt oddly serene.

Slowly, he reached out and took her face in his hands. The coolness of his fingers against her much warmer skin might have felt nice under different circumstances, but in the moment it felt wrong. Despite everything, Ali stayed calm, allowing him to turn her head this way and that as if inspecting her. She kept her eyes on his face, closely watching the subtle changes in his expression as his fingers traced over her features and down the length of her neck.

Ali kept her breathing slow and even as he rested his hands on her shoulders. He lifted his eyes back to hers. "You are quite different than the others."

Was she?

He leaned in close and drew a slow, deep breath in. He hummed his appreciation and whispered, "Your scent is intoxicating."

Ali wouldn't know how to respond to that even if she wanted to.

His hand caressed her cheek and along her jawline. "So lovely."

Ali studied him as well. All his masculine features. Those sharp angles and hard lines. His intricate blond plaits hung over his lean, toned shoulders. And his incredibly pale skin almost luminous, even in the dark alcove.

"Tell me your name."

"Ali," she answered without hesitation. "What's yours?"

"I am Tiago."

Ali felt the forced calm lift from her, but she still wasn't angry or frightened. "Why am I here, Tiago?"

"Because I need you."

The hint of sadness in his voice intrigued her. "Why?"

"My people are dwindling fast. We only have three breeding females left. One is still young, not yet in her breeding years. And I share a mother with the other two. I want to do my part to keep our blood alive, but there is no other way for me to help."

She didn't like the sound of that, but she forced herself not to react. "That's why you want me? To help increase your people's numbers."

"Partly. But I think you are a beautiful creature and smell good enough to eat."

Ali took a deep breath, letting it out slowly. "Are you going to hurt me?"

"Why would I hurt you? I need you, Ali. I want you." He tilted his head. "You are afraid of me?"

Uh. Yeah. She was terrified. The guy was insane. He'd hunted her down, attacked her and her friends. Taken her deep into the bowels of the jungle. All because he wanted to have a companion. And breed with her.

Bad enough he'd been able to snatch her up so easily. Ali didn't want to show him any weakness or fear. So, keeping her tone as steady as possible, she reluctantly admitted, "I've heard things about your people."

"From the Jagara, no doubt."

Ali nodded.

"Not all my people are animals. Desperate, perhaps, to keep our lines going. Some are violent, angry because the

Jagara have plenty of females, and they feel that Jagara men should share."

"And which are you, Tiago?"

He looked her in the eyes. "I want to have children and keep my blood alive, but I also want a female to claim as mine. I do not want to share her with the other males."

"But why me?"

"You appeal to my every sense. You stir me." He leaned toward her again and whispered, "I could please you, Ali. I could make you happy. And maybe, you could learn to love me."

No matter what Ali had been told about the Naymati, a small part of her felt sad for Tiago.

"I know your people think we are all bad, but we are only desperate to keep our people alive."

"I don't think you are a bad person." Ali murmured. "But you can't expect desperation to bring you the happiness you're after."

She caught a flicker of something in his expression, but it was gone as quickly as it had appeared. On a whim, she tentatively reached out and placed a hand on his forearm. His dark eyes followed the movement.

"I understand your wanting someone of your own. Of needing someone. And I hope somehow you find a female that can be all yours."

His gaze slowly returned to hers. Silence hovered between them for several heartbeats before he rasped, "I have that female. I have you."

"Tiago." Ali shook her head. "I'm sorry. I can't be yours. I belong to someone else."

"No. You are mine."

The steady, certain tone he used made Ali hesitate, but she swallowed her unease and tried another approach. "If I was your female and you'd spent your entire life waiting for me, would you be upset if someone took me from you?"

Tiago's dark eyes searched her face, but he remained quiet.

"My mate has waited his whole life for me, and he is so happy now that I'm here. I'm happy." When Tiago still said nothing, Ali continued. "The last ten years have been so hard because I thought something was wrong with me, but now that I'm with my mate, I'm finally happy."

Tiago looked her right in the eyes, unwavering determination. "But I want you."

Ali's heart stuttered, but she swallowed the growing alarm and tried again. "Do you really want to hurt someone else just so you can be happy?"

Every ounce of vulnerability she'd sensed in Tiago disappeared like it had never been. His presence instantly turned menacing as he leaned in close and growled, "I do not care about anyone else. You are mine because I want you to be. I will do anything to keep you and I will take what is mine whether you like it or not."

NICOLAI RAN hard through the jungle, fear and fury driving him forward. He couldn't believe the Naymati had the audacity to come so far into Jagara territory, but taking his mate was unforgivable.

Nicolai didn't want to think about all the vile things

that might happen to his mate if he didn't reach her in time. Nicolai's sanity depended on his mate's safety. So, he could only hope Greg was quicker and stronger than the average human. Prayed his history with playing football meant his endurance was better as well.

Nicolai followed the scent trail all the way to the central river, running straight to a fallen tree half-submerged in the water and leaping off the far end. For a few aggravating minutes, he frantically searched the opposite bank for her scent.

Instead, two hundred yards down, he found the Naymati's scent and Greg's heavy footprints. He followed them both at full speed, trying to make up for the time he'd lost recovering the trail.

Nicolai soon found himself standing at the entrance of a hidden cave. The Naymati's earthy musk was stronger there. Growing even stronger as he crept forward into the darkness. No way was it residual from passing through once or twice. The male had used the entrance regularly.

A hint of Ali's subtle jasmine scent lingered in the air. Like she'd passed through, but her feet hadn't touched the ground. The Naymati must have been carrying her. Just the thought of the enemy touching his mate infuriated him. But knowing she'd been unconscious since the bastard had snatched her only made Nicolai murderous. No way would the male have been able to make off so easily with a conscious Jagara female.

More determined than ever, Nicolai shifted his focus back to Greg's prints. He followed them through the caves, weaving in and out of every alcove he came across. The human was thorough, for sure.

The gradual downward slope led Nicolai deeper, and with every step he took, the temperature dropped even more. By the time the scents grew stronger again, there was a chill in the air that might have bothered him had the adrenaline not skyrocketed his body heat.

His mate was close. And though he still couldn't connect with her through their mate bond, he could feel her. Forcing himself to take slow, steady breaths, Nicolai crept down the narrow corridor, careful not to make any noise to alert anyone of his presence.

Every step closer to his mate made his muscles tremble with the need to race toward her, but he knew he had to keep himself under control. He must maintain his calm. For her sake and his own.

Nicolai froze when Ali's soft voice carried through the passageway. He couldn't make out her words, but her tone sent a chill up his spine. That tone was reserved for him alone, not for a depraved Naymati male…or for any other male, for that matter.

Nicolai's lips peeled back from his teeth in a silent snarl. He itched to rush around the next bend and rip the Naymati apart. Or better yet, crush his skull for daring to take his mate. But no matter how much he craved violence, he knew he had to keep a level head. For Ali.

Nicolai moved again, creeping forward. Then he froze the second he heard the distinct click-click of a gun being cocked. And then Greg's deceivingly calm voice. "Get the fuck away from her."

ALI COULD BARELY BREATHE with Tiago's long, cool fingers gripping her throat. But she managed to stay calm, because she was no longer alone with him. Greg stood in the narrow entrance, a gun in his hand and a determined look on his face. Tiago wouldn't be going anywhere without a fight.

But Greg's expression faltered when a low, menacing growl rumbled from behind him. He slowly turned his head, his eyes grew wide, and his face paled noticeably. That's when Ali saw it. A big, black jaguar stalked into the dimly lit alcove with his teeth bared and his eyes focused on Tiago. Even without their mate bond, Ali knew it was Nicolai. She would know him anywhere.

Greg took a cautious step to the side, his eyes bouncing between the Naymati and what he thought was a wild animal. Ali knew she couldn't tell him the full truth, but she could reassure him.

"Greg," she rasped. And when his focus jumped back to her, she nodded toward the jaguar. "He won't hurt you."

She could see the doubt in his eyes when he whispered, "How the hell do you know that?"

"Just trust me."

"Shut up!" Tiago hissed.

Nicolai's growl intensified.

Tiago leaned down and whispered next to her ear. "Tell them to let us pass."

"No," she breathed. Because she knew if Tiago took her away again, Nicolai might not have another chance to save her. She suspected that if the male was desperate enough, things might not turn out so well for her.

"Tell them to move away or I will make you my meal

instead of my mate." He ran his nose up the side of her neck. "You will be quite tasty either way."

Nicolai inched forward, his vicious, throaty rumble growing louder.

Tiago tensed, the hand on her throat flexing. "Tell them," he gritted out, and Ali felt the tip of a blade tear through her shirt and break the skin at the small of her back.

She gasped, her heart leaping into her throat. "You have to let him take me."

Greg shifted his weight and said through gritted teeth, "There's no way I'm letting that happen."

Nicolai snarled and inched forward.

"Nico, stop." Her gaze shifted back to Greg. "Please, put the gun away."

"Not a fucking chance." He hesitated and then blinked. Ali could see the moment her words registered, and his eyes went back to the jaguar. "Did you just…"

Ali nodded. Confirming he'd heard her right. "I'll explain everything later."

Greg scoffed. "You go with him, and you won't be explaining shit."

His protective instinct was in overdrive. She could see that, but he looked to her for guidance on what to do. She could see the pleading in his eyes, but she didn't know what the hell to do.

"Enough," Tiago hissed. "Make room or your precious mate suffers."

Nicolai's glowing eyes stayed hyper-focused on Tiago, and Ali knew he was trying to come up with a solution. Some way to get her away from Tiago without her getting hurt.

"It's okay, love."

She could feel Nicolai pushing at whatever barrier had been erected between their minds. Finally, his voice broke through. *Are you hurt, love?*

Relieved to hear him again, Ali closed her eyes and answered. *No. But he has a knife at my back. So, you gotta let us go.*

I cannot do that.

Ali exhaled a ragged breath. "You have to let him take me."

No, he growled. At the same time, Greg spat, "Fuck that!"

He will kill me if you don't.

Alessandra, I cannot do that. The potent combination of his fear and anger scared her. But she knew she had to convince him to back off and find another way.

Nico. "Please. You need to let me go." *For now.*

After a long, painful silence, Nicolai's posture eased noticeably. *I will be with you, amor. Stay strong and brave. I will come for you.*

KNOWING it was the only way to convince the Naymati that he yielded, Nicolai shifted back to his human form. He ignored Greg's startled gasp and took three steps backward into the tunnel. It allowed the cave-dwelling fiend plenty of room to slip from the alcove with Ali still in his grasp.

It took every ounce of restraint Nicolai had not to follow them. He watched, feeling utterly powerless as the Naymati left with his mate. He acknowledged the possibility that he might never see her again, but even the most miniscule of chances was better than the alternative.

When they disappeared around the bend, Nicolai turned his focus back to Greg, who stared at him for a long moment, his expression blank. Thankfully, his gun hand lay limp at his side with the business end pointed at the ground as if entirely forgotten.

Nicolai waited, watching the guy process what he'd witnessed. It didn't take long. The faraway expression soon melted away and Greg cleared his throat. "I'm not even going to pretend to understand what the fuck I just saw. Or what episode of *The Twilight Zone* I stepped into. But I know one thing for sure. You've lost your damn mind if you think I'm not going after them."

"I know."

"I get why you let them go. I didn't have a clear shot at the guy, but I have never wanted to shoot somebody so bad in my life."

"And I have never contemplated ripping out a man's throat before this night."

Greg gave a nervous laugh. "Yeah, well, I just hope we can find them again. Every second we stand here talking, the farther away they get."

"Trust me. So long as I can scent them, I can find them."

"And how long do we wait before we hunt this fucker down again?"

Nicolai nodded toward the dark corridor. "Can you keep up?"

With a humorless smirk, Greg motioned for him to lead the way.

They traveled through the maze of tunnels, delving

deeper into Naymati territory. The farther they went, the stronger the Naymati's scent grew. But the more underground pools and rivers they crossed, the weaker Ali's scent became.

Panic and anger threatened to take him over, but he knew if he let his emotions win, he would never find his mate. Nicolai closed his eyes, reaching out to Ali through their mate bond. Nothing. She'd gone silent again, and that terrified him.

Behind him, Greg panted. "Why are we stopping?"

Nicolai tried over and over to make the connection. "It's gone. I can't sense her anymore."

"Nothing?" Greg pressed.

Nicolai shook his head. "All I smell is the Naymati. His scent is everywhere. And strong. This is his domain. He has traveled each of these tunnels many times. I cannot tell which he took most recently."

"What are we going to do?"

Nicolai didn't know. But giving up was not an option no matter how bleak it looked.

With a startling roar of frustration, Greg slammed his fist into the cave wall.

Nicolai closed the distance between them and laid his hand on Greg's shoulder. "You must stay focused."

The fire in his eyes didn't die down. The guy's outburst only seemed to enrage him more. "How the hell can you be so calm? That is your girlfriend out there with that psycho."

"Yes. But losing my temper does not help her."

Greg clenched his fists and closed his eyes.

Nicolai gave his shoulders a squeeze, and when Greg

made eye contact, Nicolai kept his tone even. "I know you are upset, but we will get her back."

Greg took a deep breath and exhaled slowly. "I don't think I could face Maggie if we couldn't bring Ali home."

"You will not have to worry about that. We will find her." He patted Greg's shoulder. "Come, now. Let us try again to catch her scent or a sign that she has been through here."

23

Tiago tossed Ali onto a bed platform, leaving her to pace the rough stone floor. He'd dragged her through winding tunnels, crossed underground springs, and delved even deeper into the earth. Ali wasn't sure she could find her way out again, but she'd damn well try if she got the chance.

She shivered as she studied her surroundings, looking for a way to escape him. No such luck. There was only one way in or out of the spacious hideaway. And her captor stood between it and her.

The chamber looked lived-in, and judging by the smells, it had to be Tiago's personal space. His scent was everywhere. It made her incredibly uneasy to be where he slept. It felt too intimate, and the last thing she wanted was to be intimate in any way with the guy. Though that's exactly what he wanted from her.

With her heart in her throat, Ali kept her eyes on him, watching him carefully. She'd never been so scared in her life, but the second he tried to do anything she didn't want, she would fight with all her strength. If she thought she might be able to shift efficiently enough to get the upper hand, she'd do it. But she didn't feel confident enough to take on such a strong, quick, and more experienced opponent. She could only hope Nicolai had a plan and he would rescue her soon.

When Tiago finally looked at her again, he hesitated, studying her for a moment before he moved to the opposite corner. He snatched up a bundle of cloth from the neat stack and tossed it at her.

Ali's quick reflexes allowed her to easily catch the bundle before it hit her in the face. She glared at him, her earlier need to mollify him gone after the shit he'd said and done.

He held her gaze and snarled, "Put it on."

Ali didn't reply. Instead, she sat the clothes beside her and lifted her chin. She wasn't putting his damn clothes on.

Tiago stalked forward, and she fought not to back away when he crouched in front of her. "It is for your own good. It is too cold down here for you to stay in those wet clothes. Now, change."

That much was true. She was freezing, but no way was she getting naked in front of him. "Can I have some privacy?"

"You are mine. You need no privacy."

He had the nerve to look offended by the reasonable request. But Ali refused to budge, holding his stare until he backed away.

With a little breathing room, Ali stood and unfolded the soft fabric. A flowy robe-like frock much like Tiago's. The material was thin, but it had to be warmer than her drenched jeans and t-shirt. The only problem was how vulnerable it left her.

Knowing what he had in mind for her, she'd much rather stay in something that provided a little protection. Unfortunately, she knew he was right. She needed to change into something dry.

Ali turned her back to Tiago before she pulled the wet, clinging shirt over her head and tossed it onto the floor. Shivering, she slipped her arms into the dry sleeves, covering some skin before she peeled off her soaked pants as well. Once completely covered, Ali turned back around to face Tiago. "Happy?"

His dark eyes drifted over her, a wicked smile slowly forming, and Ali knew she'd messed up.

"Come to me, my female."

Ali tensed. "I told you. I'm not yours."

With a subtle tilt of his head, Tiago leveled his eyes with hers and murmured, "Come to me."

The logical, stubborn part of her refused. She didn't want to be there. Much less do what he wanted. But her body obeyed him. Like a puppet, she sauntered forward until she stood before him.

A wicked, satisfied grin pulled at Tiago's pale lips. And with excruciating slowness, his chilled hands caressed her face. Gentle fingers stroked down the soft curve of her neck, and an unexpected shiver of arousal raced through her.

Ali drew a shuddering breath, confused by her body's sudden, intense reaction. Though his touch was pleasurable in the physical sense, the whole thing felt wrong. She wanted to pull away from him, but her traitorous body wouldn't listen. She just stood, frozen in place while the terrifying male touched her.

"You are a beautiful female," he rasped, his voice little more than a whisper. "I am a lucky male to have you."

Ali closed her eyes, painfully aware of his body shifting closer to hers. And when she opened them again, Tiago leaned in as if to kiss her. Just before his mouth met hers, a voice broke through the hypnotic haze. *Alessandra, please hear me. I am coming for you.*

Whatever compulsion Tiago had over her, it shattered the moment she heard Nicolai's voice in her mind.

Angry that Tiago had been able to control her so easily, Ali bared her teeth, a vicious growl escaping her throat.

He jerked back, a stunned expression flickering over his features a moment before he smiled. "Get angry all you like. It will only make for a more satisfying victory when I take what is mine."

Both terrified and disgusted, Ali held his amused gaze. She didn't know where the confidence came from, but she lifted her chin and informed him. "I will never be yours."

Tiago gripped her face, his fingers digging into her cheeks as he forced her back toward the bed. "Fight me or give yourself freely. It does not matter," he said through his clenched teeth. "But either way, you are mine."

On instinct, Ali snatched her face from his grip, but the move threw her off-balance. She fell backward onto the bed, and Tiago was on her before she could recover. He tried to push himself between her thighs, but she squeezed her legs together so tight there was no way he was getting in.

"Do not deny me!" he roared in her face.

Though terrified, adrenaline coursed through her,

giving her the strength she needed to fight him. Ali refused to let him win. No way would he take something from her that was meant only for Nicolai. For her mate.

She had a brief thought to unleash her jaguar and rip him to shreds, but she couldn't calm herself enough to make that happen. She may not have been able to summon the full transformation, but her claws emerged. It gave her a slight advantage, but Tiago was still stronger than her.

He grappled with her, trying to gain control of her hands. But Ali's nails ripped into the pale flesh of his forearms like sharp little daggers. The scent of his blood filled the air around them. And it might have given her some small bit of satisfaction if she hadn't seen the frustration in his black eyes turn to pure, unbridled fury.

Tiago rose above her, and with unfathomable speed, he reared back and struck Ali across the face. Pain burst in her cheek and her vision blurred. Her body went slack for little more than a heartbeat, but it was time enough for Tiago to shove a knee between her thighs and gain control of her hands.

He gripped both her wrists with one hand, pinning them over her head. With the other, he yanked the thin material separating them, and sheer panic set in the second the cool cave air hit her bare skin.

In all her life, Ali had never felt so helpless. No matter how hard she struggled, she couldn't get free. Pinned beneath him as she was, she could do nothing to stop Tiago from taking what he wanted.

He shoved her legs farther apart and wedged himself between her thighs. The sick bastard was fully aroused, and she could feel every hard inch of him pressed against her most sensitive flesh. One shift of his hips and that would be it.

Ali wanted to scream and cry and plead for him to stop, but the words froze in her throat. Her heart thundered so hard in her chest she could barely draw a breath.

Then it happened. The most terrifying roar she had ever heard echoed all around them. Tiago stiffened above her, genuine fear blooming in his dark eyes. One second, he was there. The next, a massive body slammed into him, knocking him off the bed.

For a moment, Ali was too stunned to move. But then, the vicious sounds of fighting registered, and she knew the distraction was her chance to escape.

Before she could gather her composure, a pair of big hands grabbed her and dragged her off the other side of the bed. Survival instinct finally took over and her body reacted without conscious thought.

Fighting like a madwoman, Ali squirmed and kicked to get free. When her foot connected with the edge of the bed platform, she shoved as hard as she could, knocking both her and her new captor backward. They crashed to the floor with a hard jolt, his arms loosening just enough for her to slam an elbow into his ribs.

With a pained grunt, he demanded, "Ali, stop."

She went still in an instant, the familiar voice washing over her like a soothing balm. Hardly believing her ears, she looked over her shoulder.

"Greg," she breathed, her vision blurring with unshed tears.

Ali sank into his arms, and he hugged her close. "It's okay. I have you."

The chaos that had erupted in the chamber suddenly

went quiet with one last sickening snap. And though terrified to see what had happened, Ali couldn't stop herself
from looking.

Tiago lay motionless on the chamber floor with his
throat ripped out and his black eyes unfocused. And
Nicolai stood over him, his chest heaving, and his
gorgeous mouth covered in thick crimson blood. But all
that wasn't what frightened her most. It was the savage
expression on his face. Though in human form, there was
nothing human in his eyes.

24

The trip to Marius's home was a blur. It took forever, but having her thoughts so consumed with the night's events and the absolute emotional rollercoaster she'd gone through, Ali couldn't recall a single step of the journey.

It was dawn when they finally arrived. Marius met them at the door, looking as tired as Ali felt. He took one look at Nicolai and nodded, his expression one of approval. Ali couldn't look at him though. Every time she did, all she could see was the savage, inhuman expression. And the blood.

Marius turned to Ali, his eyes sweeping over her. She knew what he saw. A broken woman dressed in the enemy's clothes. But he didn't give her a pitying look. He simply asked, "Do I need to have my doctor friend come back and look you over?

Ali shook her head. "I'm fine. I just need to check on Maggie."

"Your friend is resting. Zev checked her out. He

suspected she might have a few cracked ribs, but after a thorough exam, he said they were only bruised. It was a struggle to get her to take something for the pain, though. She wanted to be awake when the boys brought you home."

Greg spoke up. "Where is she?"

Marius nodded toward the room to his right. "Through the dining room and down the hall. First door on the left."

Greg stepped close and offered Marius his hand. "Thanks for taking care of her. I owe you."

Marius clasped his hand. "Not a problem. She is a strong woman. And brave. Ali is lucky to have a friend like her."

Greg disappeared around the corner and Marius glanced at Nicolai before turning back to Ali.

"After the night you had, I am sure you would like to get a bath. You can go get cleaned up while I talk to Nicolai. Then you two can get some rest."

Though a shower and some rest sounded amazing, she didn't know how restful she would be sharing a room with Nicolai. She hated that she felt that way, but her anxiety began to build again just thinking about being alone with him.

"Kesara?" Marius called over his shoulder.

A soft voice answered from around the corner. "Yeah?"

"Can you show Ali to the guest room and get her a change of clothes, please?"

The petite woman that came into view took one look at Ali, her eyes widening almost imperceptibly, but she nodded. "Of course." She offered Ali a warm smile. "Come on. I think I have something that will fit you."

Ali glanced at Nicolai, but he was staring Marius

down, his expression unreadable. She wanted to reach out through their mate bond to see if he was okay, but after everything that had happened and what she'd witnessed last time she'd connected with him, she was afraid of what she might see or hear. So, she left him alone with his friend and followed Kesara through the house, to the room across from where Maggie was fast asleep.

It was like stepping into another world when they walked through the door. Though a little bit messy, the space still felt cozy and cheerful. Velvety blankets covered the bed and fluffy pillows were everywhere. All of it pink. Not a soft pastel pink. A deep, vibrant fuchsia.

Kesara went straight to the dresser, retrieved a couple items, and handed Ali the neatly folded stack. "You are a bit taller than me, so the pants will probably be a little short."

"It's okay. I just want to get the hell out of this damn robe."

Kesara showed her to the room next door. "You have your own bathroom. Fully furnished. Fresh towels in the cabinet behind the door. If you need anything, do not hesitate to ask."

Though she knew she wouldn't, Ali nodded. "Thank you."

Kesara lingered for a moment as if she wanted to say more. But then she turned without another word and left Ali alone.

Ali took in her surroundings. The room had minimal furniture. Only a small dresser to her left and a double bed on her right with an old oak trunk in front of the footboard. With the warm, neutral décor, the space felt inviting. Like a sanctuary. Like no one could get to her there. Especially not Tiago.

Closing her eyes, Ali stood in the center of the bedroom and drew a deep breath. On an ordinary day, she would savor finally being alone. But after the night she'd had, she just wanted to go snuggle up next to Maggie and sleep for a week.

But first, she needed to get rid of the Naymati's lingering scent. Despite having dredged through three separate rivers, she could still smell him, and it made her sick to her stomach.

With her borrowed clothes in hand, Ali made her way into the bathroom. It was nothing fancy. Just a toilet, a small basin sink, and a free-standing soaking tub.

Ali ran her bath, climbing in while the tub still filled, and scrubbed every inch of herself with soap that smelled of coconut and sweet almonds.

Once clean, she sat for a long time, playing over and over the night's events. Hard to believe that less than twelve hours had passed since she'd fallen asleep in Nicolai's arms. Somehow, it felt like a lifetime ago. It was the happiest she'd ever been. Now, she stared down at the murky bathwater, heartbroken by the distance between her and Nicolai.

She knew it was mostly her fault, but Nicolai hadn't spoken a word to her since they'd left the caves. In fact, he hadn't said a word to anyone. And that made it worse somehow.

Just as her eyes began to burn with unshed tears, she thought she heard a soft knock on the door. She held her breath, waiting. Had she heard a knock or was it only sound carrying from somewhere else in the house?

"Ali?" Kesara called from the other side of the bathroom door.

Blinking the tears away, she ran her palms over her face and cleared her throat. "Yeah?"

The door opened a crack. "Are you okay in there?"

"Yeah. I'm good."

After an awkward silence, Kesara said, "Nicolai is worried about you. You have been in here for quite a while and he wanted me to check on you."

"Really?" Ali ignored the shaky, uncertain sound of her own voice. Of course Nicolai was worried. How could he not be after what happened?

Besides, Kesara was right. She had been in the bath long enough for her fingers and toes to prune. It was beyond time for her to get out.

Clearing her throat again, Ali said with a little more strength, "Tell him I'm fine. I'll be out soon."

"If you are hungry, I made egg muffins for everyone."

"I'm good. Thanks." Food was the last thing Ali could think about.

Since she'd finally gotten rid of the Naymati's unwanted scent, she only had two priorities. Checking on Maggie and getting some sleep. She felt bone tired, but she'd never be able to rest without seeing her friend first.

Once Kesara left her alone again, Ali climbed out of the bath and dressed in her borrowed clothes. The t-shirt fit perfect, but Kesara was right. The flowy lounge pants were a few inches too short, but Ali didn't care. She was clean and comfortable.

She hesitated with her hand on the doorknob, torn between not wanting to be around anyone else and desperately needing a distraction. Because no matter how hard she tried, she couldn't stop playing over and over everything that happened in the caves. What she could have or should have done different.

Giving herself a shake, Ali pulled the door open and stepped into the hall. She could hear quiet chatter at the front of the house. She couldn't make out the conversation, but she recognized the voices. Kesara and Marius. Where was Nicolai? With them, she hoped.

The door across from her opened quietly and Grandi stepped into the hall, closing the door behind him with a gentle click. He hesitated the moment he saw her hovering in the hallway. And without a word, he pulled her into his arms.

Ali didn't know what to think. Grandi had been so reserved until that moment. Even during the mad dash through the jungle as they tried to escape the Naymati, he had remained calm and steady.

But all that composure disappeared. He squeezed her tight, holding her against his chest like he thought she might disappear. And Ali couldn't hold back the tears. All she could do was press her cheek to Grandi's sturdy chest and let herself be surrounded by his warmth and comfort.

When he eventually eased back, his expression softened. And with gentle fingers, he wiped the twin streams from her cheeks. "I cannot tell you how grateful I am to those boys for bringing you back home."

The slight wavering of his words had Ali fighting back another wave of tears, but she sniffled and cleared her throat. "Me too."

Grandi cupped her cheek and offered her a faint smile. "How are you feeling?"

Ali shrugged one shoulder. "Exhausted, but I wanted to check on Maggie."

"She is sleeping. You should get some rest as well."

"I can't sleep until I see her with my own eyes."

Understanding, Grandi nodded toward the front of the house. "I will be with the others if you need me for anything."

Ali offered him a watery smile. "Thank you. For everything."

Grandi gave her shoulder a gentle squeeze and headed down the hall.

The moment he was out of sight, Ali slipped into the dimly lit room. The faint glow didn't come from a lamp, but the morning light seeping in around the edges of the heavy curtains. She could just make out two bodies lying close on the double bed. Greg lay next to Maggie, his head on the pillow and his fingers entangled with hers. Even in her sleep, Maggie had turned her head toward him.

Witnessing such intimacy made Ali feel like she was intruding. She had a fleeting thought to back out of the room and come back when they'd all had some rest, but she couldn't make herself leave.

"You look exhausted."

Startled by Greg's rough whispered words, her eyes jumped to his face. "I'm sorry. I didn't mean to wake you."

Greg let out a quiet laugh. "You didn't. After a night like tonight, I don't think I'll be sleeping for a while."

Ali snorted. "I know the feeling."

He eased into a sitting position and nodded toward the opposite side of the bed. "Come sit."

Ali shook her head.

"If you're worried about bothering Maggie, don't.

Whatever the doc gave her, it knocked her out. She probably won't wake until tomorrow." His gaze shifted toward the window. "Well, later today, I guess."

Ali moved closer and eased onto the edge of the bed. Maggie didn't budge. Her breathing didn't even change. Greg was right. She was out cold.

Even with Ali's human eyes, she could see the damage done to Maggie's pale skin. Scrapes marred her delicate jaw and her cheek showed signs of bruising.

Ali hated that the night had taken such a turn. It seemed like a lifetime ago that they were all laughing as they strolled down the jungle path, joking about Maggie's strong dislike of birds. Tears welled in Ali's eyes again, and she cleared her throat. "I'm sorry your vacation was ruined."

"It's not ruined, Ali. Everything will be okay." Greg leaned toward her, drawing her attention fully to him. With his dark expressive eyes, he assured her. "She'll be okay."

25

Nicolai sat at the kitchen island while Marius and Kesara chatted quietly. He didn't hear much of their conversation. He was too deep in thought about Ali and whether she would ever let down the impenetrable wall she'd erected around her mind.

Grandi said to give her time, but Nicolai wanted nothing more than to barge into that room and drag her into his arms. He couldn't do that though. He had to give her the space she needed, and knowing she was safe would have to do. For the time being.

Thirteen minutes after Grandi joined them, Greg came walking into the kitchen as well. Before Nicolai could even ask, Greg informed him, "Ali's in bed with Maggie. I figured I'd let them both get some rest."

Great.

Kesara shoved the plate of muffins toward Greg. "Want some?"

"Sure." Greg took one. "I'm starving."

She'd already offered some to Nicolai, but he wasn't

hungry. He didn't want anything. No food. No drink. No conversation. Just his Alessandra.

He knew she was physically okay, aside from the slight bruising on her cheek. But he wanted to hold her close. Problem was, he didn't know when he would get to, or when she would let him near her again. He felt gutted every time he thought about the way she'd cringed away from him and turned to Greg for comfort instead.

Greg settled on the stool next to him. "So, I know we're all exhausted, but can we talk about what the fuck happened tonight? Because I have some questions."

Marius and Kesara both looked at Nicolai. He had the answers, of course. He just wasn't sure he was ready to give them. But after everything Greg did to help, Nicolai owed him that, at least.

"What do you want to know?"

Greg glanced at Kesara and Marius. "Are they like you?"

"Yes. You can speak freely here."

Greg seemed to contemplate that for a moment before he asked, "Not to be offensive or anything, but what are you exactly? Shapeshifters?"

"One species, yes." Marius spoke up. "Our people are Jagara."

"Jaguar shifters," Nicolai added.

Greg snorted. "Yeah. I remember that part. Scared the shit out of me when it…you…walked into that cave."

"It must have been shocking." Kesara's tone was full of sympathy. "Here in the village, it is a common occurrence to spot a jaguar. Even the locals who are not Jagara know they have nothing to fear when they see one. They keep their distance and let them be. Which helps us blend in."

"The locals know about you?"

Marius leaned back against the fridge and crossed his arms over his chest. "If they do, they will never say. But they do leave offerings near the edges of the village."

Greg's brows furrowed. "Offerings?"

"People out here have superstitions that run deep. They have stories passed down for many generations. Stories about the ones they call the *Onça Guardiãos*: Ancient spirits that take the form of jaguars to protect the native people and animals. They believe if you honor the spirits with an offering, you earn their protection."

"Protection from what? Assholes like that Naymati guy?"

"Yes. They believe his kind prey on the innocent and drink their blood."

Greg's eyes grew wide. "Wait. Do they?"

Marius nodded. "Among other things."

Nicolai could feel his anger rising just thinking about the Naymati asshole, as Greg called him.

"So, you're telling me vampires are real?"

"The locals call them *bruxso*. Their lore says *bruxso* were once men who sold their souls to a woman of darkness to become immortal. And in the process, gained a hunger for blood. But we know they are something else. A species as old as the Jagara."

"And your people have been enemies the entire time?"

Marius shook his head. "Our Elder, Bazyli, has told us stories about the rocky past between our people and theirs. His grandfather was a young boy when the last falling out happened. And it was all over a woman. The Jagara leader's daughter, to be exact."

Nicolai could see Greg's interest grow. He leaned forward, resting his elbows on the counter. "What happened?"

"Despite a longstanding truce between their families, the Naymati king's son tried to claim her as his mate. Though she had been friends with him, he tried to take her. And her true mate was forced to kill him."

"Oh shit."

"His father came into Jagara territory demanding he be allowed his vengeance. And when the leader refused, the king was furious. The leader was forced to reinstate old boundaries and banned his longtime friend from our lands. Those boundaries are still enforced to this day, but on occasion, a brave male will venture into our territory. Usually out of curiosity. But that hasn't happened in years."

"That we know of," Kesara spoke up again, giving Marius a pointed look.

The room went quiet, and Marius just stared at her. Nicolai didn't say a word. He knew his friend didn't want to discuss his missing sister. The subject was too sore.

Greg, picking up on the undercurrent of the conversation, cautiously asked, "What do you mean?"

Marius glared at Kesara, but she shook her head. "He asked."

Shoving away from the fridge, Marius cursed under his breath and stalked from the room.

Greg glanced between Nicolai and Kesara, but he stayed quiet until the front door slammed. The loud clap reverberated through the house. "He gonna be okay?"

Kesara sighed. "Eventually. He is having a hard time. His sister, Mina, went missing around the beginning of the year. Like the others, she disappeared without a trace. And to make it worse, her mate recently called off the search for her."

Greg blew out a rough breath. "Damn. No wonder he didn't seem very happy."

"Yes. Marius is furious. Though there is no real hope, he refuses to believe the worst."

In the silence that lingered, Nicolai thought about going to check on his friend. But he knew Marius well enough to know he needed some space. If he wanted to talk, he would.

Studying Greg's expression, Nicolai figured he had more questions, but he might as well leave that to Kesara, since she seemed so willing to talk. Nicolai just wanted to go to Ali, even though he knew she was most likely asleep.

Sliding off the stool, Nicolai stretched, feeling the ache in his tired muscles. He was exhausted. "I am going to check on the girls and then try to get some rest." He clapped Greg on the shoulder. "Thanks again for everything. I truly appreciate all you did tonight. I owe you, my friend."

Greg clasped Nicolai's forearm, holding him in place. "You don't owe me shit, man. And if you need anything else, ever, don't hesitate to ask."

The sincerity of his words and in his steady stare had Nicolai nodding in agreement. "Same goes to you."

Greg nodded, not moving from his spot at the counter.

Kesara offered a friendly smile. "Sleep well."

Nicolai made his way down the hall and slipped silently into the dark room. It only took a moment for his eyes to adjust. On the bed, Ali lay facing her friend with her hand resting on Maggie's arm. Both women were fast asleep.

Careful not to disturb either of them, Nicolai snagged the straight-back chair from beside the bed and positioned it across from Ali. He sat for a long time and watched her sleep. She was safe. That's all that mattered for now. They could work through the rest later. Until then, he needed some sleep too.

ALI TOOK a leisurely stroll along her favorite path. The only reason she could relax was because she knew it was a dream. The dull, hazy world around her gave that away. It lacked the detail of real life. But that didn't stop the fear from racing through her when a tall shadow crossed the path nearly twenty yards ahead of her.

Every ounce of survival instinct told her to turn and run, but some unseen force dragged her forward.

A sudden blur of disorienting movement brought her face to face with the Naymati male that had taken her. He grabbed her around the waist and took her mouth by force, pressing his body against hers.

Though she wanted desperately to get away from him, wanted to be strong and fight, Ali couldn't move. She was frozen.

Tiago took her down to the ground, and when his body covered hers, they were both completely naked, and the cool press of his body sent a shiver up her spine. He pulled her hands above her head and held them there while he moved against her. Tears streamed down her face as he shifted against her, and the hard length of his arousal slipped easily between her legs.

Ali felt betrayed by her own body. How could she be so utterly terrified by what was happening and her body still be responding to his? Why was she drenched with arousal? And why were soft, satisfied moans bubbling up from her own throat? Though horrified, she couldn't stop herself from making little noises as his mouth and hands roamed her body.

The tears fell harder when he pushed inside her. She'd never felt so violated in her life, but she could do nothing to stop him. And though she knew she belonged to someone else, she couldn't keep her body from responding to Tiago's deep, sure thrusts.

Then everything changed in an instant. Tiago bared his razor-sharp teeth, a cruel smile on his pale face as his fingers wrapped around Ali's throat. He squeezed until she couldn't breathe, until stars danced along the edges of her vision. Her body tingled all over. And just when she thought she might pass out from the lack of oxygen, Tiago thrust harder into her unwilling body.

Pain ripped through her, like a hot blade repeatedly stabbing her in the most sensitive part of her body. All the while, those pitch-black eyes of his held her captive, nothing but pure evil staring down at her as he took everything he wanted.

The torture felt never-ending, gaining intensity until she thought she couldn't take any more.

Tiago hissed and his back arched with unmistakable pleasure. But then his pleasure suddenly cut short. His eyes widened with surprise when a big hand gripped his throat and yanked him backward.

Before Ali could fully register what happened, Tiago was on the ground next to her, and she had an up-close view of the carnage that took place next.

Nicolai ripped the other male's throat out without hesitation, and blood spurted everywhere, getting all over her.

When she made a sound of distress, Nicolai shifted his focus her way, and Ali nearly stopped breathing for a whole new reason. His savage expression was terrifying. He snarled as he eased closer, keeping his eyes on hers as he took Tiago's place above her. His eyes were ferocious, but Ali's gaze was stuck on his mouth. Tiago's blood covered his beautiful lips and dripped from his sharp teeth.

She shook uncontrollably as Nicolai dropped down and kissed her. Tiago's blood was a fiery tang on her tongue, and she gagged hard. Blood didn't usually bother her, but this did. She pushed against Nico with all her strength and…

ALI SCREAMED AT HIM. "Get off of me!"

Nicolai could only guess what caused the blind panic in her unfocused eyes. Though he couldn't read her thoughts, he could see that she was in full defense mode. Her teeth were fully extended, and her claws ripped into his chest.

"Fuck," he muttered and took her wrists and pinned them over her head. "Calm down," he said as gently as he could while she struggled so hard against him. "Alessandra. Please look at me. You were only dreaming."

She continued to fight until he let out a growl of frustration and her eyes finally focused on his.

He could see the terror there, and he tried to reassure her. "It is all right, love. I have you."

Fresh tears spilled from her eyes, and as she turned her head away from him, she sobbed, "Let go of me."

Nicolai sat back on his heels, his heart breaking for her when she rolled away from him and sobbed harder. He tried to comfort her by laying a gentle hand on her back, but she shrugged him off and pushed herself off the floor. She made a beeline for the door, and when she crashed through it, Nicolai gave a quick glance toward Maggie. Miraculously, she was still asleep.

"Nightmare?"

Nicolai turned to the sound of Marius's voice. He stood in the doorway, dressed only in his boxer briefs. Nicolai didn't miss the blade in his hand.

With a heavy sigh, he got to his feet. "Yes." He should have known Ali's outburst would draw someone's attention.

"Would you like me to talk to her?"

Nicolai scoffed. "Not dressed like that."

Marius looked down at himself and smirked. "I guess not."

Nicolai followed Ali outside and found her leaning against the waist-high wall bracketing the patio. Bent at the waist, she sucked in erratic breaths between harsh sobs.

Seeing her so upset ripped Nicolai's heart out and he didn't know what to do. His instinct was to go to her. Wrap his arms protectively around her and let her cry all she wanted if that's what would help. But the way she'd pulled away from him before, he suspected that was the last thing she wanted.

Ali leaned further forward and retched hard. No matter

what she wanted, Nicolai's need to take care of his mate had him racing forward. Without hesitation, he stepped up behind her and caught her hair in his hand, pulling it back out of her way.

The second he brushed his palm down her spine she gasped, "Don't touch me."

"Shh, it is all right," he tried, but she slapped his hands away. "Amor, please…"

Ali moved away from him, avoiding eye contact, and Nicolai was unsure whether she was fully awake yet. He stepped to her again, this time pinning her between him and the wall by placing a hand on either side of her. She cringed and squeezed her eyes shut.

"Alessandra." He spoke softly. When she kept her eyes averted, he took her chin in his hand and tilted her head back. "Look at me."

With tears still streaming down her face, she finally lifted her wet lashes and Nicolai's heart shattered on the spot. Complete and utter fear shone bright in her amber eyes. It wasn't just the nightmare. His mate was truly afraid of him, and he knew he could do nothing to change that.

Over the last couple months, he'd witnessed Ali come out of her shell, watched her gain confidence. But all that progress no longer mattered. The Naymati had taken all that from her.

Furious and devastated at the same time, Nicolai dropped his hold on Ali's chin and took a step back. No matter how much he wanted to wrap her in his arms and tell her everything would be okay, he couldn't. He didn't know if that was true. Besides, he doubted she would even let him.

Nicolai wanted to apologize. Wanted her to know how sorry he was that all this happened to her. That he'd allowed it. Sorry that he'd ever brought her to the homeland. But he couldn't speak. The words got stuck in his throat.

Stepping around her, Nicolai headed for the tree line. He desperately needed to get away. Needed to clear his head. And maybe if he ran enough, he could figure out a way to fix everything that was broken.

ALI SQUEEZED her eyes shut the second Nicolai left her alone. Seeing the devastated look on his face made her want to cry all over again, but she couldn't keep doing this. She had to get a hold on her thoughts and emotions. And then figure out where the hell she and Nicolai went from there.

Not wanting to let herself be consumed by everything that had happened, she squared her shoulders. She had to do something, or she knew she'd lose her mind. Though she'd never been much of a drinker, she was ready to try anything to calm herself down. Including slinging back glassfuls of whiskey. It probably wasn't the best idea, but she had to do something to get those images out of her head.

Wiping beneath her eyes, Ali drew a deep, calming breath. It helped a tiny bit, so she did it again. And again, until the tears stopped coming. When she finally felt like she had some semblance of control, Ali slipped inside and went straight to the sitting room where she knew Marius kept his alcohol. Bad idea? Sure. But it was better than having those vivid images flashing through her mind. If she could just blur them, even a little, she'd be grateful.

Ali grabbed the first bottle she found and poured herself half a squat glass. She didn't hesitate or allow any time to second-guess her actions. She just tossed her head back, downing the whole thing in three gulps. And instantly regretted it. The smoky flavor burst on her tongue, and she could feel the burn all the way down her throat and into her empty belly.

She shivered, breathing through the burn as she poured herself another. She hoped it would kick in fast because she didn't know how much she could stomach.

She managed to choke down the second glass before Grandi found her. His concerned expression should have been enough to make her stop, but she couldn't. She needed a distraction.

"Ali, what are you doing?"

His gentle yet firm voice gave her pause, but she couldn't speak. She just poured a third and drank it down like she had the others.

With a heavy sigh, Grandi crossed the room and took the glass from her hand before she could fill it again. "This is not what you need."

"Don't tell me what I need!" she snapped, trying to take the glass back.

Shifting it out of her reach, he spoke in an infuriating calm tone. "I understand that you are upset. You have been through a terrible ordeal, but alcohol is not the answer. Doing this will not make you feel better."

Tears welled in Ali's eyes. She didn't understand how she could feel so frustrated and weak, yet so out of control at the same time. Embarrassed by the flood of emotions, Ali turned her back to Grandi.

She knew he was only trying to help, and he didn't deserve her attitude. He'd been nothing but sweet to her. Besides, he was right. Alcohol was not the answer. She knew that, but she didn't know what else to do.

"You want to talk about it?"

Trying to calm herself, she pushed her hair from her face. "About what?"

"What is going on with you and Nicolai?"

Ali rubbed her eyes and leaned against the table. Avoiding making eye contact with Grandi, she stared at the candles, contemplating how much she wanted to tell him. She didn't know what to say. Didn't know how much he knew. Or wanted to know. Most of what happened was humiliating or just plain traumatizing and she didn't care to relive any of it. In fact, the whole reason she was downing alcohol in the first place was so she could try and forget.

When she didn't answer him, Grandi pressed. "Yesterday you two were inseparable. And now, you are avoiding each other like the plague. Why?"

That was easy enough to answer. "Because he scares me."

Ali's admission took Grandi by surprise, but he assured her, "You have no reason to fear Nicolai. He would never harm you."

"You didn't see him. He looked insane. He wasn't my Nico."

"Ali, he loves you more than life itself."

She squeezed her eyes shut. "I know."

"Do you?" Grandi pressed.

"How he feels about me isn't the problem. And it isn't that I'm afraid of him, exactly. More like terrified because I know the uncontrollable violence that he's capable of. I saw him rip a man's throat out, for fuck's sake. I can't just be okay with that like it's a common, rational reaction." Did Grandi not understand how distressing it was to witness her sweet, loving mate kill a man?

"I do not know everything that happened out there, and I do not want to know, for fear of my own reaction. But I am certain of one thing. If Nicolai, of all people, responded the way he did, there was good reason."

Again, her mind flung images at her, and she fought to shove them away.

"If your places were reversed, would your reaction not be the same? Would you not behave just as fiercely to protect him?"

Ali turned to look up at Grandi. He was right. She would have destroyed anyone who tried to hurt Nicolai. Even now, she'd go to battle for him. How could she expect him to be any different? And if Nicolai had that in him, she had no doubt the rest of them did as well. Even Grandi. Despite his gentle nature and his soothing voice, she could see an underlying aggression shimmering in his eyes that she'd never noticed before.

He held her stare, his square jaw flexing before he spoke again. "Last night was the most terrifying night I have had since I lost you and your mother twenty-four years ago. Believe me. If I had the chance to defend you and my Gianna back then, there would have been nothing recognizable left of the one who took you from me. So, trust me when I say, Nicolai spared that Naymati. He had a far easier death than the one I would have given him."

26

Grandi was right. Nicolai loved her. He would never do anything to hurt her. Ali knew that deep down in her bones. And the nightmare? Ridiculous. She knew it was triggered by the trauma of what happened. Nicolai would never be so cruel to her. Still, when he'd tried to comfort her, Ali's body rebelled against his touch. She hated it. Hated the hurt in his eyes every time she pulled away from him. She wanted to be stronger. Wanted to shove all that shit away and take comfort in Nicolai's arms. But she just couldn't.

Needing a distraction, Ali made her way back down the hall to check in on her friend. The second she pushed open the door, she stopped in her tracks.

Maggie was awake and propped up with a stack of pillows behind her. She looked paler than usual, but at least she was showing signs of life beyond those slow, shallow breaths she'd been drawing all day.

Ali wanted desperately to rush forward and drag her

friend in for a tight hug. But she knew Maggie was still in pain. Instead, she hovered near the doorway.

Maggie gave her a tired smile. "Hey."

Tears welled in Ali's eyes. She wanted to return the greeting, but her throat suddenly felt clogged.

Greg cleared his throat, rising from the chair he'd pulled close to the bed. "I'm gonna go get some water."

Though certain Maggie was thirsty, Ali had a feeling Greg chose to give them some privacy to talk. Sure enough, he closed the door behind him with a soft click, leaving them alone.

After an awkward silence, Ali took Greg's place in the chair. She studied Maggie's features, noting the slight haziness lingering in her midnight blue eyes. "How are you feeling?

"Better, now that I've seen your face."

Trying to hide the emotion threatening to bubble out of her, Ali scoffed. "Seriously. How are your ribs?"

Maggie let out a weak, humorless laugh. "It only hurts when I breathe."

"Do you want something for the pain?"

Maggie shook her head. "Whatever they gave me made me feel loopy. I'd rather deal with this than feel so out of it." She grimaced as she readjusted on the pillows. "What about you? How are you doing?"

Not wanting to worry her friend over the drama between her and Nicolai, Ali shrugged her shoulder. "I'm okay."

Maggie reached out, giving Ali's hand a squeeze. "Are you sure?"

Ali forced a smile and nodded. She didn't have the heart to tell her friend what a mess she was on the inside.

"I've just been worried about you. I heard you took a helluva hit for me."

"Yeah, well. I couldn't just let that fucker kidnap you without putting up a fight."

Tears stung Ali's eyes again. "I just hate that you got hurt."

"I'll be good as new soon enough," Maggie chuckled. Then sucked in a short breath and grabbed her side. "As long as I don't laugh too much. Or make sudden movements."

Ali felt useless knowing she could do nothing to help her friend, but she understood Maggie's reluctance to take anything for the pain. She hated that feeling of not being in complete control of her body. That's why she refused anxiety medication. And why she didn't usually drink.

The rest of the night was relatively uneventful. Greg eventually returned to check on her and Maggie. The three of them sat and chatted about mundane things, easily filling the relative silence and distracting Ali from the chaos of her mind. Mostly distracting.

Come midnight, her eyes grew too heavy to keep open any longer. So, she said goodnight to Maggie and Greg, then made her way to the room across the hall. The one she was supposed to share with Nicolai. But when she pushed into the room, she knew he still hadn't stepped foot into the space. It still smelled vaguely of Kesara. And an old, distant hint of Marius's scent lingered. He likely hadn't been in that room in months.

Ali had a hard time wrapping her head around how she knew those little details. She knew her senses grew stronger by the day, but she never thought she'd be able to identify a person simply by their scent. Let alone, tell how long it had been since they'd been in a space.

Giving herself a shake, Ali climbed into the bed and curled on her side, facing the door. After the conversation she'd had earlier with Grandi, part of her hoped Nicolai would come back and join her. They could talk. She could apologize for the way she'd reacted. For pushing him away.

But he never showed.

The next morning, Ali woke to the sound of soft chattering across the hall. Greg and Maggie were already awake. And judging by their tones, it was a very private, intimate conversation. Ali envied them that. It had barely been twenty-four hours, but she missed having that kind of connection with Nicolai. Still, she was happy Maggie had found that with one of her oldest, closest friends.

With a sad smile, Ali rolled onto her back and stretched. As her muscles relaxed again, she drew a deep breath in, only to freeze when she detected a hint of Nicolai's all too familiar scent in the room. She knew he wasn't there, but she could tell by the fading potency that he had been there only a few hours ago.

He'd slipped into the room while she slept. If it was anyone else, she would have found the idea thoroughly creepy. But it was Nicolai. Her mate. And even though she'd closed herself off from him completely, she knew he only cared about her wellbeing and happiness.

Sitting up, Ali breathed in the lingering scent, savoring it for a moment before she forced herself to get out of bed. As tired as she still felt, she needed to get up and get something to eat. She hadn't eaten much of anything the last couple days, and her stomach was making audible demands. But first, she needed a bath.

In the bathroom, a neatly folded bundle sat beside the sink. For a moment, she thought to thank Kesara for another fresh change of clothes, but then, Ali recognized the items. Her own clothes. Ones from Nicolai's house. And resting on top were her toiletries bag and a note that read:

Though the distance between us kills me, I will give you all the time and space you need. I do not fully understand why you have shut me out, but when you are ready to let me back in, I will be here for you. Until then, I thought you might want some of your own things.

Nico

Ali's heart did a funny little flutter and she sat on the edge of the bathtub. She already felt terrible for pushing him away. But staring at his bold, precise handwriting and his heartfelt words made her feel impossibly worse.

She was terrified of letting him in. Of letting him see the things that had happened, both in the caves and in her nightmares. But no matter how scared or uncomfortable she felt, she needed to fix things between her and Nicolai. Soon.

Ali didn't waste time in the bath. She rushed through her usual routine and then made her way into the kitchen. An odd mix of disappointment and relief rushed through her when she saw Marius sitting alone at the counter. He looked up from his coffee and offered her a warm, gentle smile. "Morning."

She returned the greeting as she grabbed a bottle of water from the fridge.

"Kes made banana bread, if you are hungry."

"Thank you, but I'm okay." Ali was hungry, but she had other things on her mind. Like her mate. "Have you seen Nico?"

"Not since yesterday evening."

Well, that sucked.

"I did hear him come in early this morning. I assumed he stayed with you."

"No." Not while she was awake, at least. "He brought some of my things from his house, but he was gone when I woke up."

Marius grunted in response and then went back to reading the book on the counter in front of him.

Ali didn't mind the silence that followed. She wasn't the best at small talk. So, she leaned back against the counter and sipped on her water.

Down the hall she heard a door close and a minute later, Greg strolled into the kitchen. "I thought I heard you in here. You sleep okay?"

Ali lifted one shoulder in a noncommittal shrug. They all worried about her enough. They didn't have to know that she spent much of the night tossing and turning. So, she smoothly changed the subject. "How is Maggie this morning?"

She could see by his expression she didn't fool him. Or Marius for that matter. But at least they didn't call her out on it.

"Cranky, but better. She sent me to scrounge up some food when I told her she didn't need to get up and move around too much yet."

That made Ali laugh. She could see that. Rest was a foreign concept to Maggie. Even on her rare day off, she was always on the go. The most downtime she got was when Ali stayed the night, and they watched movies. Even then, there were breaks for more snacks or drinks. Or whatever other reason Maggie's active mind would come up with to keep her from sitting still for too long.

"Even with freshly bruised ribs, she still refuses to lay the fuck still. The woman is a menace. She's sitting her ass up in bed this very moment, waiting not-so-patiently for me to get back in there with some food."

Ali's smile widened. "How'd you get her to stay in bed?"

Greg hesitated, cutting his eyes from her to Marius and back again. Grabbing a plate from the stack on the counter, he added a couple muffins before he admitted, "I told her if she didn't behave and listen to the doc's advice, I'd withhold sex."

Marius didn't respond. Didn't make a sound. But Ali didn't miss his amused smirk when he took another sip of his coffee.

Ali stared at Greg's profile, surprised by the faint hint of color growing on his cheeks. She didn't know him all that well, but shyness wasn't something she would have ever associated with him.

Greg cleared his throat, avoiding eye contact. "Well, I better get this to her before she changes her mind and comes to get it herself."

Ali agreed. "And I should find Nicolai."

"You might check out back. I saw him out there earlier this morning."

With a nod of thanks, Ali sat her drink on the counter and made her way to the back door. With her heart racing, she scanned the cozy yard and surrounding flora. She didn't see Nicolai. But, as her senses flared and expanded, she knew he was close.

Ali stepped onto a wide covered porch that hugged the entire back of the house. To her left, she could see the edge of the patio just outside Maggie and Greg's room. In front of her, the forest was partially obscured by the rain cascading off the slanted roof over her head.

Ali closed her eyes, taking in the sounds and scents around her. Between the pouring rain and the forest creatures calling to one another, it was chaos and calm all rolled into one.

But despite the sensory overload, she knew the moment Nicolai joined her on the porch. He didn't make a sound, but his delicious masculine scent drifted to her on the light breeze.

Without opening her eyes, Ali drew in a ragged breath. "I'm sorry about yesterday."

"As am I."

Though his voice was little more than a whisper, her heightened sense of hearing picked up the quiet words. And the intense emotion behind them.

There was so much more they needed to talk about, but she wanted to skip forward in time and sink into his warm embrace. There was no place on earth she wanted to be more than in his arms. Still, something held her back.

As the silence hovered over them, the tension in the air grew like static just before a lightning strike. And when she thought she couldn't take it anymore, Nicolai spoke again.

"Talk to me, love."

Tears stung her eyes and guilt weighed heavy on her.

She hated how heartbroken he sounded. And after the connection they'd shared, the wall she'd erected must have unnerved him. She wanted to talk to him, but she didn't know what to say. Where to start. How could they get past this if she couldn't even talk to him?

He took a step closer. "Alessandra."

She drew a ragged breath and forced herself to just say how she felt. "It's hard for me to look at you after what I saw you do."

He stayed quiet for a long time. And despite the mental barrier still standing firmly in place, Ali could feel the emotion coming off him in waves.

"I know you were protecting me, but it was too much for me. The sickening sounds. The blood everywhere." Ali squeezed her eyes tight and continued, the words spilling out of her. "The worst part was the look in your eyes when you turned to me. The kind, affectionate man that I grew to trust and love was gone. In his place was this vicious savage that I didn't recognize."

"I am sorry, love." His words came out as a pained rasp. "You have to know that I would never hurt you."

"I do, but I can't get those vivid images out of my head."

"I never want to frighten you like that again. But I cannot lie to you. I will always fiercely defend and protect you. It is in my nature. And if I had to, I would tear the entire world apart to get to you."

Oddly enough, she felt a peculiar sense of comfort knowing he would always come for her no matter what. And now that she knew what he was capable of, heaven help anyone who endangered her in any way.

Nicolai moved to stand beside her. "I hate the distance between us. The silence is torture."

In her periphery, she could see him turn his head toward her. She felt the heat of his stare but kept her eyes straight ahead.

"I grew so accustomed to having our minds so effortlessly connect. So, when you severed the bond, it felt like I lost a part of myself. Like I lost you."

The strain in his voice made Ali's heart ache. She felt the same way, but she didn't want to connect with him again if it meant him seeing how she felt. Or worse, what she'd experienced.

"Let me in, love."

Ali missed that connection with Nicolai, but a part of her felt ashamed of how easily she'd been manipulated by Tiago. The things he'd said and done to her. What he'd almost done to her.

And though Nicolai saw her at her lowest, most defenseless moment, she didn't want him to witness it from her perspective. Somehow that seemed worse.

With tears burning her eyes, Ali shook her head. "I don't think I can."

"Look at me," Nicolai whispered.

After a long hesitation, she reluctantly turned and met his pale green eyes.

"There is no reason to endure this alone. I am your mate. Let me shoulder some of it for you."

Ali squeezed her eyes shut to keep the tears contained. She knew if even one drop escaped, she wouldn't be able to stop the flood.

She managed to hold it together until Nicolai pulled

her into his arms. Unlike the last time he'd tried to comfort her, this time felt different. It felt like coming home. And for a moment, every bit of tension between them melted away like it had never been.

27

"Can I ask you something?"

Hearing the underlying concern in Maggie's voice, Ali looked up from the book in her lap.

"Do you know what's going on with Greg?"

Ali arched a brow at her friend. "What do you mean?"

Maggie sank back against the pillows with a heavy sigh. "He's been acting a bit strange lately. Sort of distant. He won't talk about what happened out there the other night. And judging by how everybody seems to be tiptoeing around, I'm almost scared to ask."

Guilt flooded Ali. She hadn't realized the weight of her secrets sat so heavy on Greg's shoulders. She'd been so consumed by her own thoughts and fears, she hadn't even considered how Greg might be affected by what he'd witnessed. Or what carrying that might mean for him and his relationship with Maggie.

Forcing him to keep secrets from Maggie would only

hurt their relationship, and Ali couldn't do that to them. They deserved better.

Then tell her, love. Tell her everything.

Ali closed her eyes, grateful to have Nicolai right there with her. Much of what she needed to fill Maggie in on wasn't just about her. It was about him too. About all the Jagara people. A shared secret that didn't often include anyone outside of the tribes.

Drawing a calming breath, Ali sat on the edge of the bed and took Maggie's hand. "I have so much to tell you."

"Okay." The subtle shift in Maggie's tone gave away her nervousness, but she sat patiently waiting for Ali to continue.

Unsure where to start, Ali's mind raced. She could feel the anxiety building. The fear that Maggie might not understand. That she might not believe her. Or worse, think she'd finally gone off the deep end.

Breathe, love, Nicolai whispered, his soothing voice bringing her back from the edge of the approaching panic attack.

She did as he said, taking a deep breath, before she met Maggie's worried stare again. "You know more than anyone how much I've struggled. With everything."

Maggie nodded.

"I've always known I was different. But I assumed I had something wrong with me. Something broken. And because I knew absolutely nothing about my birth family, I had no clue how different I really was. How different I am."

Maggie gave her hand a gentle squeeze.

"Then Nico came into my life. Just stepped out of my dreams and opened my eyes to a whole new world. One where so much suddenly made sense. Even if it's been unnerving at times."

"I can imagine. But as strange as your meeting was, I've never seen two people so in tune with each other."

"You have no idea." Ali shoved her free hand through her hair and decided to just go for it. "It's called a mate bond. It happens with the Jagara people—my people— when we come into our Awakening. Between the dreams and the pull of the bond, that's how Nico found me."

Maggie's brows pulled down tight. "Awakening?"

Ali nodded. "It's a transition period when a Jagara gains the full strength of all their senses and abilities."

She could see Maggie's wheels turning. Her thoughts had to be utter chaos.

"The ability to change," Ali added. "Like a shapeshifter."

Maggie blinked. Then stared at her as if waiting for the punchline, so Ali continued.

"The night of the party, when I left without telling you, I went through my first change. I took my other form. My jaguar form."

After a beat of silence, a doubtful laugh burst out of Maggie. "I must have rattled something loose when I hit that tree, because I swear you just said that you're a jaguar shifter."

"It's true. I've seen it with my own eyes."

The sound of Greg's voice startled them both.

Whether distracted by her conversation with Maggie, or Greg was just that light on his feet, Ali hadn't heard a sound until he spoke up.

Maggie stared at him with wide eyes. "You're serious."

Greg nodded, his expression remaining neutral.

Maggie cracked up. Both hands pressed to her ribs, but whatever pain she felt didn't stop her hysterical laughter. "Right. My best friend can turn into a jaguar?"

"Yes."

Maggie motioned toward her. "Go ahead then. Show me."

Ali exchanged a glance with Greg. He made a move to leave, but Ali stopped him. "You should probably stay. You know. Moral support. Just in case she needs you."

Maggie laughed again. "Really. This is ridiculous."

Greg leaned back against the wall by the door, and when Ali stood, he let his gaze drop to the floor. He knew she was about to get naked, and Ali was grateful for the consideration. Nudity didn't bother her all that much, but the thought of Greg seeing her like that felt a little too personal. Especially after everything that happened. And considering he and Maggie were more than just friends now.

Maggie's expression of amusement faded when Ali began to undress. "What the hell are you doing?"

"I don't want to ruin my clothes, so I'm taking them off."

"Ali, come on."

"We've always known I was different. Now we know why. And even though it's not something people outside the tribes are supposed to know about, I can't keep this from you any longer." Ali took a deep breath and slipped out of her comfy pants. "Now, don't freak out, okay. I'll still be me. I won't hurt you. I promise."

Maggie sat a little straighter, her nervousness growing.

Ali took a deep breath and crouched beside the bed.

The second she shifted, Maggie's eyes grew wide, and she breathed, "Holy fuck."

Greg crossed the room and sat next to her on the bed. When his fingers wrapped around hers, Maggie threw him a quick glance, barely taking her eyes off Ali. "You saw this?"

"Not Ali. Only Nicolai."

Maggie stared at her for a long time, her hands fidgeting in her lap. "Can I...can I touch you?"

Careful not to make any sudden movements, Ali slowly padded forward and rested her chin on the edge of the bed. Maggie drew a shaky breath before she slowly reached out to brush her fingertips along the soft fur on the side of Ali's feline face.

"You know..." Maggie managed a grin. "I've always liked cats."

Ali's snorting laugh came out as a low chuffing sound.

Greg stood. "If you're good, I'm gonna go help Kesara with lunch. She promised to teach me to make those fluffy cheese roll things." He gave Ali a pointed look. "You two should talk more."

"Definitely," Maggie agreed.

He leaned down and kissed Maggie on the forehead. Once he left them alone, Ali took her human form again.

As she dressed, Maggie relaxed back against the pillows. She stayed quiet for a long time, staring off into space.

Ali settled on the edge of the bed. And when Maggie still didn't speak, she asked, "You okay?"

"Yeah. Still processing. I can't believe all this is real."

Ali nodded. "I know the feeling."

"Are you okay? After what happened the other night, I mean."

Ali's first instinct was to say she was fine. But she didn't want to lie to her friend. She was far from fine. "I will be."

"Do you want to talk about it?"

No. She didn't. Mostly because she didn't want to relive what had happened beneath Maylanju. But also, because she didn't want to burden her friend with the mess. She'd been through enough on her own. She didn't need to hear about Ali's trauma as well.

Maggie gave her hand a squeeze. "I understand if you don't. But if you ever need to, I'm here."

"I know." Ali offered her an appreciative smile. "Thank you, Maggie."

28

Ali had terrible nightmares for weeks. And every time she tried to be intimate with Nicolai, she either pictured Tiago's cruel face or the nightmare version of Nicolai with blood covering his mouth and the crazed look in his eyes.

She tried so hard to remind herself that none of his aggression had been—or would ever be—directed at her. But she had trouble separating that version of him from the calm, loving man she knew him to be.

Nicolai must have been the most patient, understanding man on the planet, because he never once got mad or frustrated with her. Still, Ali felt guilty every time she became overwhelmed and pulled away from him.

She tried so hard to get beyond her trauma, but she finally admitted to herself that she couldn't do it on her own. That's when she decided to give Jeff a call. She figured if anyone could help her get back to some semblance of normal, it was her therapist friend.

Even after months of countless emails and phone calls

twice a week, she still had that nagging worry that she'd never be free of the trauma. That she would never be wholly happy again. She had numerous setbacks and seemingly endless frustration, but Jeff reminded her many times that everyone's battle was different, and she needed to be patient with herself.

But Ali was done being patient. She'd spent too many years a slave to her anxiety already. And she was determined not to let what happened pull her back into her old habits. She had to regain control of her life before the darkness dragged her so deep that she couldn't climb back out again.

That morning had been the pivotal point in her healing process. And though awkward and slow-going at first, she and Nicolai finally reconnected on a physical level. The emotional aftermath of their lovemaking was unexpected. But she needed the release.

Nicolai held her close while she cried. He never said a word, but she felt him there in her mind, the perfect combination of tenderness and strength she needed in that moment.

When the tears finally dried, Ali rolled onto her back and let out a long, shuddering breath. She felt bad for losing control of her emotions like that. But she fought the overwhelming urge to apologize for ruining the moment between them.

Nicolai propped himself up on one elbow and cupped her cheek, forcing her to meet his intent stare. "There is no need for apologies, love. I promise you nothing is ruined."

Despite all the tears she'd already cried, Ali's vision grew misty again. "What if one day you get tired of me and all my baggage?"

Nicolai snorted. "Trust me. That will never happen. You are stuck with me, Alessandra. No matter what this world throws at us, I will never give up my beautiful, brave, sweet, resilient mate."

The sincerity in his words made her heart ache. She should have instinctually known that he'd never let anything come between them. Especially after everything they went through together already. They were mates. She was his and he was hers. Regardless of where life took them, they would always be together. And that simple thought made her deliriously happy.

Ali brushed her thumb across Nicolai's stubbled chin and smiled up at him. "I love you, Nico."

His pale sage eyes sparkled with pure joy. "And I love you."

"Then let's do it. Let's get married."

The words came out before Ali had time to think too hard about it. What was the point of waiting if they were destined to be together? She knew it was far too soon in their relationship for something so permanent, but Nicolai didn't think so. He instantly responded with a wide smile on his handsome face. "Nothing would make me happier."

"You don't think it's too soon?"

Nicolai snorted. "Maybe by human standards, but we are not bound by those same ideals, are we?"

Ali shook her head. "I guess not."

He tilted his head a scant inch and studied her for a long moment. "I must ask one thing of you first, though."

Ali shifted uncomfortably beneath him. "And what would that be?"

He brushed her hair back and tucked it behind her ear.

"Take me to see your mother's friend. I would like to meet the woman who took you in when you had no one else."

Relieved that's all it was, Ali snorted. "I can do that."

———

ALI STARED at the charming little cottage across the street. The front gate stood open, as if saying "Welcome home."

All week, she'd looked forward to introducing Nicolai to Deanna, but the moment they pulled up in front of the house, Ali suddenly felt nervous. She didn't know why. She knew Deanna would love him. How could she not?

It could've been the fact that she hadn't visited Deanna in almost two years. And with only thirty yards or so separating them, guilt reared its ugly head. Sure, they had the occasional phone call or text to stay in touch. But even that had grown less and less over time.

Nicolai squeezed her hand. "Come on, love. We cannot sit in the car all day."

Ali scoffed. "You underestimate my powers of procrastination."

He brought their joined hands to his mouth and placed a gentle kiss to her knuckles. The movement was so controlled, she almost missed the subtle little smile tugging at his gorgeous mouth. "You worry too much."

With a heavy sigh, Ali climbed out of the car and led Nicolai up the stone path to the cheery purple door. Before she could even knock, the heavy wood panel swung open. Deanna greeted them with a wide smile.

Ali gave her an awkward grin. "Hi."

Deanna didn't even wait for them to come inside. She

stepped onto the narrow porch and dragged Ali into her arms. "It's so good to see you, sweet girl."

Though Ali had never cared much for physical affection, she'd always appreciated a hug from Deanna. Because, like Ali's mother, she gave the warmest hugs. The kind that made you forget the rest of the world for those few short moments. Made you feel loved and protected.

When she finally pulled away, Deanna's ice-blue eyes shifted to Nicolai, and she gave him a onceover. "Well, now. I can see why you willingly let him drag you out of your comfort zone."

Nicolai smirked. "Trust me. It took a bit of convincing."

"I can imagine. She doesn't let people in so easily. But I can see how special you are to her." Deanna smiled at Ali. "She is glowing like a woman in love."

Ali and Nicolai exchanged a secret little smile. While Deanna was right, their connection was about so much more than just love. They had a bond that went soul deep. After everything they'd been through in the short time they'd known each other, she knew nothing could ever tear them apart.

When Deanna led them inside, Ali was struck with a strong sense of nostalgia. It had been a long time since she'd last stepped foot in the house. But nothing had changed. In the living room, the same burgundy crocheted blanket draped over the back of the sofa. And the coral-colored papasan chair still sat in the corner near the wood-burning stove.

A familiar blend of scents surrounded her, and Ali closed her eyes and took them all in. She could smell the orange-scented furniture polish. The unlit incense bundle in the dish on the windowsill. And most prominent, the delicious aroma emanating from the kitchen.

Deanna's famous sweet cinnamon apple bread. Ali would know that scent anywhere, and just thinking about the fluffy, crumbly goodness made her mouth water.

"You two want some tea? Rosa's got the kettle on."

Ali smiled. "I would love some."

They followed Deanna into the kitchen, and Ali felt that old familiar comfort the second she stepped through the archway. Just being in the cozy space brought back memories. Days she'd sat at that little bistro-style table, devouring whatever tasty treat Deanna had baked. She would sit for hours, listening to her mother and Deanna catch up on life and the latest gossip.

After introducing Rosalinda and Nicolai, the four of them settled at the table and chatted over tea and sweets. Deanna, Rosalinda, and Nicolai did most of the talking. And Ali sat quietly, listening to them.

Just hearing how both women spoke about her with Nicolai made Ali's eyes water. All the energy she'd spent trying to keep her distance from people after her mother died was for nothing. She should have known that just because she put up a wall, it didn't mean others had. Despite all her efforts to not get close to Deanna, she failed to realize that it was too late. They'd formed a bond a long time before Ali lost her mother.

Tears welled in her eyes and though it felt awkward, Alli reached over and took Deanna's hand. Ali hadn't initiated physical contact for years, and Deanna's startled expression made Ali's heart ache. The woman loved her.

Clearing her throat, Ali forced out a long-overdue

apology. "I'm sorry for being so difficult. And distant. I know it must have been frustrating that I kept you at arm's length all these years."

Deanna shook her head. "Sweet girl. You were not difficult. You were hurting and lost without your mother."

Ali nodded. "But I wasn't the only one who lost her. You lost your best friend. And then got stuck with a grieving teenager."

"I was never *stuck* with you, Ali. Being there for you through all the hard days helped me survive my own grief. I was lost without Filipa, but I was blessed to have you in my life. I still am."

Tears spilled over Ali's lashes, and she opened her mouth to speak. No words came, though. What could she say in response?

Deanna gave her hand a firm squeeze. "I love you, sweet girl. Never doubt that."

Ali was up out of her chair in the next breath. She all but flung herself into Deanna's lap. Which probably looked ridiculous considering Deanna's much smaller frame. She wasn't bothered, though. She embraced Ali and held her tight.

When Ali finally regained composure, she pulled away. Wiping the tears from her cheeks, she gave Deanna a watery smile. "I love you, too."

29

Three months later, Ali brushed at the wispy waves framing her face. She studied her own reflection and tugged at the scrap of fabric criss-crossing her chest. It didn't leave much to the imagination, and the flowy, ankle-length skirt wasn't much better. It was made of the sheerest of fabrics and the twin slits on either side went clean up to her hip bones. Traditional tribal attire clearly wasn't meant for modesty. She might as well be wearing a bikini with a filmy coverup skirt.

Ali met Maggie's gaze in the mirror. "I know this is a tribal thing, but I don't think I can wear this in front of everybody."

"You look beautiful."

"I look like a virgin sacrifice," she complained, tugging at the top.

"More like an island princess," Maggie assured her and then smirked. "I think I might have to steal that from you and wear it for Greg later."

Ali snorted. "Be my guest."

"Are you decent in there?"

Greg's cheeky tone made them both smile and Maggie chuckled. "Yes. Just taking care of finishing touches."

Greg stepped inside, his eyes jumping straight to Maggie. He took a moment to appreciate the sight of her before he said, "You look beautiful, as always."

Maggie smirked. "This day isn't about me, remember."

He pulled her in close and whispered something Ali couldn't hear. Maggie blushed and gave him a playful shove.

When Greg finally turned to Ali, he hesitated, his eyes flaring. "Oh wow. You look amazing."

Ali's cheeks grew warm. "Thanks."

Greg approached and offered her a vibrant orange flower as big as his fist. "A gift from Nicolai."

"Thank you. It's beautiful."

Greg and Maggie exchanged a look before Maggie smacked his butt. "Okay, get out of here. She needs a minute."

Once he was gone, Maggie turned back to Ali and after a moment, she asked, "Are you sure you want to do this?"

Ali laughed. "Without a doubt."

"Well, then. Let me see this thing," Maggie said as she reached for Nicolai's flower. She tucked it into the twisted golden strands pulled back from Ali's face.

Ali watched Maggie as she fussed over her hair, trying to arrange the flower in precisely the perfect spot. This was a true friend. She'd helped Ali through some rough times before, and when Nicolai had stepped from her dreams and into her life, Maggie was there to try to keep her firmly gripping reality. The only problem was that Ali and Nicolai's reality wasn't like everyone else's, but Maggie saw how good it could be for Ali.

"Thank you, Maggie," Ali said softly.

"Not a problem. I want today to be perfect for you."

Ali took her friend's hand and met her gaze. "Not just for today, but for everything you've done since the day we met."

Maggie opened her mouth but closed it again.

"You've been a good friend to me when you didn't have to be. And despite all my issues, you stuck by me. You didn't try to force me to be anything other than me. And during the scariest time in my life, you risked your life to protect me."

Maggie's eyes suddenly shimmered with unshed tears. "Fat lot of good that did. I didn't stop him."

Ali gave her a chiding look. "That's not the point. You went up against a scary-ass kidnapper guy in the middle of the dark jungle. Armed with nothing but your determination and a mean right hook."

With an almost timid smile, Maggie said, "Yeah, well. Just be glad it wasn't another one of those demon birds. You woulda been on your own."

Ali snorted. "Somehow, I doubt that. But either way, I'm thankful to have you in my life."

Maggie blinked as if trying to hold back tears.

"I know we come from two vastly different backgrounds, and I don't really know what it's like to have siblings. But I imagine you are the closest thing to a sister I'll ever have."

Maggie gave her a watery grin and cleared her throat. "Sweetie, we may not be blood, but you are most definitely my sister. Heart and soul."

Overcome with emotion, Ali rested her forehead against Maggie's, gently clasping her nape. "I love you."

Maggie gave a rough laugh. "I love you too, girl."

RESTLESS AND WAITING for the ceremony to begin, Nicolai paced the claustrophobic confines of the hut. Not that it was excessively small, but his patience wore thinner by the second.

D'mitri sat calmly in the corner, watching him pace, and Marius stood near the door, looking out at the gathered crowd. They'd both tried to get him to sit and relax, but they gave up trying after he'd refused for the tenth time.

He couldn't wait for Ali to be his wife. The silence between them drove him nuts. Ever since the incident in the Naymati cave, they'd promised not to shut each other out again. But Jagara tradition demanded that on the day they spoke their vows, they were not to speak through their mate bond until after the ceremony. Though he despised it, Nicolai kept the barrier between their minds firmly in place.

It wouldn't be for much longer though. In a handful of minutes, he and his Alessandra would speak their vows in front of all the tribes. And they wouldn't be forced to keep each other in the dark again.

Greg came striding back in, a wide smile on his face. "You ready?"

Nicolai nodded. "What did she say? Did she like the flower?"

Greg laughed. "She loved the flower."

Nicolai knew she would. "How does she look?"

"Man, I don't have the words. Just wait and see."

"I am tired of waiting." Nicolai shooed him back toward the door. "Come now. Tell them I am ready."

Once Greg left Nicolai alone with his best friend and his brother, each of them clapped him on the shoulder on their way out to join the others. When Nicolai was alone, he took a series of deep breaths to ease his nerves.

And when the ceremonial drum began its slow, steady rhythm, Nicolai exhaled and straightened his spine. It was time. When the beat stopped, he stepped out into the warm evening air. His gaze flew to the hut across the ceremonial grounds, eager to see his mate.

The moment their eyes met Nicolai forgot how to breathe. Ali looked like a goddess. Her golden hair was pulled back from her face, and his flower sat tucked into the twisted strands. Bright white fabric wrapped around her slender neck, crisscrossed over her chest and tied at the small of her back. A sheer white skirt wrapped around her curvy hips and flowed all the way to her bare feet.

Under the skirt was a small scrap of fabric that only covered the junction of her legs…the sweet spot he'd been happily buried in just the night before. Nicolai couldn't wait to get there again and seal their union with the ritual mating. He couldn't wait to sink his teeth into her shoulder again while he dove into that sweet heat he'd grown to know so well.

Nicolai never took his eyes from her as they took their places on either side of Bazyli.

When the drumbeat stopped, Nicolai heard nothing but

the sound of his own breath and the excited pounding of his heart. Until the elder spoke.

"My Jagara friends. This day is a joyful one. We gather here on our ceremonial grounds to join these two souls and bind their tribes. On this day, the Montez tribe comes before the rest of us to welcome a Zendori female as one of their own. Let us each pay witness."

Everyone remained quiet.

"Alessandra Zendori. You have come this day before all the tribes to take this male as yours. You have proven your love for Nicolai by standing proudly before us. Give me your hand as a symbol of that love you offer Nicolai."

Ali held out her hand, and Bazyli took it in his.

"Nicolai Montez," Bazyli said, turning towards him, "You have come this day before all the tribes to take this female as yours. You have proven your love for Alessandra by standing proudly before us. Give me your hand as a symbol of that love you offer Alessandra."

Nicolai held out his hand, and Bazyli took it in his.

"Alessandra Zendori, do you vow before all gathered here this day to love Nicolai with every fiber of your being for all the days you walk this earth?"

Tears dropped from Ali's face, and she said proudly, "Yes, I do."

"Nicolai Montez, do you vow before all gathered here this day to love Alessandra with every fiber of your being for all the days you walk this earth?"

Nicolai smiled at Ali and said in a clear, proud voice, "Yes, I do."

Bazyli raised both their hands, clasped them palm to palm between his own hands, and continued. "With great joy, I join these hands."

He closed his eyes, tilted his head toward the sky, and blessed them. As he spoke the warm words, Nicolai and Ali stared at each other, happier than they had ever been in their lives.

"May these two always be as joined at heart and at spirit as they are this day and let none ever come between them. May they be blessed with long lives and an endless amount of joy for all their years." He looked back at them both and smiled. "May you produce an abundance of youngling to help replenish our tribes."

Bazyli dropped his hands, but Nicolai and Ali held tight, twining their fingers together.

"I now give you Alessandra and Nicolai, the newest mated pair in the Montez tribe." He lifted his hands and said with immense joy, "You may seal this claiming with a kiss."

Ali smiled up at Nicolai. *Make it a good one.*

Nicolai arched an eyebrow. *When is it not?*

Ali grinned, knowing every kiss made her knees weak. Still, he left her breathless every time. And that first kiss as a mated pair was no different. Nicolai pulled her flush against him, one hand on her hip and the other at her nape. He held eye contact for a long moment before he dropped his mouth to hers. He branded her with his kiss, and Ali melted into him, meeting his aggression with a bit of her own.

They were so lost in each other that they barely heard the elder clear his throat. Or the buzz of the gathered crowd.

When they finally came up for air, Bazyli said, "If you are done, we will close the ceremony with the mate marking."

MATE MARKING WASN'T what it sounded like. At first, Ali thought they would have to mark each other with a mate bite like the ones they given each other before. But, turned out, it was more permanent than that.

Tattoos. Hand-tapped tattoos. It hurt like a bitch, but the end result was worth it. A series of symbols that spelled out Nicolai's name in Old Jagara script were etched forever into her skin. And on Nicolai, her name, a stunning display of bold lettering that started at his thick wrist and traveled up his forearm.

Ali loved the traditions of their people. The ceremony was beautiful. Just like human vows, the declaration was an important part of binding the two of them together. That part hadn't taken long at all. But the mate marking lasted well into the evening.

By the time they finally emerged from the scribe tent, the celebration was well under way. Laughter filled the tribe grounds. Some people stood around talking while others drank and danced.

Nicolai introduced her to so many new people. And though the sheer number of Jagara overwhelmed her, it was nice to be among her kind for the evening.

The party was still going strong when Ali and Nicolai slipped away for some alone time down by the river. They could still see the tribe grounds in the distance, and Ali couldn't help smiling at the antics of some of the partygo-ers. "Are they really this happy for us, or are they just grateful for an excuse to celebrate?"

Nicolai wrapped his arms around her from behind and placed a kiss against her nape. "Jagara take any chance we get to celebrate. Especially since events like this are few and far between. Do not be surprised if the next gathering is for our first child's naming ceremony."

Ali turned to look at him over her shoulder, her heart in her throat. "What?"

Nicolai chuckled. "No need to look so terrified. We have plenty of time before that happens."

Ali turned in his arms. "You're thinking about kids already?"

He lifted a shoulder in a casual shrug, but she could see an underlying emotion in his eyes.

Ali arched a brow at him. "Nico. Don't hold back on my account."

"I was not actively thinking about children. But yes. It is something I have always wanted. A family of my own. My beautiful mate and a handful of rowdy little ones that look just like her."

Ali's eyes grew wide. "A handful?"

Seeing her panicked expression, Nicolai let out a snorting laugh. "One at a time, love. One at a time."

THANK YOU FOR READING!

I hope you enjoyed Ali and Nicolai's story.
Up next…
Cherished One

Also, check out my other books.
Given
Assertion Trials
The Betrayal